The Canal Boat Killer

A Detective Inspector Benedict Paige
Novel: Book 5

Joshua Black

Rathbone Publishing

Copyright © 2023 Joshua Black

All rights reserved.
ISBN- 978-1-8384993-9-6

All rights reserved.

No part of this publication may be reproduced, distributed, or transmitted in any form or by any means, including photocopying, recording, or other electronic or mechanical methods, without the prior written permission from the author except for the use of quotations in a book review.

This is a work of fiction. Names, characters, and incidents portrayed in this production are fictitious. Any resemblance to actual persons (living or deceased), or actual events is purely coincidental.

Joshua Black

Joshua Black is the pen name of Rupert Colley.
Rupert is the author of ten historical novels, all set during the 20th century.

The Love and War Series
The Lost Daughter
Song of Sorrow
The White Venus
The Woman on the Train
My Brother the Enemy
The Black Maria
Anastasia

The Searight Saga
This Time Tomorrow
The Unforgiving Sea
The Red Oak

rupertcolley.com

The Canal Boat Killer

Rathbone Publishing

rupertcolley.com/joshua-black/

Prologue

June 2023

She hurried along the towpath, keen to put as much distance between herself and what she'd just seen on that canal boat. A fine drizzle fell, dampening her mood further on this Tuesday morning. A small boy in a Harry Potter outfit said hello, his mother not far behind. She ignored him, her head down. She passed several more barges, all painted bright primary colours. Her head spun; nothing felt real.

She emerged on Gray's Inn Road, relieved to be back in 'civilisation'. She saw the red bus that would take her home. She ran for the bus stop but just missed it. 'There'll be another along soon,' said an older woman wearing a headscarf. A man in dungarees hawked and spat. She turned away from him and wandered towards King's Cross.

She'd never seen a dead body before and now she'd seen two in the space of a couple of days. Maybe she'd imagined the second one, lying face up on the boat; perhaps he wasn't dead. She clamped her hand over her mouth to muffle her scream. She should have made sure he was actually dead but the shock had made her bolt. She didn't want anyone to see her there.

She put her hand on her heart. She still felt sick. She didn't know what to do. All she wanted to do was to go home and forget she'd seen him there. But she'd never forget, she knew that. And if she did nothing, she'd never forgive herself.

She saw a red telephone box, an old-fashioned one. She checked her pockets for some change but found none. That, she thought, gave her the excuse not to do anything until she remembered one didn't need money to phone the emergency services. Would they ask for her name, her number? They were bound to but surely she wasn't obliged to furnish them with her information. The last thing she wanted was to have the police knocking on her door asking all their questions. What if they thought she'd killed him? No one could vouch for her.

She stepped inside the telephone box, ignoring the numerous cards posted up advertising sexual services. Did men really respond to these seedy-looking offers? How pathetic men are.

She dialled 999. A female operator answered.

'Hello? Hello. I'd...' She wasn't sure if she could do this.

'You alright, miss?' came the voice. 'How can I help?'

She had to stop herself from putting the phone down. She noticed someone outside, a man with a dog waiting for the phone box.

'Miss, are you still there? Is there something you need to report? Hello?'

She held the mouthpiece closer to her mouth. 'Yes, I...' She needed to do this. 'I'd like to report a murder, please...'

Part One

2005
Eighteen years ago

Chapter 1: Ian

April 2005

Ian Turner always rather enjoyed making love on a boat. A canal boat to be precise. But now, he was itching to leave but to do so too quickly would come across as a little impolite, or seedy. Or both. 'So, how's Julia?' asked Beth, sitting up and pulling up the duvet to preserve her modesty.

'Juliet.' They may not have met but Beth knew full well his wife's name. Did she really need to ask after her? They'd just had sex, for God's sake, couldn't she think of a more suitable topic for their first post-coital conversation?

'Oh, she's alright, you know.'

'She must be due soon.'

Don't remind me, he thought. 'Not for another couple of months.'

'How far is she gone?'

'Erm, twenty-three weeks, I think.'

Beth stretched. 'What are you hoping for? Boy or a girl?'

'Don't mind, really.' He did know, the doctors had told

them – Juliet was carrying a boy but he didn't want to tell Beth. 'Listen, what time did you say Kris will be back?' He was due back at ten, he knew that, but he needed to change the subject.

'About ten. So, plenty of time. I'll give you ten minutes and then how about another pop?'

'T-ten minutes? Christ, Beth. I need longer than that. I'm not so young these days.'

She laughed. 'We're not yet thirty, you fool. Well, go put the kettle on. Make yourself useful.'

'Erm, yes, sure.' He reached for his pants.

'No, don't.'

'What?'

'I want my tea served by a man in the buff.'

'Yeah, right, not happening, love.' He pulled his clothes on.

They heard Beth's baby make a noise. Ian paused at the bedroom door. Beth swore. They waited, hoping for Baby Harry to settle. 'Go back to sleep,' Beth whispered. 'I can't be arsed tonight.' Luckily, he soon did.

'He sleeps well, doesn't he?'

'Normally. That's one thing I will say for him. Slept the night through from day one. Nothing wakes Harry up.'

Ian padded through to the little kitchen and flicked the kettle on. He always wondered how Beth and Kris survived on this barge, all four of them. They had the one chemical toilet between them, the place was cramped. Yet, Beth kept a tidy boat, much tidier than home. There was no clutter on this boat, everything had its place, it was clean, the surfaces shone. The kitchen had one shelf that sported statuettes of the famous Three Monkeys: See no evil, Hear no evil, Say no evil, each with a silly expression.

'What hospital are you going to?' Beth called from the bedroom.

Ian answered and they continued the conversation between the two rooms, all about Juliet's impending day, whether she was going for gas and air, or pethidine or an epidural. Having only given birth herself three months before, Beth took an unhealthy interest in Juliet's birth plans. It didn't please Ian at all. Didn't Beth realise that whenever she brought up Juliet's name, that needle of guilt pressed down a little further into his flesh. He'd told Juliet he was at the pub with colleagues from work. But he'd had enough of Beth now, he wanted to get home, away from this boat. He wondered how he could make his escape now without causing offence. Why were women always so darn needy?

He took Beth's mug of tea through to her. She thanked him. 'You must be excited, first baby and all.'

'Yeah, yeah.'

'You don't sound sure.' She sipped her tea. She was right, though, he wasn't sure at all. In truth, the doctors had warned them things were not going well. Halfway through the pregnancy, they told them that something was seriously wrong. A scan showed too much fluid on the baby's brain and that he wasn't growing as well as he should. They knew the baby was a boy. The best-case scenario, so they were told, was that he'd be born prematurely. Ian preferred not to dwell on it; he'd worry about it when the time came.

'No, it'll be fine. It'll be cool.'

'Cool?'

'Yeah, as in… cool.'

'It's a baby, Ian, not a new pair of trainers.'

'Actually, talking of Juliet, I ought to be going, you know.'

'Oh.' Yes, she looked offended, as predicted. 'OK, wipe

your dick on the curtain as you leave, why don't you?'

'No but, you know, I shouldn't leave Juliet too long, what with… you know.'

'Oh, aren't you the considerate husband? How nice.' She shook her head.

They were both startled by a knock on the cabin door. 'Shit,' said Beth, sitting up, spilling her tea.

'Hello?' came a distant voice, a man's voice. 'Hello?'

'Fuck,' mouthed Beth, jumping out of bed, reaching for her dressing gown. 'That's Ethan. Shit. Give me a minute, Ethan,' she shouted.

'Who?' whispered Ian.

'Don't make a sound. Just coming, Ethan. Just a mo.'

She ran her hand through her hair and tightened the cord on her dressing gown. She puffed out her cheeks. 'Right.'

Ian stayed in the bedroom, listening to the conversation happening outside. So, it seemed Beth's son, Dan, was meant to be having a sleepover with his friend but the friend was sick so his dad, Ethan, had brought Dan back. 'Didn't you get my text?' asked the man.

'No, sorry, early night. Knackering day. I was out like a light. Sorry.'

Ian heard Dan coming into the boat, making a lot of noise and stamping around. Beth and Ethan continued talking. Ian's phone pinged. Bound to be Juliet, he thought, wanting to know what time he'd be home. But it wasn't Juliet, it was his mate, Alan Milner. **You free?** it asked.

Now, that was worrying, thought Ian, what did Alan want? He wasn't really a mate, just a bloke he knew, and he was generally bad news. Truth was, Ian was rather in awe of Alan. Alan was hard. No one messed with Alan. He could ignore it and pretend he hadn't seen it. But that wouldn't wash. **Give**

me ten, he responded. He got a thumbs-up emoji in return.

'Ian's here,' he heard Beth say loudly to her son. 'Ian? Where are you?'

As if he could get lost on a canal boat. Ian stepped through to the little kitchen. Daniel was there, removing a Transformers rucksack. Ian said a sheepish hello and got nothing in return. 'Well, thanks for fixing the toilet, Ian,' said Beth.

'The what? Oh yes, sure. No problem.'

'See you around then?'

'Yeah. Sure.' Daniel threw him a sullen look.

Ian skipped off the boat, happy to get away. He wasn't so happy about the prospect of having to phone Alan Milner. He didn't like having him in his life but both Juliet and Beth were friends with Lana, Alan's on/off girlfriend.

He trotted along the towpath, making his way back towards Kings Cross. It was April. The days may have turned warm, but this time of night, it was still cold, the ground damp after an earlier downpour. Slowing down, he rang Alan.

'Ian, my old mucker. You up for some easy money?'

'No.'

Alan laughed. 'Of course not. But this really *is* easy cash.'

'How much we're talking about?'

Ian heard Alan suck his breath in. 'We're talking a hundred K between us.'

That stopped him. '*How much?*'

'Thought you'd be interested.'

'A hundred grand.'

'Yep. Straight up.'

'No, it sounds too risky–'

'You don't know what it is yet.'

'If it's worth that much, it's got to be dodgy as fuck.'

'Kris is in; at least he wants to hear my plan first, but he will be, mark my words.'

A man walking a cocker spaniel passed, muttering a good evening. The dog sniffed at Ian's trouser leg. 'Kris?' he asked, as in the man married to the woman he'd just had sex with or another Kris / Chris?

'You know, Beth's husband.'

'Don't really know him, to be honest.'

'They live on that boat on the canal near King's Cross. *The Purple Mermaid* or something.'

'Do they?' Ian glanced back at the said boat. 'I had no idea.'

'So, we're meeting on the boat tomorrow evening at seven-thirty. Be there.'

'No, hang on, Al, I'm not sure… Hello? Alan, are you there?'

But he wasn't; he'd hung up.

'Shit.' Ian put his phone in his coat pocket and walked on.

.

Chapter 2: Ian

Ian Turner woke up wondering why his stomach was churning with anxiety. According to his digital alarm clock, it was still only six in the morning; this anxiety had woken him up early but it still took a few seconds for his brain to catch up with his body – he'd agreed to meet Alan tonight. 'Shit,' he said aloud. Juliet slept on her side beside him, cradling her belly. By the time Ian had got home the previous night following his evening of passion with his former girlfriend, Juliet was asleep. But she was five months pregnant, she tired easily.

The Turners lived in a small, two-up, two-down terraced house in London's Camden Town area. The house had been paid for by their deceased parents but, having spent it all on the house, they had precious little left now and money, or the lack of it, was a constant source of worry for Ian.

Why had he agreed to meet Alan? He had agreed to meet him on Kris and Beth's boat to discuss a job worth a lot of money. A lot. He lay in bed watching the shadows of a tree branch dancing on the bedroom wall to his side. He didn't really know Kris, the man who, a few years back, had stolen *his* girlfriend and married her. By rights, Beth was his, not knobhead Kris. Which is why he enjoyed shagging Beth on Kris' boat on a regular basis. Karma, Knobhead Kris. Karma. And what sort of Chris spells their name with a K anyway, the idiot?

He wasn't too worried about Kris, but he *was* worried about Alan. Alan Milner was a different matter entirely. The man was a beast and as unpredictable as one. Not only was Ian *not* friends with Alan Milner, he was actually frightened of him and the less he had to do with the man, the better. But a hundred thousand? It'd be silly not to hear what nefarious scheme Milner had come up with now. God, he needed the money. Juliet had a job in a café, a job she recently had to give up because she tired too easily and not the sort of job that paid maternity leave. And his job at the furniture store was hardly well-paid. Still worrying about money and worrying about Alan Milner, Ian drifted back to sleep.

Seven a.m. Ian got up for work and, the dutiful husband he was, brought his wife a mug of tea in bed. She asked after his night out, whether he enjoyed meeting his friends in the pub. 'They're not really friends, they're just blokes from work. How are you feeling?' he asked, even though he knew the answer but he needed to change the subject.

Hauling herself up on the bed, and not without some difficulty, Juliet listed the woes of being twenty-three weeks pregnant. 'You keep your phone on you at work, right? In case anything happens.'

'It's far too early.'

'I've got a horrible feeling, Ian.'

'Look, Jools, I've got to go out again tonight. Not for long,' he added quickly, anticipating her objections.

'What the hell for? You went out last night, you can't–'

'I'll be back by half eight, all right?'

'Ian, I need you *here*.'

'Christ, Jools, anyone would think no one's ever given birth before–'

'Oh great. Thanks a bunch, Ian. Thanks so much.'

Hell, was she going to cry? He should know by now… women and their hormones… 'Shit, look, I'm sorry.' He sat next to her on the bed, taking her hand. 'Sorry, Jools. I didn't mean that. Of course, you're worried. I'm just… I don't know. I'm worried about stuff too, you know.'

'About money.'

'Yeah.'

'And fatherhood.'

'Yes.'

'Work.'

'Yes, yes, all right.'

'That you got shit for brains.'

He laughed, despite himself. 'I've got to get ready for work.'

'Seriously, Ian, keep your phone on, will you? I can't do it by myself. I'll need you there.'

'Of course, I'll be there. I'm not a total bastard.' Well, he was, he thought, he was having an affair with his first love while his wife was pregnant. On a bastard scale of one to ten, he was damn well near the top. Still, he'd brought his wife tea in bed this morning so he couldn't be all bad.

*

Ian hadn't enjoyed his day at work at the furniture store, too distracted by everything happening in his life. He'd gone to the nearby greasy spoon café for lunch, Total Nosh, and sat with Manish at the table nearest the aquarium. The café owner liked his boxing, there were framed prints of the greats – Muhammad Ali, George Foreman, Sugar Ray Robinson and others. Ian liked Manish, he was a decent bloke. Having only recently been promoted, he still acted as if he was still one of them, a shop floor employee, not the suit-wearing manager he was now meant to be. Looking at the aquarium, Manish said, 'I used to keep fish when I was a kid…'

That morning, Manish had sent around a memo in which he wrote that the printout from the till for the previous couple of days hadn't matched up with the takings and could all staff be more vigilant when taking cash and using the till. 'So,' said Ian. 'That memo you sent, what do you think? An honest mistake or is someone fiddling?'

Manish shook his head. 'I don't know but I hope to God it's the former.'

'You ought to set up a secret camera.'

Manish laughed. 'Let's hope it doesn't come to that.'

*

Ian hadn't expected to be back on *The Purple Mermaid*, the name of Kris and Beth's boat, so soon but here he was, on a cold April evening with Kris and Beth. Alan hadn't turned up yet. Kris seemed agitated, not that Ian blamed him, a meeting with Alan always had that effect on people, especially those who'd known him long enough.

'You got any idea what this is about?' asked Kris, handing Ian a canned beer.

'No clue, mate.' He didn't know why he was calling the man 'mate'; they'd only met a couple of times.

Beth was in the bedroom breastfeeding Harry, yet to show

her face for which Ian was thankful. He couldn't face seeing her in the presence of her husband. He opened his beer.

Kris was about to light a cigarette but stopped himself. 'Better not,' he said, putting the unlit cigarette back in the pack. 'Beth's banned me from lighting up indoors what with, you know, Prince Harry in there.'

'She's probably right, to be fair.'

Dan came through, wearing a Pokémon tee shirt. On seeing Ian, he about-turned and returned to his room.

'Hey, Dan,' shouted Kris. 'Come say hello to Ian.' He received no response. 'Beth says your missus is doing OK.'

'Yeah.' He couldn't tell him that their chances of a healthy baby were slim. 'I've got my phone on so if I get the call, I've gotta go.'

'But you got ages to go yet.'

'I know but Jools gets a bit…'

'Ha, you're under orders. I know what it's like.' Kris paced his tiny kitchen. 'I wish he'd hurry up.' With quick movements, he dragged a chair over and sat uncomfortably close to Ian. 'Listen, Ian, can I speak to you about something?' Ian realised the man was sweating.

'S-sure. Why, what's up?'

Kris glanced around the kitchen as if checking it out for eavesdroppers. 'I don't want this to go further but…'

Ian had a nasty feeling about where this was heading. 'Something wrong, mate?'

'Yeah, you could say that. See, don't say anything but I reckon Beth's playing away.'

'Beth?' Shit, how did he know? 'Nah, mate, you've got that wrong. You must have. There's no way Beth would do that.'

'She is. I'm sure of it.'

'What makes you so sure?'

'I came home early last night and she looked guilty as hell and–'

'What time did you get back?'

'What time did I get back? What does that matter? Anyway, Beth was acting all weird on me and I could smell it, you know.'

'No. What?'

'Sex. I went into the bedroom and I could smell it.'

'Oh. Right. You sure? I didn't know–'

'Has she said anything to you? Or to Jools perhaps?'

'Beth?' He forced a laugh. 'No, of course not. Nothing. Look, mate, I reckon you've got this all wrong.'

'I don't know.' He shook his head, looking down at the floor, the picture of a despondent man. 'All I know, if I catch the bastard, I swear I won't be held accountable. I'll chop his fucking balls off.'

Ian gulped. He took a swig of beer to cover his nervousness. 'I'm sure it won't come to that.'

'Don't tell her I said anything, right?'

Beth chose that moment to come into the kitchen, Harry in her arms. 'Hello, Ian,' she said with a fake smile. 'How goes it? How's Julia, I mean Juliet? Baby due soon?'

'Oh, you know…' He told her in great detail, trying to talk his way through his embarrassment while Beth jiggled Harry on her hip. But he couldn't look her in the eye and after a while realised he was talking to the Three Monkeys.

As soon as Beth placed Harry in his high chair, the boy jammed his thumb into his mouth. Without Harry to distract her, Beth looked awkward. 'I'm making tea. Fancy one?'

'No, you're alright.'

She went to the sink and filled the kettle. Ian could see Kris watching her intently, looking for signs. He needed to distract him.

'A hundred grand, Kris. It's a lot of money.'

'Depends on what needs doing.'

'We need to hear him out.'

'What time is he coming around?' asked Beth.

Kris looked at his watch. 'Any minute.'

Just as he said it, the boat rocked as Alan jumped on the deck. 'I think that's him,' said Kris. 'Let's see what he's got to say for himself.'

The door opened, and squeezing himself through, came Alan, with his shiny, bald head and his Popeye-like arms. 'Bloody freezing out there' he said, in his booming voice. He looked at Kris and Ian watching him with their expectant faces. 'All right, girls? Who wants to make a shedload of money?'

Chapter 3: Ian

'Shall we go for a walk, girls?' asked Alan.

'Sure,' said Kris. 'Is that OK, Beth?'

'Don't mind me. How's Lana, Alan?'

'Yeah, she's alright. Shall we go, girls?'

Ian didn't want to go for a walk, it was bloody freezing out there but he shrugged in a 'don't mind either way' manner.

They stepped outside, their breaths clear in the cold, night air. They stepped off the boat onto the towpath.

'So, what's all this about?' asked Ian. He'd known Alan long enough to know Alan didn't do small talk; he wouldn't be interested in Juliet's pregnancy or Kris' kids or the football or anything, frankly. Straight to business, that's how Alan liked it.

Kris stopped and lit a cigarette. 'Wow,' he said, once he'd taken his first draw. 'Been needing that. Don't tell Bethan. She'll go nuts.'

Alan waited until a jogger passed. They started walking slowly. 'Right, this is the thing,' said Alan quietly. 'I know this fella and the fact is, he's rich. When I say rich, I mean stinking rich, like a Bentley on the drive, and another around the back, you know what I'm saying? Niall Greene is his name. He owes this haulage firm. You've probably heard of it – Greene Haulage.'

To be fair, thought Ian, he had heard of Greene Haulage.

'I looked them up at Companies House,' said Alan. 'And it's worth some six mil. Now, his girl goes to this posh school in Hampstead. But he lives in Highgate and she walks to and from school every day.'

'How do you know that?' asked Kris.

'I've been following her.'

'You perv. Didn't she notice?'

'Nah, of course not. Kids these days, they got their noses in their bloody phones every minute, haven't they? Wouldn't notice a herd of elephants on the rampage. Too busy gossiping with her friends and crap.'

Ian had a nasty feeling he knew what Alan was planning here, and he didn't like it one bit. 'How old is she?' he asked.

'Sixth former, so what's that? Seventeen, eighteen? Nice looking girl, as it happens. So, this is the idea. We nab her and keep her entertained for a day or two, at least until Daddy hands over the dosh.'

'Christ, Alan,' said Kris. 'This is a bit of a step up, ain't it?'

'Bloody risky,' added Ian.

'Not if we do it properly.'

'So, a couple of questions,' said Kris. 'Like how do we nab a girl in broad daylight in the middle of a busy London suburb?'

Alan tapped his temple. 'You think I haven't thought this through?' They passed a barge blaring out music, lights flashing inside. 'Fancy gate-crashing a party, girls?'

'Go on,' said Ian. 'How do we take her?'

'She's called Amy, and young Amy walks across a park. So, she goes to school, walks across the park and as she comes out of it, there's a small muddy space where people park their cars for free. But there's only room for three cars. It's unmanned. So, at first light, we park our van—'

'Do have a van?' asked Ian, knowing this is where he came in.

'That's why I'm bringing you in, mate,' said Alan.

In a past life, Ian had been a veteran of car thefts. 'I feared as much.'

'So, five in the morning, we park the van—'

'You're not asking for much.'

'Let the man finish, will ya?' said Kris.

'Then we put tape over the rest of the spaces, like no entry tape, and cones and such like. Then, at eight-fifteen, as precious Amy ambles along with her headphones, texting her friends, we bundle her into the van.'

'Brilliant,' said Ian. 'What could go wrong?'

'What happens if she's not by herself?' asked Kris.

'Then we call it off but I've been watching her, like I said, and she's always by herself so no probs.'

'Where do we take her?'

'My mate's house in Camden Town. He used to rent it out but the council slapped a ban on him, said it was *unsafe* for commercial renting.' He said 'unsafe' with air quotes. 'He's in Scotland at the moment, some shit about his mother, so he's asked me to keep an eye on it, make sure no squatters go in, that sort of thing. I've got the keys,' he said, holding up a set of keys with a grin on his face.

'I'm not sure,' said Kris.

'Once we've got the cash, we give Mr Greene his girl back, using a different van.'

'How much are we asking for?' asked Kris.

'A hundred grand.'

'Thirty-three each,' said Ian.

'No, piss off. My idea and I'm the boss here. Nah, forty for me, thirty each for you.'

'We could ask for more,' said Kris.

'Aren't we the greedy one? I thought of that, cupcake, but no. The greedier we are, the higher the stakes–'

'I'd say kidnapping a kid goes fairly high on the stakes front,' said Ian.

'Shut up, you tart. A hundred grand is like small change to the likes of Greene. Trust me, he'll find it stuffed down the back of his sofa. He won't even notice it. He probably makes that in a month.' Alan stopped talking while a giggly couple passed by, unsteady on their feet.

'When are you thinking of?' asked Ian.

'My mate's back from Scotland this weekend, so–'

'Within the next three days then,' said Ian.

'No time like the present, mate. The longer we leave it, the more we'll worry.' Alan stopped walking. 'So, girls, what do you say?'

Kris and Ian looked at each other. 'Yeah,' said Kris. 'We'll need to discuss it in more detail but in principle, I'm in.'

'Good man.'

'But on one condition.'

'Being?'

'We don't harm the girl. We don't touch her, we don't hurt her.'

Alan laughed. 'Oh, you and your bleeding heart. Don't you worry. We'll treat her like a princess. It'll be like home from home. I'll order in some caviar.' Adopting a more serious tone, he added, 'We'll take her turns looking after her. She'll be OK.' Turning to Ian, he said, 'And you, cupcake? What do you reckon?'

Every nerve in Ian's body was screaming no, this was mad, no way, this was a one-way ticket to a decade or more in prison. And yet… and yet… Thirty grand. Tax-free. What a thought. It'd make a world of difference. It'd take him over two years to earn that much at his pissy job at the furniture store. And now with Juliet out of work and with the baby on its way…

Acutely aware of Alan and Kris awaiting his answer, he said, 'I don't know. I…'

'Yes? Hurry up, I'm freezing my tits off here.'

His mobile rang, Juliet's ringtone. 'Oh, shit, I'd better get this.' He stepped away from the others. 'You alright, Jools? What's up?'

She was crying. 'Ian? Ian, oh Christ, Ian, I think my waters have broken…'

Chapter 4: Ian

Ian had never run so fast, leaving Alan and Kris behind. 'I need to know,' shouted Alan, his voice fading. 'Are you in or what?'

Ian didn't have time to answer, his mind focused entirely on the fact that his wife was about to give birth. He'd agreed to meet Juliet at St Cuthbert's Hospital.

'But you're only twenty-three weeks,' he'd said to Juliet.

'I know, Ian, I know. They said this might happen. Help me, Ian. I'm frightened.'

'Hold on. I'll be right there.'

He hurtled down the towpath while grappling with his phone, trying to order an Uber. He passed Kris and Beth's barge on the way back. Just twenty-four hours before, he'd been in Beth's bed while little Harry slept in the room next door. He stopped short for a moment, the guilt swinging at him like a sledgehammer. He put his hand on his chest. What a bastard. How could he have done that? Now, especially, given Juliet's condition, given that they were, in all likelihood, about to lose this baby. How could he have cheated on her like that?

At that moment, the barge door opened and out came Beth. She jumped on seeing him. 'Ian, what's the matter?'

'Juliet's waters have broken.'

'What? Are you sure? I thought you said…'

'I know. It's come early.'

'Oh my. You'd better get on. Where's Kris? What have you done with him?'

'He's… he's still talking to Alan. He'll be back shortly.'

'OK. Well, look after yourself. I hope it goes well.'

'Yeah. Sure. Thanks.'

'You'd better go, Ian. We can't stand here gawping at each other.' She flashed him a smile.

'You're right. I'd better… Look, Beth…'

'Yes?'

'About you and me…'

'Don't worry, all's good.'

'It's not that. Kris knows.'

'Fuck.' Her hand went to her mouth. 'How do you know? Has he said something?'

'Yes. Earlier on. He said you looked guilty as hell last night when he got back and that…'

'What?'

'He said he could smell it, the sex, I mean.'

'He said that? Oh hell.'

'Maybe, we should… you know…'

'No. No, Ian, not at all. We just need to be more careful, that's all. Don't throw it all in, not now. We go back a long way.'

'I know. I'd better go.'

'Yeah, of course. You go. I hope everything goes well.'

Back to the street, Ian paced in front of the shops and a

Burger King, stepping back a little while a rowdy group of lads passed. That was him not so long ago, a lad on the town, getting pissed with his mates, looking for girls. A different lifetime. A different person.

Juliet needed him. Beth needed him. It was too much. He was weak, he knew that, always had been. His father always levelled that at him. 'You're spineless, that's your problem. Spineless.' How could he cope with the expectations of two women? He was bound to disappoint; he always did, always let people down.

He received a notification on his phone – his Uber driver had bailed out on him. 'Shit.' He didn't know they could do that, and now, of all times. It took him an age to book a replacement. Eight minutes, it said. He swore again. He rang Juliet but received no reply. He sent her a quick message saying he was on his way.

He looked up at the London sky, almost devoid of stars, and cursed at his stupidity, his selfishness. What did Beth mean she needed him? He hadn't expected that, didn't know she still felt that way about him. They'd been an item once, a long time ago. Back in the day. He liked her. He could envisage them settling down together, having a family. It was all going well until he made a mistake, got caught up with the wrong type and ended up in a drugs gang. Beth had moved on. He didn't blame her; but the flame remained, flickering all this time. Two years back, they bumped into each other outside a supermarket. They were both married now but the attraction to each other was still there. The progression to Beth's bed was shockingly rapid. He loved Juliet, for sure, but Beth had been his first real love and if he hadn't been such a dick back then, they'd still be together now.

He needed to stop feeling sorry for himself, he had to get

going and catch that Uber to the hospital. Juliet needed him.

Thankfully Ian's Uber finally turned up. He sat in the back of the Kia, silently urging the driver to put his foot down, cursing when he stopped for a red light when he could easily have sped through on the amber. It wasn't too far a journey but, boy, it seemed to be taking an age. He tried Juliet's number again. Still no reply.

Having arrived at the hospital, he rushed to the maternity ward, down unending corridors with large directional signs hanging from the ceiling, through several heavy double doors. He'd been here before, he knew where to go. He almost slammed into an orderly pushing a large trolley of medicines. Apologising, he pushed on. Out of breath, he stormed into the Mary Keats Maternity ward and skidded to a halt on seeing Juliet in a bed surrounded by various medics, including the head paediatrician, a woman he'd met before, Dr Ahmed. Juliet had her eyes closed, tears coursing down her cheeks.

And that was when he knew – he was too late, the baby had gone. His body sagged. She'd lost the baby and she had to do it by herself; he hadn't been there for her, hadn't held her hand.

They all turned to look at him. Dr Ahmed shook her head and gently took him to one side. 'I'm so sorry, Mr Turner. We did everything we could but…'

'He's dead? Is he dead?'

'I'm afraid so, yes.' She touched his arm, a gesture that almost reduced him to tears. 'It all happened so quickly. We had to induce labour as a matter of urgency. The labour was over in no time but unfortunately Baby didn't make it. I'm sorry.'

'How is she? How's my wife?'

'She's doing fine, Mr Turner. All things considered.'

He thanked her and walked up to Juliet's bed, the medics stepping away. He sat on the bed and took her hand.

She opened her eyes. 'He didn't make it, Ian.'

'I know, love. Dr Ahmed told me.'

'I gave birth to him, Ian. You weren't here.'

Her words cut into him. 'I'm–'

'He looked like a normal baby, Ian. Just a little baby. They let me hold him for a few moments and then…'

He waited while she fought for breath.

'Then they took him away, and that was it. I saw him, I held him and I kissed his little, soft head. And then he was gone. Gone, Ian.'

'Oh, Juliet.'

'Where were you?'

'I…' There was no point bombarding her with his excuses of cancelled taxis and delays, and so on. 'I got here as soon as I could. I'm just so sorry I missed…'

'It all happened so quickly.'

Did that mean she was forgiving him?

'Toby.'

'I'm sorry?'

'What do you think? Do you like it as a name?'

'Toby? Yes, that's a great name. Toby Turner.' He liked it. He smiled. Little Toby Turner. The little boy that never was. His smile dissolved and, without warning, Ian sobbed. 'I'm sorry, Juliet. I'm so, so sorry.'

'It wasn't to be.'

'No.'

They gripped hands, both crying for Toby, the little boy who never stood a chance.

Chapter 5: Ian

Friday morning, Ian set his alarm for four thirty a.m. As it was, he was so darn nervous about everything, he woke up ten minutes beforehand. He crept out of bed despite knowing that nothing would awaken his wife. He'd told her he was doing the early shift at the furniture store. But the real reason was that he had to go out and steal a van. He couldn't believe he'd agreed to participate in Alan's madcap idea but the fear of losing out on thirty thousand pounds was greater than his fear of it all going wrong. He blocked out the numerous scenarios of it failing. He had to trust Alan. The man was a seasoned crook and, to be fair to the man, a good one. He had nerves of steel, he wasn't frightened of anyone, and he knew how to deal with people, how to intimidate them into submission by the sheer force of his physical presence and personality. But this had to be his most audacious plan to date.

It was still dark this April morning but even here, in an inner London suburb, the birds were awake and making an incredible racket. Ian drove the five miles to Newham where late the night before, he'd scoped a couple of potential vans, vans without alarms or any form of security.

Unsurprisingly, the streets were deserted save for a milk float. He parked up a few streets away and walked the last stretch, his head down, his hoodie up, his clothes dark. He carried a rucksack with a folded blanket, a round of sandwiches and a crowbar poking out. He walked down the middle of the deserted streets, a safe distance, he hoped, from any potential doorbell cameras. He had a new mobile in his pocket, the most basic model available, a pay-as-you-go. He left his proper mobile on silent hidden at home.

He reminded himself why he was doing this – this was for Juliet, to ease the pressure of their financial situation, to give them a monetary buffer, a future of sorts. He needed to take Julie away for a few days, something to help ease her pain, a few days by the sea. He'd not been a good husband and it was time to put that right.

It was half five now. He found the first van still parked in the same place from late last night down a narrow down-at-heel street. It was old and battered, just the way he liked it, easier to break into. But it didn't stop the nerves almost crippling him, conscious of every noise. It was a plain white van, spotted with rust, no writing on it, nothing to mark it out. He had to be quick but the circumstances were in his favour – still dark, not a single light on in the surrounding houses, the van parked under a tree. Back in the day, he'd stolen plenty of vehicles but he'd put his life of crime behind him. And yet, several years later, here he was again – about to steal an old white van, and that was just the start of it. Breaking into the van was child's play. The owners were asking for it to be nicked. They'd probably thank him while claiming on the insurance. Next bit was to hotwire the engine. He always hated this part because of the noise. What if the exhaust backfired, waking the whole damn neighbourhood? What if it was right out of petrol? What if it didn't start?

The engine sputtered into life, and thank the Lord, it wasn't too noisy. Oh, the relief. He eased the van out and made his escape.

Half a mile on, Ian drew to a halt and texted Alan with a thumbs-up emoji.

Ian drove the van the five miles back towards Hampstead. Even at this early hour, the roads were getting busier. London was waking up. Six-fifteen, he arrived at the park and, sure enough, found the small parking area, taped off with tape and cones. Kris appeared from nowhere and, removing a couple of the cones, allowed Ian to park up. He jumped out of the van.

'Any problems?' asked Kris, hopping from one foot to the other.

'Nope. Easy-peasy.' He took the crowbar and easily snapped open the lock of the van's back doors. Kris jumped in, Ian following. Inside was empty save for three empty crates and the stench of rotting fruit.

'So, I'll sit in the back and make sure the doors don't fly open?' said Kris.

'That's the idea. So, what now?'

'Now? We wait. What do you think?' He looked around. 'Follow me.'

Kris led the way.

'How are you feeling?' asked Ian.

'Seriously? Scared shitless.'

'Me too. So, why are we doing this?'

'Because we need the money?'

'Yeah. We need the money.'

They found Alan waiting in an old Ford Cortina parked up alongside a run of lock-up garages. Ian got into the back and passed him the blankets. Kris sat in the front.

'All right, girls?' asked Alan.

Kris and Ian grunted.

'You got the van?'

'Yep, all parked up and ready.'

'Good, that's what I like to hear.' He drummed his fingers on the steering wheel. 'If anyone comes, we'll drive off. Three blokes in a car at this time of the morning looks a bit dodgy. But we should be OK.'

'God, it's cold in here,' said Kris.

'Is everything ready?' asked Ian.

'Of course it is. The house is ready, I got Niall Greene's telephone number and I've scoped out somewhere where he can collect the girl. Stop worrying, girls. Look at you both, you look like shit.'

'That's because I feel like shit,' said Kris. 'God, Alan, there must be an easier way. Can't we just rob a shop or something?'

'Funny you should say that. That's the next job if you're up for it. There's this mini supermarket I know of. They make a killing there. I know, I've been scoping it out as well. One old security guy, crap cameras and dozy staff. Piece of piss.'

'Christ, Alan, one job at a time.'

Alan laughed.

'What's so bloody funny?' said Kris.

'You look like you're about to puke, mate.'

'That's because I'm not used to kidnapping kids. Funny that.'

'Sometimes we have to do things out of our comfort zone.'

'Oh right. Thanks for that. Did you hear that, Ian? Are you out of your comfort zone yet?'

Ian didn't answer but yes, he thought, he was way, way beyond his comfort zone.

They had almost two hours to kill. The time passed with excruciating slowness. Ian ate his sandwiches and afterwards wished he'd brought a flask of coffee. Alan had forbidden them from bringing their phones. Alan, sitting at the wheel, read a newspaper, tutting at regular intervals while Kris flipped through a fishing magazine. Ian dozed off. He'd barely had four hours of sleep and he was knackered.

He woke up, his feet frozen. Looking at the car clock, he saw that it was almost time. Alan and Kris were both asleep. Ian woke them up.

'Shit, it's time,' said Kris.

'Calm down, mate,' said Alan, stretching.

'I don't know if I can do this.'

Ian was relieved that he wasn't the first to break.

'You what?' snapped Alan.

'Look–'

'No, no, you look here. We've come this far. You ain't backing out now. You know the plan. Ian sits in the van ready to drive off, you approach the girl from behind, me from the front.'

'I know, it's just–'

'Thirty grand, mate. Remember that. That's a lot of dough for a morning's work. Come on, let's go.'

It was a five-minute walk from the lock-ups to the park. On Alan's instructions, they walked separately on different sides of the street, Ian in front. Someone might remember three blokes together at this hour. Ian reached the park, everything was the same, the van parked, no other vehicles around. A boy on a bicycle whizzed by. The sun was making an effort to break through.

Ian checked his watch – eight-thirteen. Two minutes. Young Amy Greene was due any moment. His heart was going like the clappers. He felt sick. He got into the van and waited. Alan and Kris appeared within the minute. Kris looked white as a sheet. He could see Alan telling Kris to go into the park. Kris scuttled off, throwing Ian an anguished look. Alan ambled down the street a little, his little phone at his ear, pretending to be talking to someone.

From his high vantage point inside the van, Ian saw her. His heart stopped. At least, he had to assume it was her, and yes, sure enough, she was on her phone with a pair of headphones, totally distracted. She was a tiny little thing, long, gangly legs, her hair in bunches, her school satchel on her back. She wasn't a sixth former like Alan had said, she was much younger than that. She couldn't be more than twelve or thirteen. And Kris was following her, a mere few feet behind. Alan, off his phone, a large blanket at the ready, was coming back towards the park entrance.

This was it; they really were within seconds of kidnapping a child off the streets. 'This is insane,' said Ian. 'We can't do this…'

He could see Alan tensing himself up, ready to pounce. Kris, behind, was within touching distance of the girl.

Ian beeped his horn. Both Alan and Kris jumped out of their skins. Alan shot him a filthy look as Ian leapt from the van. The girl just glanced up at him and wandered on, oblivious to everything. 'I heard a siren,' he said.

'Where?' said Alan, his eyes darting everywhere.

'I can't hear nothing,' said Kris.

'I heard it. We've gotta go.'

Alan glanced at the girl, a hundred thousand pounds walking away without a care.

He stamped his foot. 'Shit.'

'He's lying,' said Kris.

'No, I heard it.'

Alan stepped right up to him. 'You bloody bottled it, didn't you? You were inside the van and you heard sirens. So how come we didn't?'

'I don't know. I got good hearing–'

'Like fuck you have.' He lifted Ian by his collar and slammed him against the side of the van. 'You spineless tosser.'

The punch took the wind out of him. Ian fell to his knees, clutching his stomach, struggling for air.

He heard Kris say, 'Leave him, Alan. People are coming.'

'Get up,' said Alan. 'Hurry up, get on your feet.'

Rubbing his stomach, Ian struggled to stand.

'You useless idiot.'

'I heard a siren, honest to God. I panicked. I'm sorry.'

'No harm done,' said Kris. 'He's probably right, Alan. Better safe than sorry and all that.'

Ian glanced up the street, and the girl, Amy, was standing there, her earphones around her neck, watching them. He caught her eye and it was as if she knew. On seeing him, she turned and hurried off.

'There goes one lucky girl,' said Kris.

'There goes a hundred thousand pounds,' said Alan.

Chapter 6: Kris

Kris traipsed home dodging all the rowdy kids making their way to school and the commuters and travellers heading for King's Cross. The earlier promise of sun had given up and now it was raining again, adding to Kris' misery. He was furious that Ian had bottled it. He hadn't heard a siren, he'd made it up. He simply saw the girl, felt sorry for her, and beeped his horn in order to scupper the whole operation. Kris truly thought Alan was going to throttle Ian there and then. And he wouldn't have blamed him. What a wuss, what a total waste of space.

Alan could barely contain his anger after their failed attempt to snatch the girl. He paced up and down and punched the side of the van. 'You twats,' said Alan. 'You utter twats.' He bundled up the blanket he'd dropped and stuffed it into Ian's arms.

'It might be for the best, Al,' said Kris. 'We had left a lot to chance.' He had wanted to say, '*You* had left a lot to chance' but didn't have the courage.

'Next week, we're going to do that supermarket, OK?'

'Yeah, yeah. Sure,' said Ian, still caressing his stomach.

'Think you can manage that?'

Ian shook his head.

'What about me?' asked Kris.

'This is a two-man job. But don't worry, cupcake, you can come to the party after. Right, let's get out of here.'

'What about the van?' asked Ian.

'Take it back if you want to but, you know, I suggest you leave it here.'

Still only nine o'clock, Kris was exhausted. The whole morning had taken it out of him – getting up at an ungodly hour, waiting in that cold car for two hours and then the adrenalin as he stepped up to the girl, ready to pounce. He reckoned they could have done it as well. He could have been on his way to thirty grand now if it hadn't been for Ian's weakness.

But the truth lay further back in his mind, and he was trying his damnedest to suppress it – the utter relief. The thought shamed him but the fact was, he was grateful to Ian. He, himself, had come within a hair's breadth of bottling it several times. Those last few moments creeping up on the girl were terrifying. And what if they'd gone through with it? What if she fought back? What if she'd screamed the place down? What if a passer-by had seen them?

He should never have got involved in the first place. He should have known better. He'd known Alan for years – and it was typical Alan. The man was good at coming up with these grand plans but the detail bored him or eluded him, Kris was never sure which. The operation had more holes in it than a sieve. Alan would never admit it in a thousand years but frankly, Ian had saved them from disaster. The more he thought of it, the more convinced he was. But he didn't want to think of it in that way, he preferred the former scenario – that Ian had fucked up the whole shebang and if it wasn't for his cowardice, they'd have made a success of it. There was no way he wanted to feel as if he was in Ian's debt, that was not a narrative he cared to entertain.

He arrived back at *The Purple Mermaid* and was surprised to see his son sitting slouched in the kitchen watching TV, an empty bowl on his stomach. 'Why aren't you at school?'

'I'm not feeling good.'

'Really? You look alright.'

'I was sick in the night,' said Dan, his eyes fixed on the television.

'Were you? I didn't hear you.'

'You weren't here.'

Beth came through, baby Harry on her hip. 'Where the hell have you been?' she asked.

The baby had food smeared all over his mouth and down his bib. 'None of your business.'

'Tell me.'

'Business.'

'What? At five in the bleeding morning?'

Dan got up and, dumping his cereal bowl in the sink, went to his little room at the back of the boat.

'Well?' said Beth, cuddling Harry.

'Well what?'

'I got up to see to Harry at half five and you weren't here. So where was you at that time?'

'I couldn't sleep so I went for a walk.'

Beth laughed and pointedly looked at her watch. 'What, for five whole hours? Pull the other one.'

'I'm going to bed.'

'You're up to no good, aren't you?'

'Oh, just leave it, will you? I can't be bothered.'

Beth handed Harry a plastic beaker of milk without looking at him. 'Oh, by the way, I'm going out Thursday night.'

'You what?'

'So, I'll need you to be here for Harry.'

'Can't Dan look after him?'

'He's only ten, Kris, as if you didn't know.'

'Who are you going out with?'

'None of your business,' she said with a smirk.

'Oh, very funny. Well? Tell me. It's *him*, isn't it?'

'Eh? What are you talking about?'

'You think I'm stupid, don't you?'

'I don't know what you're talking about.'

But she did, Kris knew by the way her voice faltered just a fraction. He'd rumbled her.

'I'm going out with Angela. I used to work with her and we sorta bumped into each other on Friends Reunited, so we said we'd meet and have a chat about old times – if that's OK with you.'

'I've never heard you mention anyone called Angela.'

'Yeah, well, now you have. Thursday night, OK?'

'Are you going to wipe that muck off his face?'

Taking a wet wipe, Beth went to clean Harry's face. Swinging his pudgy arm out, Harry dropped his beaker of milk, the lid coming off on impact, spilling milk all over the linoleum floor. 'Oh, bloody hell, Harry. Look what you've gone and done.' The baby, frightened by his mother's outburst, began crying.

'So, who is he then?' Kris shouted over the screaming baby.

Beth, on the floor, dabbing the milk with kitchen roll,

ignored him, ignored both of them.

Kris could feel the anger rising within him. 'Answer me, damn you.'

'I don't know what you're talking about.'

'You're sleeping with someone. You've got a fella on the go.'

'Don't talk rubbish.'

He stepped over her, his fist clenching. 'Don't lie to me. I'll teach—'

'Dad, stop!' Dan had appeared. 'Just stop shouting at each other all the time.' He looked close to tears.

Beth stood, her knees creaking. She scooped Harry up from his highchair. 'We weren't shouting—'

'You were. You're always shouting at each other. Why are you even married if you hate each other so much?'

Beth shot Kris a guilty look. 'I'm sorry, Dan.'

Kris snatched a clump of his own hair. 'I've gotta get some sleep.' He pushed his way past them.

He collapsed on his bed. His son was right, he knew that, but he wasn't man enough to admit it.

Chapter 7: Ian

Toby Turner. The name kept pinging around Ian Turner's brain. Juliet spent that night in hospital and the following day, Ian picked her up, booked an Uber, and took her home. There, they stood at the door of what was to be the nursery, freshly decorated, a crib at the ready with a mobile dangling above it, and Ian held Juliet as she wept into his chest.

In the couple of days since, she'd barely left her bed. Ian had to talk her into opening the curtains to allow some light in. If only there were someone he could call, someone who could come and look after her. She had a sister in Scotland and thus impractical. Her parents were both dead, as were his. No, all this fell on his slender shoulders and he was finding it difficult. He didn't know how to comfort her, what to say. He wasn't emotionally equipped to deal with this much pain. She didn't say it but Ian knew she was angry with him for not being there. He could hardly tell her he got caught up in a nefarious plan to kidnap a girl.

Ian went to work worrying about Juliet and thinking about Amy Greene who had been within a whisper of being bundled into the back of a van and held hostage for goodness knows how long. The more he thought about it, the more he knew they'd dodged a bullet there. Why had he agreed to the plan in the first place? He must've been mad. Truth was, he'd always been rather in awe of Alan Milner, even frightened of him.

Lunchtime, Ian made his way to Top Nosh, the greasy spoon café just around the corner from work. His manager, Manish, arrived at the same time and they took the table next to the aquarium.

'How goes it?' asked Manish.

'Cool. Have you sorted out the mix-up with the till yet?'

'No, but it was alright yesterday. Everything added up so I'm hoping the problem's sorted itself out.'

'Cool.' They talked shop briefly before ordering a full English breakfast each. The conversation moved on to boxing and football, as it always did. Ian silently toasted the photo of Muhammad Ali staring down at them.

Their breakfasts had only just arrived when Beth walked in. What the hell was she doing here? She stood at the table, looking flustered. 'Beth, you alright?'

'Yeah,' she said, glancing to the side. 'Can I…'

Manish, picking up on the vibe, stood. 'Do you want to sit?' he asked her.

'Well…'

'It's fine. I'll go sit over there.'

Beth shot him a smile. 'Thanks.'

Manish picked up his tray and winking at Ian, moved off, joining another table of colleagues. Beth sat opposite Ian. She looked washed out, her hair lank, hanging over her eyes.

'What's up?' Ian asked. 'You look…' He didn't want to say it but she didn't look well. 'Do you want a coffee or something?'

'I heard about Julia.'

'It's Juliet, Beth. Bloody hell, it's not that difficult.'

'All right, I'm sorry.'

'Why are you here?' He pushed a sausage around his plate. 'How did you know where to find me?'

'One of your workmates told me I'd find you here.'

'So?'

She ran her fingers through her hair. 'I want to leave him.'

'You what?'

'You heard.'

'But… but…'

'I've had enough, Ian. I've had enough of living on that shitty boat, I've had enough of his moods and always shouting at me. I actually thought he was going to hit me yesterday. The baby's driving me insane, he never stops crying. It's doing my head in.'

'What about Dan?'

'He's alright, that is whenever I can get a word out of him. He doesn't actually speak to me unless he wants something.'

There was something wild about Beth that Ian hadn't seen before and he didn't like it. He glanced over at Manish's table, envying their easy banter. He didn't want Beth here, he wanted her to go and frankly piss off out of his life.

'Like you said, Kris knows I'm seeing someone.'

'Exactly. Which is why perhaps I think we should, you know…'

Beth shook her head. 'Christ, my life is such a mess. I can't stand to spend another minute with him.'

'I'm sorry.'

'I'm pregnant.'

'Oh shit.' He choked on a mouthful of baked beans.

'I thought you'd be pleased.'

'Pleased? You mean… Is it…'

'Yes, it's yours, Ian.'

'Oh. Right.' He put his knife and fork down. Christ, this was awful. He felt sick, physically sick. This couldn't be happening, she was testing him, that was all it was. 'Beth, are you, erm…'

'Yes, Ian, I am sure. Kris and me haven't, you know, for weeks. Months even.'

'Right.'

Manish's table exploded with laughter.

'So,' said Beth. 'What do you think?' He withered under the intensity of her fierce eyes.

'Think? Me?'

'Yes, you, Ian.'

'I suppose… I don't know, Beth. This has come as a shock. Do you…' He hesitated; he knew he was entering delicate territory here. 'Are you planning on keeping it?'

'What sort of question is that?' she said loudly, drawing attention from Manish's table. She leaned forward, her eyes boring into his. 'Of course I'm planning on keeping it.'

'Right. Yes, of course. Sorry, I'm… I don't know. I thought we'd been careful,' he whispered.

She shrugged. 'Accidents happen.'

She was enjoying this. It was obvious. She enjoyed seeing him squirm.

'But, you know, Ian…' She leaned back on her chair and folded her arms. 'I see it as a sort of blessing in disguise.'

'You do?' He didn't like the sound of where this was going. 'How do you mean?'

'Well, you know how unhappy I've been and you know how Kris treats me. So, this forces it all out into the open.

So, this is what I think we should do.'

We? She said *we*.

'I've thought it through. I'll leave Kris. He can look after Dan and I'll take Harry. Then we can rent somewhere out while you arrange for Jools to move elsewhere—'

'You're bloody joking,' he screamed, jumping out of his chair. The whole café fell silent. A smile crossed her face. Oh, Christ, she was being serious. He sat again, glancing behind him. He caught Manish's eye. Leaning forward, he repeated it: 'You have to be joking.'

'This is our baby we're talking about, Ian, yours and mine.'

'No, no, no. What about Juliet?' He pushed his breakfast plate to the side. 'She's just lost a baby, she's all over the place, she needs me.'

'And I need you.' She reached for his hand but he snatched it away. 'And your missus will get over it soon enough, but this…' She patted her flat stomach. 'This is for real. This is forever.'

Ian put his hand on his chest. His heart was beating furiously. She grinned at him, an evil, calculating grin. She'd planned this from the start. Hell, they'd been her condoms, not his. He remembered the first time, he'd come prepared and had a condom in his back pocket but she insisted on using hers, saying they were more comfortable. He remembered saying, 'But, Beth, they're the same.' But she was adamant. 'Oh my God.'

He felt a hand on his shoulder. Looking up, he saw Manish's smiling face. 'We'd better get back to work.'

'Yeah, yeah. Sure.' He was more than happy to go. 'That's my new boss,' he said to Beth, standing and gathering his coat from the back of the chair. 'So, I'd better go.'

Beth caught his hand. Pulling him down, she said, 'Look,

I'm not such a heartless bitch, I know Julia is suffering, so how about we give her a week and then we'll start looking for somewhere nice she can move to, hey? What do you say, darling? That sounds fair, don't you think?'

He shook his hand free from her grip. 'You're mad. You're actually bonkers.'

'Ian—'

'I've gotta go. Really, I can't be late.'

*

The rest of Ian's working day passed in a haze. God, he'd done some stupid things in his life but this, this took the biscuit. Manish came up to him and asked if he was OK. He said he was fine. Manish placed his hand against his arm and Ian found his touch so reassuring he almost broke down there and then. He thanked the man and for a few moments, felt a little better.

Ian was leaving work and wishing the security guy a good evening when he remembered he'd left his coat in the staffroom. He swore and, flashing an apologetic smile at the security guy, went back upstairs. He found his coat in the staffroom and, having the place to himself, sat down for a moment. These last couple of days had been draining but he knew his troubles were only just beginning. He texted Juliet, saying he was on his way home.

Passing Manish's office, he realised Manish was still there, his outline clear through the frosted glass. Manish had been kind to him today, he thought he'd go and thank him. He knocked on the door and without waiting for a response, walked in.

Manish staggered back, shocked by Ian's presence. His eyes darted to his desk. Ian followed his gaze, and there, on

Manish's desk, a small pile of ten and twenty-pound notes. 'You alright, Ian?' he stammered. 'I th-thought you'd gone home.'

'Yeah, I, erm, I forgot me coat.'

'Right. I see you have it now.' He glanced back at the money, he couldn't stop himself.

'Yeah.'

'Did you… did you want something?'

'Oh, no. I… I just p-popped in to say, you know, good night.'

'Yes, right. Well, good night then. See you tomorrow.'

'Sure, yes. See you tomorrow.'

Ian walked back downstairs, heading out, his head spinning. So it was Manish after all. Who'd have thought it?

Chapter 8: Ian

Ian Turner didn't know what to do with his wife. She seemed comatose with grief. She wouldn't get out of bed and hadn't stopped crying for two days straight. She needed to have a shower but he couldn't bring himself to mention it. He tried to get her to eat, but she refused all his offerings. He needed to get to work but before doing so, he went upstairs to see her, hoping for a slight improvement in her mood. He sat on the bed and reached for her hand but she snatched it away. Without looking at him, she asked, 'Can you phone the hospital and ask them if we could have Toby's certificates?'

'Certificates?'

'His... I don't know, birth certificate? His death certificate. I want there to be a record of him.'

'But...' He couldn't say it.

'What?'

He wanted to say that Toby never lived, not even for a second, so how could there be any certificate recording the fact? 'Sure,' he said. 'I'll do it today.'

'Thanks.'

'Jools, look, let me ring your sister,' he said. 'I know she's in Scotland but she'll come down, she'll look after you.'

'No, no,' she said, shaking her head. 'Don't call her.'

'But you'll be able to talk to her, you'll–'

'No, Ian. No. I can't tell her. You know what she's like.'

'No. What do you mean?'

She didn't answer.

'Let me open the curtains, love. Let a bit of light in. You're turning into a vampire.'

She didn't object so he opened the curtains for the first time since her return from hospital. She blinked several times while her eyes adjusted.

'I don't understand, love. She's got kids; she'll understand.'

She stared beyond him for an inordinate amount of time before answering. 'She's got kids but she's never lost one, has she? She'll think me a failure, she always has. I can't even bring a baby to term while she pops them out like candy, lots of bonnie Scottish babies.'

'No, that's not true–'

'It is, Ian. Look at her, three healthy kids, a house the size of a castle, a husband with a six-figure salary, foreign holidays every year, whilst I…'

Ian had heard this before, this listing of everything his sister-in-law had that his wife didn't, and each time the implication made him wince. *He* didn't have a six-figure salary, they couldn't afford to go on holiday and they lived in this crappy two-up, two-down with its rising damp, and grotty garden overgrown with weeds and god-knows-what.

'There must be someone you can talk to.'

'No. I don't want to see anyone.'

'Jools, please–'

'I said no, didn't I?'

'You haven't failed here, Juliet. How about Lana?'

'Who?'

'You know. Lana. Alan's girlfriend.' He couldn't believe he was recommending Alan's girlfriend but at that moment, he couldn't think of anyone else.

'God, no.' She turned her head to one side. 'I'd like to be left alone now, please.'

He stared at her. Was she really dismissing him like a servant? Was she shunning him? 'Jools–'

'Leave me.'

He returned downstairs, his heart heavy.

He plonked himself in the armchair and stared into the distance. He loved his wife, he did, but she'd always had this capacity to make him feel like a failure and never more so than now. Was it his fault that she'd lost the baby, even though they knew they probably would from about week seventeen? It wasn't his sperm - not according to Beth. He still couldn't absorb the fact that Beth was pregnant. It seemed so unfair that Beth was pregnant while Juliet lost the baby. But if Beth really thought he was going to discard Juliet and start afresh with her, she was totally mad. But if she really was pregnant, if the child really was his, he was fucked – there was no way he could afford to pay Beth, he and Juliet struggled as it was. He rubbed his eyes. Why did life have to be so damn hard at times?

He rang the hospital and after hanging on for an age, he was finally put through to a Sister O'Reilly, the ward sister in the Mary Keats Maternity Ward. He asked whether he could have Toby's certificates.

'Certificates?' she said. 'Erm, not sure. Give me a minute.'

Two minutes later, Sister O'Reilly was back. 'Mr Turner, I'm afraid your wife miscarried–'

'No, she had a stillbirth.'

'I'm sorry, Mr Turner, but when a baby dies before twenty-four weeks of pregnancy, it's officially a miscarriage, not a stillbirth, so there is no legal recognition of his life.'

'Oh. Are you sure, I mean–'

'Quite sure, Mr Turner.'

'So… so there won't be a birth or death certificate?'

'I'm afraid not.'

'Oh. OK.' He put the phone down and wondered how in the hell he was going to break this to Juliet. He had to leave for work. He called up the stairs, saying goodbye but received nothing in response. He paused at the front door, wondering whether he should call in sick so he could stay at home for the day and look after her. But what was the point? She'd made it abundantly clear she didn't want him around. He checked nonetheless. 'I'm going to go to work. Is that OK?'

No response.

'Jools? Is that–'

'Just go,' came the curt reply.

And so he did.

*

Several hours later, Ian was on his way home, hoping he could persuade Juliet to eat something. He walked quickly, his shadow ahead of him when he heard his name being called. His first instinct on seeing Alan was to run. Alan came pounding up the street towards him, his bulky coat impeding him somewhat, his bald head reflecting the sun. 'So, you're still on for the supermarket job?' he asked without preamble.

It took a moment for Ian to remember what he was referring to. 'You think I bottled it last time so why in the hell would you want my help?'

'Did you bottle it?'

'No,' he lied. 'I told you. I thought I heard a siren. I was only trying to help.'

'There you are then.'

'A small supermarket's not gonna have that much cash on them. Everyone pays by card these days.'

'You're right but I sneaked a look in their till earlier. It's more than you think. They had stacks of notes in there. It closes at eleven on weekdays so we do the job just before closing.'

Ian shook his head; it was a ridiculous idea.

'Look,' said Alan. 'I know we're not talking thousands here but still, it'd be any easy job—'

'No job is easy what with CCTV and stuff.'

'Relatively easy.'

'No, you're alright. Count me out.'

'I need your help. I can't do it by myself.'

'Ask Kris then.'

'You're more reliable.'

'No can do.' He turned and walked away pleased to have the last word with Alan for once.

But Alan shouted after him. 'I'll tell her.'

Ian stopped. He didn't like the sound of this. Turning, he said, 'You'll tell who what?'

Alan walked up to him, a smirk on his face. 'I'll tell your missus that you're playing away, mate.'

Ian's mouth dropped.

Alan laughed. 'I'm not wrong, am I? Your face, mate. You've given it away.'

He had to brazen this out. 'You're talking out of your arse.'

He tried to walk away again but Alan hadn't finished. 'Beth told Lana. Lana told me.'

Shit. 'She's lying. It's not true.'

'No? I've written Juliet a text.'

'For fuck's sake, Alan. You've texted her?'

'No. Like I said, I've written it but not sent it yet.'

'You don't know her number.'

'I do, as it happens,' he said with a wink. 'Nicked the number off Lana's phone. Here.' He held up his phone for Ian to see. Sure enough, he'd written a text to Juliet's number: **Ask your fella about Beth**, it said. 'So you see, all I have to do is press send.'

'You wouldn't do that.'

'Try me. Shall we see what she has to say to this? Yeah? Do you want me to hit send, Ian?' His finger hovered over the button. 'Is that what you want me to do? Cos I will.'

Ian felt himself deflate. 'What day are we talking about?'

Chapter 9: Ian

Ian Turner sat on the bed. Juliet still hadn't got out of bed for any length of time, still paralysed by grief following the miscarriage. He started by offering her something to drink, something light to eat. She didn't want anything. He wanted to suggest that she have a shower but lacked the nerve.

'We should have had a photograph.'

'Of what?' As soon as she said it, he knew what she meant.

'The baby, of course. The three of us, you, me and Toby.' She looked hard at him. 'But you weren't there.'

He hung his head. 'No.' He knew this was a black mark against him that would never be erased; it would forever be there, hanging between them, his failure to be at his wife's side at the most important and emotional moment of her life. He wanted to say that it wasn't the end of the world, that they could try again and make another baby. But he knew that wasn't what she'd want to hear right now.

'Did you ask about the certificate?'

'Ah, yes. Not...'

'What?'

'It's not good news, I'm afraid, Jools. You see, technically you didn't have a stillbirth, you had a miscarriage.'

'So?'

'They don't issue certificates for miscarriages.'

He watched as she absorbed this, her eyes flickering, her brow creased. 'But that's bullshit.'

'I know.'

'So, that's it?'

He nodded.

'So we have nothing to show that Toby lived, that he existed?'

'No.' He didn't dare correct her, that Toby hadn't lived. 'I did try, Jools,' he added, hoping for some acknowledgement that at least he was *trying* to do the right thing.

She didn't cry as he expected her to, she simply looked drained. He wanted to leave her now, get away from this suffocating misery but he felt she needed him there.

'Why has everything gone to shit?' she said, looking through him.

'I know. But things will get better, Jools. I promise you.'

Now she looked at him. 'Oh, you do? You can promise that, can you? No money, no children, nothing to look forward to, and yet, somehow, my husband can promise a better, brighter future for us. Great. How reassuring.'

He had to stop himself from screaming at her. Why was it always his fault? Why did she always make him feel like such a failure? It was one of the reasons he reconnected with Beth. If he hadn't gone off the rails all those years ago, they could have still been together. A part of him would always belong to Beth.

He had to go. He had a supermarket to rob.

*

Spring may have been here but it was another bitterly cold night in North London on the day that Alan Milner and Ian Turner decided to rob a mini supermarket.

Ian needed to concentrate but his emotions were all over the place, all of them concerned with his wife. Yes, he felt sorry for her, she'd lost the much-desired baby, but *he* had lost a baby too. But she never once asked how he was feeling or coping with the loss. It was always all about her. His feelings didn't come into it. He felt guilty about sleeping with Beth and petrified that Alan would tell Juliet. But for now, he needed to park all this and concentrate on the job at hand. It was approaching eleven. He wore gloves and a dark hoodie, pulled up and tightened.

Alan was waiting for him, as he said, next to the park entrance, his shadow stretching before him beneath a street lamp. 'You ready?' he asked.

'Listen, if we do this, I want you to promise you'll never tell Jools about... you know what.'

'We'll see about that.' He chortled to himself.

'You said...'

'Alright, alright, don't cry on me.'

'I want you to promise.'

'Since when have I ever kept a promise? But, OK, if it makes you feel better...' Adopting a pompous tone, he said, 'You have my word on that. She'll never hear it from me. So, remember what I said?'

Ian nodded.

'Here.' He passed Ian a plastic bag. Inside was a gun. He had to admit, it looked real enough and it was surprisingly heavy. No one would know. 'We'll be in and out within two minutes. Like I said before, the staff are dozy, and they're just minimum wagers, it's not like it's a family business or anything, so they won't care. You've got your balaclava?'

'Yes.'

Alan's mobile rang. He stepped away as he took the call. Ian could hear Alan getting agitated. 'Look, I've gotta go, mate. I've got a meeting that starts in two minutes.' He finished the call. 'That's my next job,' he said to Ian.

'I don't want to know.'

'No? Could be very lucrative.'

'Go on then, what is it?'

'Babies.'

'What?'

'Apparently, there's a big demand for white babies in China and—'

'No, I don't want to know. You're not seriously thinking about it?'

'There's a lot of money involved, mate.'

'Good, so we don't need to do this job now, do we?'

'Aha, not so hasty. We're here now so, you know, might as well.' He checked his watch. 'Come on, they close in a minute. We'd better go.'

They briskly walked the three minutes to the supermarket, imaginatively called Mini Supermarket. At the last moment, they pulled on their balaclavas. Ian saw a man about to lock the automatic doors as he and Alan approached. 'Sorry, just closing,' said the man, without looking up.

'Not to us, you're not,' said Alan, pushing past him.

'Hey, you…' The man stepped back, his hands in the air, as Ian pointed his replica revolver at him.

'OK, OK,' said the man, clearly terrified.

'Lock the door,' Ian ordered.

With trembling fingers, the security guy inserted the key

into the lock above the glass doors and locked them.

Alan pointed his gun at a second man behind the counter. 'You press any buttons, mate, you're dead.' The man, a short Asian chap, no more than about twenty, shot his hands up in the air. 'Open the till. Now!' Alan placed a canvas bag on the counter.

Ian could see a man towards the back of the shop, a stooped older guy wearing a baseball cap. That was OK, thought Ian. He looked harmless.

'Come on, come on, hurry up,' shouted Alan, brandishing his gun.

'Please, don't shoot, don't shoot.'

'Get on with it then. Go on, all of it.'

Ian kept his gun trained on the security guy while Alan urged the cashier to hurry.

'That's it,' said the boy.

Alan looked in the bag, clearly disappointed. 'Is that it?'

'There's no more.'

'Fuck. Give us your cigarettes then.'

'What?'

'Your fags. Go on, pile them in.'

'We need to go,' said Ian, managing to stop himself from using Alan's name.

'What the hell's going on?' said a voice.

Turning around, Ian saw it was the old man in the baseball cap confronting Alan, behind him a younger woman in a cardigan.

'Piss off, old man.'

'For Christ's sake,' shouted Ian. 'We've got enough now. Let's go.'

'You can't rob this store. I've been coming here for years.' The words 'God's Favorite' were emblazoned in the man's baseball cap.

'I told you to piss off, didn't I?'

'Daddy, come away,' said the woman with a tremor in her voice. 'Please, don't get involved.'

'That's it,' said the young cashier.

'Put it back,' said the old man, stepping up to Alan. 'All of it. Give this lad his money back.'

'Go away before I do something I might regret.'

'It's not yours to take.'

'No, Daddy!'

The man went to grab Alan's bag, gripping the handles. Alan pushed him off. The man staggered back but righted himself. The security guy took a step forward. 'Don't move,' said Ian.

The old man lunged at the bag again. This time, Alan slammed his gun onto the side of his face, a sickening crack as the metal cracked the cheekbone. The woman screamed. The man fell back, his hand to his face, the blood pouring.

'You stupid bastard.' And with that, Alan punched him. The man fell, falling onto the magazine racks behind him, his arms flailing helplessly. The woman ran to her father, screaming his name.

'Open the doors,' shouted Ian.

The security guy hesitated.

Ian levelled the revolver at him.

'OK, OK, don't shoot.'

The old man lay on the floor, his stilled eyes staring up, the right side of his face covered in blood, and he wasn't moving. The woman, crying uncontrollably, fussed around him.

'Oh, Christ,' said Ian.

The door unlocked. Alan and Ian charged out. Removing

their balaclavas, they walked quickly back down the street, their hoodies up, their heads down.

They finally stopped at the park entrance, three minutes from the shop. 'Why did you have to hit him?' He had to stop himself from shouting. 'You didn't have to do that.'

'He was annoying me.'

'He was annoying you? Great. Just great, Alan.'

'It's done now. What is…' He stopped. They could hear a siren getting closer. 'We'd better go. I'll count this out and drop off your share in the next couple of days.'

'Don't come to my house. Meet me outside work.' Ian gave Alan his gun. 'And don't sell me short, Alan.'

'As if, mate. As if.'

'Yeah, right.'

'Let me know if you wanna help with the babies.'

Ian looked at him and realised at that moment just how much he hated this man. 'You're joking, right? Don't even think about it.'

Ian made his way home quickly. All he could think about was the horrible sound of that gun breaking the old man's cheekbone.

He just hoped to God that Alan hadn't killed him.

Chapter 10: Ian

The morning after the robbery, Ian woke with a headache. It felt like a hangover but it wasn't drink that had caused this but the stress of it all. Juliet was awake, staring up at the ceiling. He hadn't heard from Beth since she'd dropped her bombshell. Had she told Kris that she was pregnant, that she planned on leaving him? He doubted it – for Kris would have been over in a shot ready to kill him. And he knew it could happen, that Kris could come storming up here at any moment.

'You were late last night,' said the sleepy Juliet. 'Go out, did you?'

'Yes. You didn't mind, did you?'

'No. I suppose not. Who did you go with?'

'Oh, no one you know. Just Manish from work. He's my boss but he's a decent bloke.' When he's not stealing from the company till that is.

After a while, she said, 'You're not having an affair, are you?'

'No. I'm not.'

'I wouldn't blame you.'

'But I'm not.'

She didn't respond. Did she mean that? He didn't believe her; it was just her way of tricking him into making a confession. He thought of Beth. He should never have slept with her and he swore to himself that he would never do so again. He was married to Juliet and she needed him now more than ever.

'I ought to get up.'

'Ian?'

'Yes?'

'Can I have a hug?'

Oh, he didn't expect that. 'Of course you can, love.' He took her in his arms as she pressed her face into his neck. 'You really ought to see someone, you know. Get the doctor to give you some pills or something.'

'I don't want pills. I don't want to see anyone.'

'But, Jools–'

'You'll look after me, won't you?'

He pulled back to see her face. 'I thought…'

'Yes?'

'Is that what you want?'

The tears seeped down her cheeks. She nodded.

He pulled her in again. 'Of course, I'll look after you, love.' He kissed her forehead.

'I just want a baby, Ian.'

'I know you do, love. So do I.'

'Just a little baby of my own.'

'As soon as you feel better…'

'Yes. I know. Thank you.'

'Thank you? For what?'

'I don't know. For being here, I guess. Go on, you don't

want to be late for work.'

Ian walked to work with a spring in his step. The sun was out and everyone seemed a little happier as a result. Juliet had transformed his mood. One hug, that's all it took, one hug, and her need for him. Yes, he thought, he would look after her. He'd do anything it took to make sure she was safe and happy. He loved her and she needed him. And that meant more to him than anything else in the world.

During his lunchtime, Ian decided to treat himself to a fry-up in Top Nosh. A few of his colleagues were already in the café. Manish spotted him. 'Hey, Ian, mate, come join us.'

He wanted to be alone but, having ordered a full English breakfast, felt obliged to sit with them.

'You alright, Ian? How goes it?'

'Yeah, yeah.'

A television above the counter played the national news. Ian's colleagues gossiped about work while the news led on a news story about a politician being suspended following accusations that he subjected colleagues to unwanted sexual attention.

Twenty minutes later, Ian and his colleagues were gathering their things, ready to return to work when the local news began. Ian was checking his phone when he heard one of his colleagues say, 'Wait, have you heard about this?'

They all looked up at the television. And there on the screen was Ian. His legs gave way beneath him and he had to sit. Luckily no one noticed, too transfixed by the CCTV shots of the robbery. Thank God the balaclava did its job. It could have been anyone up there. 'We have to pause the footage there,' said the newswoman. 'What happens next is too distressing for television. Bernard Godwin, aged fifty-five, was taken to hospital following the vicious assault where he remains in a critical condition.'

'Shit,' said Ian.

'I know,' said Manish. 'Disgusting, isn't it?'

'I hope they catch the bastards,' said another.

The thieves, according to the news, got away with just over five hundred pounds and several dozen packets of cigarettes. 'Police are looking for witnesses.'

'Well that was well worth it, wasn't it?' said one of Ian's colleagues. 'Put a man in hospital for five hundred nicker and a few fags.'

'People like that are the scum of the earth,' said Manish.

Ian had no choice but to rush to the unisex toilets. He threw himself to the floor and puked up his breakfast into the toilet bowl. *What have I done, what the hell have I done?* The stench of vomit and piss and god knows what else filled his nostrils, his eyes watered. They'd put a man in a coma. Oh, Christ. He must have hit his head really hard on the metal of that magazine rack. Alan delivered the punch but Ian knew that if put on trial, he'd stand equally accused. The stupid, stupid bugger. Why did he feel the need to get involved? Bernard Godwin. Fifty-five. Looked about seventy-five, thought Ian. And now he was close to death. He and Alan had done that to him and for what? A few measly quid. Manish was right – they were the scum of the earth.

He wiped his mouth with the back of his hand. Flushing the toilet, he looked around. The toilet was a disgusting airless cesspit. He puked again. Finally composed, Ian returned to the café. His other colleagues had gone back to work but not Manish who was sitting next to the aquarium.

'You OK, Ian?' he asked.

'I think I may have ate something that didn't agree with me.'

'You look a bit peaky, my friend. Maybe you should call in sick for the rest of the day.'

'No, I'm alright now. Thanks anyway.'

'Come on; we're going to be late.'

The rest of the day passed with agonising slowness. He hated work at the best of times but today was the pits. He couldn't wait to get home. That name kept pounding around in his head. Bernard Godwin. Bernard Godwin. Aged fifty-five. Bernard Godwin.

Ian darted out of work as soon as he could. He'd quite forgotten about Alan but there he was, waiting for him, as promised. They walked together. 'I got your money,' said Alan.

'You almost killed him.'

'I know. Serves him right, though. He should have kept his bloody nose out.'

'Bernard Godwin. That was his name.'

'I know.' He spat. 'I saw it on the news.'

'We're marked men, Alan.'

Alan stopped. He waited while someone passed. 'We were wearing balaclavas, we were wearing gloves, we didn't touch anything, we didn't leave anything behind. The cash is used and untraceable. We'll be fine. You were at home all night last night. Just make sure Jools backs you up. But there is something.'

'Oh God, what?'

'Our shoes.'

'What about our shoes?'

'Trust me, our shoes could give us away. We need to get rid of them. And not just in the bin but properly so that no one will ever find them. Got it?'

'Yeah. Yeah, sure.' Shoes. What was he wearing? Trainers.

His black Puma trainers.

'Do it today, this evening. Here, here's your cash.'

He held out a brown envelope. Ian didn't want it, not now. Blood money. 'How much is in there?'

'Two hundred and eighty-five.'

He could have wept. They'd put a man in hospital for two hundred and eighty-five pounds. He would have to spend a third of that just to replace his black Puma trainers. Scum of the earth. But he took it, he had no choice, he took the money.

'I'll give you the rest once I've sold the cigarettes.'

'Don't worry about it. I don't want it.'

'No? Alright. Suit yourself.'

They'd reached the high street and this is where they parted. 'Right,' said Alan. 'If you're sure about not wanting the rest of it, I guess we need not see each other again. Probably for the best.'

'Fine by me.' He made to leave.

'You've always been weak.'

Ian stopped and turned around. 'What did you say?'

'You heard. Weak, sad and indecisive. That's you all over. A pathetic excuse for a man.' And with that, Alan Milner spun on his heels and walked away leaving Ian with two hundred and eighty-five pounds burning in his pocket.

Chapter 11: Kris / Ian

Kris was emptying the barge's chemical toilet, never a pleasant job but it was always *his* job. Tonight was the night Beth was supposedly meeting her 'friend' at the pub. He didn't believe her for a second. She was lying, he was sure of it. Her name, apparently, was Angela. He'd never heard his wife mention an Angela before. Beth said they'd reconnected through Friends Reunited. It was true that Beth spent half her bloody life on that site. But she hadn't mentioned how she knew this woman in the first place. She was inside now dolling herself up.

He returned to the boat, the toilet empty and relatively fresh. Dan was playing his Xbox in his bedroom, the noise of shooting guns coming through the wafer-thin walls. 'Don't you have any homework to do?' he shouted.

'I done it,' came the muffled reply.

He went through to the bedroom to find Beth applying lipstick at the mirror. 'You're putting in a lot of effort for your friend, your *female* friend.'

'Oh, do shut up about it, Kris.' She looked at him via the

reflection. 'When do I ever go out? When was the last time we went out together? Hmm? Answer me that.'

'New Year's Eve.'

'The year before last. Exactly.' She leaned forward, working on her lips.

'I'll come with you then. Make it a threesome.'

'What and leave Dan here by himself with Harry?'

'Why not? He's old enough.'

'He's *ten*, Kris. He's not old enough.'

'When will you be back?'

She huffed. 'When we've run out of things to say. So, don't wait up, basically.'

'Yeah, very funny. Be back by ten.'

'*Ten*? You're joking, right? There's no way I'll be back that early.'

Kris went through to the kitchen and made a start on the washing up. He wasn't happy about this.

*

Meanwhile, in his home half a mile away, Ian Turner was delighted to have his wife sitting on the settee in the living room with him. This, he thought, was progress. It was the first time she'd ventured out of the bedroom since *that* day. They sat silently watching TV, a David Attenborough documentary about king penguins. He could see Juliet was only half concentrating, her mind continually drifting off. He felt the same. He simply couldn't get the image of the old man collapsing like a sack of potatoes and falling, making that horrible sound as the back of his head hit that magazine rack, the man's daughter screaming her head off. If only he'd minded his own business. Why did people always want to play the hero? It was only a few quid, for God's sake, not the end of the world. But no, he had to step in like a bulldozer, like a superhero to the rescue, and look what good it did.

But what was really worrying Ian was whether they'd got away with it. They kept their hoods up and their heads down once they'd removed their balaclavas and it was dark. It was late, no one was around. No one saw them. Like Alan said, they'd kept their gloves on, they didn't drop anything, didn't touch anything. His trainers. He sat up, remembering he had to get rid of his Pumas.

'You alright, Ian?'

'Hmm. Yes, sorry, just remembered something… something I forgot to do at work.'

They were a decent pair of trainers and they weren't cheap but Alan, for once, was right; he needed to ditch them somewhere where they wouldn't be found. So, he couldn't just put them in the recycling. He could bury them in the garden, but no, too risky. If the police did come around, they might see the patch of disturbed soil. He could burn them, but they'd take an age to burn and again, it'd leave a mark on the grass and probably some form of residue. There had to be a better idea.

And then it came to him – he'd sink them in the canal. Yes, he'd do it first thing tomorrow. But no, it'd be light, the canal path was always busy with dog walkers and joggers whatever time of day. No, it had to be done late at night. But the thought of waiting twenty-four hours seemed tortuous; he needed to do it now. 'Damn. You know, I think I forgot to lock the back door at work.'

'You what?'

'I know, stupid. I popped out the back with Manish cos he wanted a smoke, and I went with him. I forgot to lock it. What an idiot.'

'Lock it tomorrow then.'

He pretended to consider this. 'I can't, love. If we're broken into tonight, there'd be hell to pay.' He got off the settee. 'It's not so late–'

'It's half nine.'

'Exactly. Not that late. I'll go now.'

'Oh, Ian, must you?'

'I know but I won't be too long. I promise. I'll be back before you know it.'

*

Beth had gone out to the pub with a skip in her step, looking like a tart, reeking of cheap perfume. 'Aren't you going to wish me a good night?' she asked as she left.

'Yeah. Whatever,' said Kris.

'Have a nice night, Mum,' said Dan.

'Thank you, my love.' She kissed the top of his head. 'Right, I think I've got everything.'

She seemed uptight about this so-called 'meeting a friend', thought Kris. She was definitely up to something. Dan sauntered back to his room while Kris settled in front of the TV with a can of lager and flipped the channels, eventually settling on some documentary about bloody penguins. 'This will have to do,' he said aloud.

No sooner as he opened his second can of lager, Harry woke up and started screaming the place down. Kris swore.

'Dad,' shouted Dan from his bedroom. 'Harry needs feeding. That's his hungry cry.'

'How do you know that?' he asked quietly. More loudly, trying to compete with the baby, he shouted, 'You do it.'

'I can't, Dad. I'm doing my homework.'

'But you said earlier…' Oh, bugger it, he'd do it. Assuming

he remembered how. 'Dan, come here and help me for a minute, will you?'

'Dad.'

'Come on, just for a minute.'

Dan padded through carrying his baby brother. 'He's definitely hungry,' he said, raising his voice.

'Here, I'll hold him and you can get his milk ready. I forgot how much powder you're meant to put in.'

'Dad, it says it on the tin.'

Kris sat on the settee jiggling Harry on his knee while Dan quietly and efficiently got the baby's bottle ready for him. Once done, Dan passed him the bottle.

"You should go to bed now. It's way past your bedtime.'

'Oh, Dad. Mum's out so–'

'No. Look at the time. Go to bed.'

Dan traipsed back to his room. But Harry struggled to settle, shaking his head, looking for but missing the teat. 'Come on, Harry. It's just here.' He looked up at the clock. It was gone ten o'clock. So where was she? She should've been back by now. If she wasn't back by the time he fed Harry, he'd go and fetch her and, if necessary, he'd pull her out of that pub by her hair…

*

Ian rushed to the canal, his favourite Puma trainers in a drawstring bag slung over his shoulder. It was only half a mile but he wanted to get it over and done with and get back to Juliet as quickly as possible. Before leaving, he sneaked the trainers out to the garden and there, with a trowel, filled them with soil and small stones, then covered each one with masking tape to ensure the soil stayed within. 'Won't be long,' he called through to Juliet still watching TV. The night had turned cold but that was OK, he reckoned – there'd be fewer people about.

Ten minutes later, he reached the canal. Now, he had to find a quiet spot and here was a problem – one he should have anticipated. This stretch of water, being near to King's Cross, was stern to bow chock-a-block with boats and barges. He could take a chance and simply throw the trainers into the canal but if someone saw him, there might be trouble. These boatowners, he knew from Kris and Beth, hated polluters and fly-tippers. But he knew there was a low bridge a little further up, a place where the boats never moored. He quickened his pace, keen to get the task over and done with. A couple walking a couple of dogs said, 'good evening'. He grunted a reply, keeping his head down. He soon passed *The Purple Mermaid* and slowed a little. He wondered what Beth was doing right now. He could see Kris in the kitchen feeding 'Prince Harry'. Well, he thought, that must be a first. Beth said he never fed the baby.

Another three minutes, Ian reached the bridge. The lights of King's Cross sparkled ahead of him. The path was always muddy here, the sun never reached beneath the low-slung arch. The place felt spooky as hell at this time of night. But no one was around. Checking left and right one more time, he threw the trainers into the water. He held his breath. Had he filled them enough? Luckily, they soon disappeared from view. The relief washed over him. Mission accomplished.

Now, at last, he could return home.

*

Harry finally managed to settle down enough to latch onto the rubber teat and start sucking. It'd been ages since Kris had last fed him and he'd forgotten what a pleasant experience it was seeing the baby's furious sucking, his cheeks plump and red. He smiled and realised he didn't smile often these days. Beth made sure of that. Harry gulped down his milk with surprising speed. Kris stood and held the warm baby against him, patting his back. Eventually, Harry burped several times. 'That's better, isn't it?' said Kris. Harry then let rip with a fulsome fart. 'Gee, that's it, Harry. Better out than in.'

Kris put Harry down in his cot. The little boy stuffed his thumb into his mouth and, turning his head to the side, looked the picture of contentment. 'Good boy.'

Back in the corridor, Kris strained his ears, trying to work out whether Dan was asleep yet. He heard a stirring. Dan was awake. He knocked on his son's bedroom door. Going inside, he found Dan in his bed, his duvet over his chin. 'I'm just popping out to fetch your mum. She's asked me to walk her home.'

Daniel nodded.

'Keep an eye on your brother. I won't be long.'

Kris returned to the kitchen. It was almost ten thirty and still no sign of Beth. He couldn't bear it a moment longer. Reaching for his mobile, he rang her. After several rings, the phone went to voicemail. He decided against leaving a message. He tapped his fingers on the table watching the second hand on the kitchen clock. He gave it another three minutes before trying Beth's number again. Still no answer. He stood and scratching the back of his head tried to come to a decision. He checked on Harry – the baby was deeply asleep, and not a peep from Dan's room. The whole world seemed silent.

OK, it was ten forty now, that was enough. He grabbed his coat and keys and locked the barge door behind him. He jumped off the barge onto the towpath. No one was around. The night was much colder than he'd anticipated and he shivered. He hesitated for a moment but decided that yes, he needed a better coat. He returned inside, found a bulkier coat and, happier, rushed off along the towpath.

*

Happy to have got rid of his Pumas, Ian was keen to get home. It was so cold and although pleased to have brought his gloves, he wished he'd brought a scarf. A couple of dodgy-looking men past him. One of them threw an empty beer can into the canal. Ian tensed up, preparing himself. But the men, laughing at something, didn't appear to notice him.

He soon passed the *Purple Mermaid* again, and there, on the towpath, was Kris. Ian darted into the undergrowth to the side of the path. He watched as Kris paused as if deciding what to do. Next moment, Kris darted back onto the boat. Ian stayed put, waiting. He was about to emerge from the undergrowth and head home when Kris appeared again. This time, with purposeful strides, Kris walked past Ian in the direction of the arched bridge and King's Cross.

That had been a bit too close for comfort for Ian's liking. He ambled past the boat, looking through the portholes. Daniel's curtains were closed. The next porthole along was the nursery but again, he couldn't see through the thick curtains. He guessed Harry would be there or perhaps Beth was feeding him or playing with him in the kitchen area. He peered through the kitchen porthole and although the lights and the television were on, no one was there. He wondered where Beth could be. She had to be in the nursery. Surely, Kris wouldn't have left the sleeping Dan alone on the boat with his baby brother?

He didn't know what to do. What if both parents had deserted their children? As a responsible adult, he needed to check. Stepping onto the barge, he knocked gently on the door. No answer. He tried again, louder this time. Still no answer, no sounds of footsteps from within, only the faint murmur of the television. He could never leave a young kid and a baby all alone so late at night. As he'd seen earlier, there were some dodgy men about. He was about to leave when he tried the door handle. The door opened. Hell, Kris hadn't even bothered locking it. The man was an utter fool.

He stepped down the four-step stepladder into the kitchen area. He called out, not too loudly. There was no one here except the Three Monkeys staring at him. He shook his head at the depth of their irresponsibility. He needed to check on Harry. He pushed open the nursery door, the light from the corridor providing enough light to see inside. And there he was, lying on his back, his wet thumb on his chest pointing up but not quite reaching his mouth. He must've been sucking his thumb, fallen asleep and the thumb slipped out. Ian smiled at the little mite. He really was the most adorable baby. It seemed so unfair that Beth and Kris, the most unappreciative and irresponsible parents in the world, should be granted this most precious bundle while he and Juliet, who would make the most wonderful and caring parents, had been denied. Juliet, especially, would make a great mum – patient, attentive and loving.

Ian stepped over to the crib and, leaning down, breathed in the baby's warm aroma. Something about it hit him in the back of the throat and he had to suppress an anguished cry.

When he thought back to this moment later, which he did continuously over the years, he would have no recollection of what he did next.

Silently, most silently, Ian carefully scooped Harry from his crib and held him against his chest. And just holding him there, this warm, gorgeous bundle of love, was like nothing else he'd ever experienced. He felt all his problems, all his worries, drain away.

*

The walk to The Red Cock was longer than Kris remembered. He was pleased he'd gone back to fetch his heavier coat. Had he locked the cabin door on leaving? He stopped short. Had he? Yes, yes, he had, he was sure of it, he remembered doing so. He saw a couple of pissed up laughing lads who were leaning in towards each other as they passed by, looking like they were up to no good.

Jogging up several stone steps, Kris emerged from the towpath onto Gray's Inn Road, and he could see the pub up ahead. A number 73 bus roared past, a couple of cyclists going at speed.

Now that he was here, Kris wasn't sure how to play this. His earlier anger had dissipated. He feared he was about to make a tit of himself. Maybe he should turn back around and go back to the boat. But he was here; it had taken him fifteen minutes; he had to see this through. He peered through the pub windows. Inside was packed but he couldn't see Beth. He pushed past the hardy smokers standing outside the pub and nodded at the security man at the door and walked in.

The place was massive and buzzing for a weekday evening. The Arctic Monkeys were blasting out over the stereo. So where was Beth? He edged around, looking for her. A young woman bumped into him and apologised. The woman was so drunk she could barely stand. She staggered away. And that's when she saw her. He stepped behind a column. She was on her feet, and so was her friend, her *female* friend, and they both had their coats on and were embracing. They were about to leave. Kris didn't want to be seen. Quickly and dodging past the numerous drinkers, he made his way back outside. He paused. Maybe, after all, he should wait for her and say he'd come to walk her home. After all, that towpath felt creepy as hell at this time of night. But no, if he did, she'd be annoyed with him for leaving the children unattended.

So, Kris rushed home.

Fifteen minutes later he was back. Everything seemed so deathly quiet here compared to the noise and the buzz of the pub and the surrounding streets. He went to unlock the cabin door but… it wasn't locked. He remembered now – he had locked the door but then, having returned for his warmer coat, he must've forgotten the second time. He cursed. Still, no harm done. He climbed down into the kitchen. The television was still on. He peered down the corridor. All quiet. All was well.

Removing his coat and shoes, he settled down and, flipping channels, found a channel showing *Pretty Woman*, one of Beth's favourite films.

Ten minutes later, Kris felt the barge rock gently as Beth stepped aboard. Coming into the kitchen, she looked flushed as if she'd been rushing. 'Alright?' said Kris without taking his eyes off the screen.

'Oh, *Pretty Woman*. Love this film.'

'Yeah, it's good. How was Angela?'

She removed her coat. 'Yeah, great, thanks.'

'Nice chat?'

'Good yeah. You think I'm bad but that woman can talk for bloody Ireland the rate she goes. She doesn't stop for breath. I'm exhausted.' She hopped on one foot as she took a shoe off. 'So, you see, Kris, the world didn't end just because I went out with a mate.'

He didn't answer.

'So, how the kids? Everything OK?'

He shrugged. 'Yeah. Of course.'

She removed her second shoe. 'Good. Harry feed OK?'

'Yeah. He drank the whole bottle.'

'He's got a good appetite, that boy.'

She walked through to the corridor. Kris could hear her checking on Harry. 'Where's Harry?' she called out.

'In his crib obviously.'

'He isn't. His blanket's gone.'

'Oh. Well, Dan must've taken him then.'

'Didn't you hear?'

'No.' He jumped up from his chair, his every sense suddenly on alert. Something wasn't right here. Daniel wouldn't have taken Harry into his bed. He stood at the kitchen door as Beth went to the end of the corridor to Daniel's room. She stepped in.

He realised he was praying, a prayer that shattered the moment he heard Beth's panicked voice. 'Dan? Dan, wake up, wake up.'

He heard Daniel's sleepy, muffled voice.

'Wake up, Dan. For God's sake, wake up. Where's Harry, Dan? Where's your brother?'

'Hey? I don't know.'

Kris felt sick. He looked in the nursery. The crib looked enormous without Harry in it. His heart was about to explode. He approached Dan's room, his legs weighed down with dread.

'He's in the bed with you,' screamed Beth. Kris saw Beth

whip Dan's duvet from the bed, exposing the huddled boy.

'Mum!'

'Where is he, Dan?' She turned and slammed into Kris. Pushing him to the side, she rushed back to the nursery, this time putting the light on. Kris followed. The crib was empty, still empty. 'Oh my God,' said Beth under her breath. 'Oh, Christ almighty. Where is he?' She looked at Kris, her eyes raw, the tears pouring, then screaming, she repeated it: 'Where is he, Kris? Where in the fuck is he?'

Kris ran to Dan's room. 'Did you take him at some point? Dan, answer me, did you?'

Dan, now sitting up, looked confused. He shook his head.

'For fuck's sake, Dan. I told you to keep an eye on your brother.' He charged back to the kitchen while Beth, still in the nursery, fell to her knees and howled. Kris looked everywhere, under the table, behind the TV, everywhere, as if he'd mislaid, not a baby, but an item or a set of keys. He truly thought his heart was going to give out on him.

Dan appeared from his bedroom, sobbing. 'What's happened to him, Dad?'

Kris couldn't speak, his legs could barely support his weight. 'I... er, I d-don't know.'

Beth staggered out from the nursery. 'He's not here,' she screamed. 'He's not here. Someone's taken him, Kris. Someone's taken my baby…'

Chapter 12: Ian

It's astonishing how heavy a baby can get after half a mile. It's like carrying a dead weight. He wrapped the baby and his blanket inside his coat. It didn't help that along the way, Harry woke up and started squirming making it all that much more difficult. Ian saw various people but no one too close. He crossed the road numerous times to avoid passing people on the pavement.

By the time he got home, Ian was exhausted. Juliet had gone to bed. He plonked Harry on the settee and caught his breath. The two of them, Ian and Harry, eyed each other. Harry started sucking his thumb and seemed to be drifting off again. Ian pulled out the bottom drawer from a set of drawers and spilt its contents onto the living room carpet. He brought down a towel and blankets from the linen cupboard upstairs and made, what he thought, a comfortable little bed for Harry. He placed the baby inside and he seemed fine enough. It was late now and, after a fretful and stressful evening, Ian was tired. He had work tomorrow; he needed to get to sleep. He decided to sleep downstairs so if Harry woke, he'd be here to see to his needs. He lay down and was asleep within seconds.

But sure enough, Ian was woken up by Harry's quiet crying. It was three in the morning. Yawning, he picked up the baby and paced up and down, jiggling Harry, but it wasn't helping. And he knew why – this baby was hungry and there certainly wasn't any formula milk in the house. He needed Juliet. It'd only been a few days since the miscarriage so he knew Juliet would still be carrying milk. He placed the red-faced baby back in his makeshift bed and ran upstairs. Juliet was asleep, naturally. He shook her gently, whispering her name. He could hear Harry downstairs getting more agitated. They needed to hurry. Slowly, she came round, opening her bleary eyes.

'Juliet, are you OK? I'm sorry to wake you but…'

'What's that noise? Is that–'

'Listen. You need to listen to me. It's a long story but I've got a friend at work…' He thought of a random name. 'Adrian. His name's Adrian. And his wife recently gave birth but the thing is…'

'A baby?' she asked, sitting up, now fully alert. 'Here?'

'The thing is, Adrian's wife is ill, I mean really ill, and she's had to go to hospital so I sort of said to Adrian that… that w-we'd look after their baby boy for a few days.'

'You're mad–'

'I know but…' Harry was building up to a frenzy now. 'But they were desperate and, Juliet, they had no one else to turn to. I couldn't say no and you're still expressing so…'

'You want me to feed him? Now?'

'Listen to him.'

'Oh my God, Ian. I can't feed another woman's baby.'

He took her hand. 'Juliet, please, you have to. Think of

that poor mite down there.'

She shook her head. 'It's not fair on me.'

'I know, I know. But… he needs you, Juliet. He's desperate. Listen to him.'

Harry was screaming the house down now. Ian realised he was sweating. He thought she'd be delighted.

'Didn't your friend have any formula or didn't his wife express?'

'I don't know. He's with her at the hospital. I didn't have chance to ask.'

'Bloody hell, Ian. You're impossible at times. All right, bring him up here.'

Oh, the relief. 'Thank you, Jools. Thank you.'

He rushed downstairs and picked up the beetroot red baby. 'There, there, little one. You'll be OK.' A name? He needed a name. He couldn't be Harry any more. He had the time it took to climb up the stairs to think of a name. Felix. He had a friend at school called Felix. They used to swap Top Trump cards. Perfect.

Carrying the baby into the bedroom, he could sense Juliet's tension. He needed this to work. He presented the squirming baby to Juliet. 'Jools, you ready? Meet Felix,' he said, trying to make himself heard above Felix's screaming. 'Felix, meet your mum for the next few days.'

Juliet held up her arms, her body stiff. 'My god, he's hungry.' She unbuttoned her pyjama top and rearranging her breast, placed the baby at her nipple. The baby shook his head, rooting frantically. Juliet was struggling. 'He can't…'

'He can't what? What's the matter?'

'He's not latching on.'

'You're too tense, Jools.'

'He's making me tense. Come on, little one. Can you put

the lamp on?'

He positioned himself behind Juliet so that he could massage her shoulders. 'Deep breaths, Jools. You can do it, you can do it.'

'Come on, Felix, it's just… oh my God.'

The baby had done it, he'd found the nipple. The sudden peace was blissful.

'Whoa, ouch. Hey…'

'What's the matter?'

'It bloody hurts.'

'It'll get better, Jools.' He climbed off the bed. 'It's because your… your nipples aren't used to it.'

'Bloody hell, Ian. I didn't think it'd be… oh my.'

The baby was making a surprising amount of noise as he suckled. But Juliet was getting there, he could sense her relaxing, the baby too. Did he see a hint of a smile on his wife's face? He hadn't seen her smile for such a long time now.

It was only now that Ian's thoughts turned to Beth and Kris. They'd be frantic. Would they have called the police already? He'd done something awful yet he was pleased. Beth didn't deserve another baby; she was forever complaining about him; she didn't appreciate him. Felix, or Harry, was unloved and unwanted. At best, he was tolerated. While Juliet was desperate for a baby; she'd never complain. She'd treasure every minute she had with him. Here, Felix would know what it was to be loved, to have a mother and father who adored him.

'You OK, Jools?'

She nodded. 'It is painful,' she said with a laugh. 'But it's bearable.'

'He's hungry.'

'He certainly is. So, how long have we got him for?'

'Oh, er. I suppose it depends on how long they need to keep her in hospital. A week or so.'

'He's looking up at me.'

Ian stretched over, and yes, Felix was staring up at Juliet and Juliet was smiling down at him, stroking his downy cheek. 'Isn't he lovely?' she said.

Ian looked at his wife and the baby gazing at each other and he knew he was witnessing a bond being forged. A bond that would last a lifetime.

Chapter 13: Kris

Kris jumped off the barge and sprinted up the towpath away from King's Cross. Part of him knew he was wasting his time but he had to try. He saw someone up ahead. Were they carrying something, a baby? He quickened his pace and turned around on passing them, alarming the man. But he wasn't carrying anything. He turned back and ran past the barge towards King's Cross. No one was around now, it was late. He drew up, catching his breath. He jogged back to the barge, hoping, praying, that Beth would have found Harry, that he'd fallen out of his crib and rolled under it, something improbable. 'Please let him be there,' he said aloud, as he stepped back onto the boat. But even from outside, he could hear Beth's wailing.

Beth saw him and knew straight away he'd not found the baby. She was cuddling Dan who suddenly looked very small and vulnerable. 'Where is he, Dad?'

He sat opposite them. 'I don't know.'

'Phone the police,' said Beth.

Kris dialled 999, his hand shaking. He could barely find his voice as he tried to explain what had happened, spluttering his way through. He tried to describe their location, but that was the problem with living on a barge on a long stretch of canal.

'I don't believe this is happening,' said Beth. 'How could he have disappeared, Kris? You were here.'

'I was.' His heart stopped for a moment. How was he going to confess this? The police would ask and he couldn't lie to the police. 'Actually…' He looked down.

'What?' asked Beth, sitting up and pushing Dan aside. 'What is it, Kris? You were here, weren't you?'

'I, er… Well, the thing is, Beth, I did step out for a few moments.'

She sprang to her feet. 'You bloody what?'

'I was… I needed a walk–'

Beth's hand shot to her mouth. 'You went for a walk? Oh my God, you… you idiot. How long for?'

'Not long, honest to God, Beth. A few minutes at the most.'

'How long?' she shouted, tearing at her hair.

'I don't know.' He calculated it in his head – he must've been gone for just over half an hour. Shit, he couldn't tell her that. 'Five minutes. Maybe six. No more than that.'

'I was asleep,' said Dan. 'Did someone actually take Harry?'

'No,' said Kris.

'But then…'

'We don't know, son,' he shouted. 'It's probably some massive mix-up.'

'A mix-up?' screamed Beth. 'Oh, like he might suddenly come back?'

'I don't know, do I?' He felt as if a weight was pushing

85

against his chest, threatening to squeeze it. He couldn't breathe. Beth stormed out of the kitchen, checking the three bedrooms again, flinging things around as if she might find him hiding somewhere.

'Did someone come on the boat, Dad?'

'No. Yes.' He couldn't talk, his head was exploding. 'Stop asking me questions. I don't bloody know. The police will be here soon.'

Dan was crying again. 'Stop crying, will you? Just stop your bloody crying.' Saying that just made it worse but he couldn't take the boy's sniffling, not now. There had to be a simple explanation for this, people don't just come along and *steal* a baby. And then, it hit him between the eyes, a massive realisation that took his breath away. Alan Milner. If the man was capable of kidnapping a child off the streets, he was capable of anything. But no, it didn't make sense. Alan knew he didn't have any money unless… Unless what? Did criminals sell babies? Did people do that? Yes, of course they did. It had to be Alan. He reached for his phone but no, maybe he shouldn't, what if it made the situation worse?

Kris heard footsteps on the barge, a voice saying hello. He opened the barge door to see two police officers, a man and a woman. 'Mr Whitehead? You've reported a missing baby.'

'Come in. Mind the step.'

The man introduced themselves but Kris couldn't take it in. Beth came through, her eyes bloodshot. 'You have to find my baby. He's–'

'Shall we sit down?' asked the woman.

They asked several questions – the baby's name and age, whether Kris had any photos of him and who was on the boat at the time. Here, Kris had to confess he vacated the barge for a few minutes. He could tell they weren't impressed. 'Exactly, what time was this?' asked the woman sharply.

'Erm, soon after ten forty.'

'Seems rather irresponsible to leave a child and a baby unattended. And where was Harry at this point?'

'Asleep in his crib.'

'And your older son?'

'Dan. In bed too.'

Turning to Dan, she asked him whether he heard anything. He hadn't.

'Has anyone shown an unusual interest in Harry?'

Kris shook his head. 'Not beyond the usual, you know.'

'Does Harry have any distinguishing features?' asked the man.

'Yes,' said Beth. 'He has a large birthmark on the back of his left leg, his thigh. A port wine mark.'

'But otherwise…'

'Just a normal, beautiful baby,' said Beth, dissolving into tears. The policewoman consoled her while the policeman inspected the lock to the door.

'Did you not lock this door when you say you popped out, Mr Whitehead?'

'Yes, I did. I thought I did.'

'It doesn't appear damaged in any way. Who else has a key to this lock?'

'No one.' He thought for a moment. 'No, no one at all.'

'No? Well, someone must have, otherwise how would they have opened it?'

'I, er…'

'Unless you went out without locking it.'

Kris glanced at Beth and saw the realisation hitting her. She shot to the feet. 'You didn't lock the door,' she screamed. Beth leapt towards him. 'You idiot, you stupid, stupid…' Kris covered his head with his hands as Beth slapped him around his head.

The woman pulled Beth back. 'Stop, stop this. You need to calm yourself, Mrs Whitehead.'

'You went out and you forgot to lock the fucking door,' she screamed, her nostrils flaring. 'I don't believe this. How could you be so stupid?'

'I thought I had.'

'But you didn't, did you?'

'OK, Mrs Whitehead,' said the policewoman. 'Please sit down. This is not getting us anywhere.'

Beth sat, looking exhausted. 'What do we do now?'

'We'll get a description out asap,' said the man. 'And we'll put the wheels into motion, as in check CCTV–'

'There're no cameras on the canal.'

'Yes, but if the perpetrator walked along the streets, I mean, it's worth a shot.' He turned to his colleague. 'OK, we'll get going.' He handed Kris a business card. 'Let us know if you think of anything else.'

'I'll see you out,' said Kris.

'No need–'

'No, really.'

The policeman shrugged. The woman, turning to Beth, said, 'I can't imagine what you must be going through, Beth, but we promise you we will do everything in our power to bring your baby back to you.'

Beth nodded, unable to speak.

Kris accompanied the officers off the boat.

'Is there something else, Mr Whitehead?' asked the man.

How did he know? 'Actually, yes. I didn't want to say this in front of the wife but I've got an idea who might have done this.'

'Oh?'

'If I tell you his name, you won't tell him I told you.'

'Rest assured, sir.'

Kris glanced up and down the towpath. A fine mist had fallen, hanging low, giving the canal a rather sinister feel. 'His name is Alan Milner.' He gave the police officers Milner's address.

'And why do you suspect this Alan Milner?' asked the woman.

'He, erm, he once talked about kidnapping a girl, not a baby, a teenager, and holding her to ransom.'

'Oh? That's serious. Did he have a particular girl in mind?'

'No. It was just an idea. He never went through with it. But I just thought, I don't know, maybe…'

'It's fine. We'll look into it. Thanks for that. Anything else before we go?'

'No.'

'OK. Thanks.'

They started to walk off through the gloom.

'Oh…' They stopped. 'You might want to ask him about that mini supermarket robbery the other day.'

The policeman stepped back towards him. 'And why would you say that, sir?'

'Nothing. No reason. Just a hunch, that's all. Please, find my son. Whatever you do, just find him.'

Kris returned to the barge, bracing himself for the torrent of abuse he knew was coming his way. Instead, he found Beth clutching her stomach. 'Oh shit, no.'

'You alright, Beth? What's the matter?'

She staggered to a chair. 'Oh God. Please no.'

'Beth?'

'Nothing. It's nothing.' Doubled over, still clutching her stomach, she hobbled to the bathroom.

Chapter 14: Ian / Kris

Ian slept on the settee that night. His alarm rang at its usual time of seven a.m. and it took a moment for Ian to remember why he was on the settee. He jumped up, remembering that there was a baby upstairs. He'd done it, he'd stolen a baby. He knew it was only the start but he'd face each hurdle as it came. Right now, he just needed to make sure Juliet was OK. He crept into the bedroom and found Juliet awake with the baby on her chest. She smiled at him.

'How did you sleep?'

'Fine. He's been asleep for over four hours now. Tell me again, how come your friend asked you to look after Felix?'

He told her, rehashing his story about Adrian's wife needing emergency medical assistance and, in a panic, asking Ian to help. 'It won't be for long,' he said. 'Just until she gets better. And then, we'll return him.'

Juliet looked down at the baby. 'What a shame,' she said. 'I shall miss him. I've got used to him being around already. What's his surname?'

'Surname? Oh, erm, King. That's it, King.'

'Felix King,' said Juliet, stroking his cheek. 'It has a certain ring to it. I like it. Felix and Toby. Toby and Felix.'

'Do you think you should change his nappy?'

'We only have newborn nappies. He's too big for those.'

'I'll go out and buy some. Anything else?'

'I think we've got everything, haven't we, Felix?'

It was true, they'd accumulated everything they thought they might need even though they knew Toby's chances of survival weren't good. They had clothing, rash cream, a cot and mattress, a Moses basket, a baby monitor, dummies, muslin squares, bibs, feeding bottles and teats, a changing mat, wipes, barrier cream, baby grows, even a baby bath and numerous other things a newborn baby needed. They'd been prepared. Ian had been gearing up to sell it or donate it to a charity shop but hadn't got around to it. He knew it'd upset Juliet had he done it too soon while at the same knowing she could be upset if she saw it all. He had been thinking of storing it all in the loft just in case they needed it at any point in the future.

Half an hour later, having bought the tiny nappies, Ian was about to leave for work. Juliet came downstairs with Felix. 'He's awake,' she said. 'Do you want to hold him?'

'Yes.' Juliet passed him the baby and Ian sat down on the settee holding Felix and marvelling at his beauty. Felix King. How were they going to register him? How were they going to get his medical records? In trying to make Juliet happy, he'd given himself a whole slew of headaches.

'I'd better change his nappy,' said Juliet. Ian passed him back, reluctant to let him go so soon.

Just as Julie made a start, the doorbell rang. Ian stiffened. 'Who could that be at this time of the morning?' asked Julie.

Surely, thought Ian, it couldn't be the police already – how could they possibly know? He felt his bowels loosen. There was no getting out of this.

The doorbell rang a second time.

'Aren't you going to answer it?'

His legs felt like lead. He answered the door and was equally shocked to see Alan Milner there. 'Christ, it's you. Jesus.'

'Nice to see you too, mate.'

'What do you want?'

'Can I come in for a mo?'

'No.'

'It won't take long.' Alan barged past him and stepped into the living room. 'Oh, Juliet, hello, didn't expect to... Oh, you've had your baby.'

Juliet laughed. 'No–'

'What is it you want, Alan?'

Alan stepped towards Juliet. Juliet was about to remove Felix's baby grow and Ian knew he had to stop Alan from seeing that birthmark. Had he seen Harry's birthmark? He couldn't be sure. 'What's his name?' asked Alan, peering at the baby. 'I'm guessing it's a boy on account of that blue thing.'

'Felix,' said Juliet, unbuttoning the baby grow. 'Ian's friend–'

'Juliet, maybe wait a second. We don't want to shock Alan with the contents of Felix's nappy.'

'Don't mind me.'

'No, but I do. Even a baby should have privacy.'

Alan laughed. 'If you say so, mate.'

'Shall we step outside a minute?'

'If you want. Nice seeing you again, Juliet.'

Ian led Alan outdoors. It was a grim, cold day, the sky a blanket of grey. 'What do you want then?' he asked for the third time.

'I've got another job. Nice easy one this time.'

'No.'

'You haven't heard what it is yet.'

'And I'm not interested.'

'It's good money.'

Ian sighed. 'Look, Alan, I can't, right? Not now I'm a family man. I've gotta keep straight. It's too risky.'

Alan considered him. 'You know, I get that. That's the problem with kids, well, babies. Makes a man go soft. It's your choice. You'll be missing out but I have to respect that.'

'Cheers.'

'You've got a week if you change your mind.'

'Fine. But I won't.'

'Alright then. If you're sure. See you around, mate.'

Ian watched Alan saunter off. Returning indoors, he batted away Juliet's questions about what Alan wanted. Wanting to change the subject, he laughed at how someone so small could make such a stink.

*

Kris woke up and was hit by the pain of remembering that his life had turned to shit. Beth wasn't in bed. She wasn't in the kitchen. Dan was in his room sitting on his bed. He'd been crying. 'Where's Mum?'

Dan shrugged; he didn't know.

Kris returned to the kitchen, his head thumping as if he had a hangover. He tried Beth's mobile but received no reply. He was tempted to go see Alan himself but he knew it'd be better if he left it to the police. With any luck, they would have arrested him by now. But if they asked him about the supermarket job, that could land Ian in trouble. He had to warn him. Ian had saved his bacon with that kidnapping malarky. He owed the man.

Beth returned to the boat, her face a mess with snot and tears. 'Where have you been?'

'Doing the police's job for them and asking all the neighbours.'

'Asking them what?'

'Whether they saw anything.'

'And did they?'

'No, nothing.' She strode up to him. 'I shall never forgive you for this, Kris. To think you left our baby on the boat unsupervised to go out for a bloody walk. What were you thinking of?'

'I'm so–'

'Don't. I don't want to hear it. All I know is that my baby's gone. Nothing else matters.' She collapsed into tears. Kris tried to put his arms around her but she fought him off, batting his arms away. 'Don't touch me,' she screamed.

Dan chose that moment to wander in. 'And you,' shouted Beth. 'You *must* have heard something?'

'I didn't, Mum. Honest. I was–'

'God, you're as useless as each other.'

'It's not my fault,' said Dan, the tears streaming down his face. 'It's not my fault.'

'Get out of my sight, go on, both of you. I can't bear to look at you. My baby's gone and I just want him back. Leave me alone, just… just leave me alone.'

Chapter 15: Ian

Ian was walking to work, knowing he'd done the right thing by Juliet. They'd been married five years already and he loved her for sure despite his occasional failings. He only wanted to make her happy. Seeing her distraught in hospital broke his heart. He knew then that he would do anything to ease her pain. Beth, on the other hand, was not a good mother – he'd seen it with his own eyes.

He was about to go to work when he heard footsteps behind him. Turning around, his heart went into freefall on seeing Kris. His first instinct was to run but it was already too late; Kris had him in his sights. He braced himself for the torrent of abuse. Instead, Kris greeted him with half a smile. 'I was hoping to catch you. I tried ringing you but your mobile's off.'

'Is there anything wrong?'

Kris stopped in front of him. 'Yeah, you could say that. A lot's wrong, as it happens. Some bastard has taken Harry.'

'Harry? What do you mean taken?'

'As in stolen or kidnapped, I don't know.'

Ian stepped back, hoping he was showing the right amount of shock. 'You're joking. Bloody hell, Kris.'

'We'll get him back, I know we will, but Beth's beside herself as you can imagine. So am I.'

'Don't blame you but…'

'The police are on it and I reckon I know who's done it.'

'What… who?

Kris looked around, making sure no one was within earshot. 'That sodding Alan.'

Ian felt a surge of relief. 'Why do you think that?'

'Well, it's obvious, isn't it? He wanted to kidnap that girl, and Christ, Ian, we almost did. If he's capable of that, the man's capable of anything.'

'Hell.'

Ian heard his name. It was Manish, greeting him with a smile that couldn't hide his anxiousness. Ian hadn't properly spoken to him since the day he saw Manish with all that cash on his desk. 'I'll be in in a minute.'

'No hurry. See you in a bit.'

'My boss,' said Ian to Kris. *My hand-in-the-till, thieving boss.* 'Did you tell the police?'

'About Alan? I sort of hinted at it, yes. But see, this is why I needed to see you, to warn you, like. That morning we almost nabbed that girl, I know nothing happened–'

'Apart from the fact I stole a van.'

'Yeah, but we left it there, didn't we? The owner would have got it back within a few hours. So, the police will ask him about his plan and cos nothing happened, they'll have nothing to go on, so they'll let him go. I need them to keep him and grill him, get him to crack. So, er, I mentioned the supermarket.'

'You what? Oh, shit.'

'I know. I'm sorry, mate, but I've got to think of Harry first.' He paused. 'I don't understand. Why would someone steal my baby? It doesn't make sense. You should see the state of Beth. Who'd do such a thing?'

Ian tried to make a sympathetic noise but all he could think about was that Kris had dropped him in the shit. 'What did you say about the robbery?'

'Nothing much. I just told them they should look into it. I'm sorry, mate. But look, all you need to do is find yourself a solid alibi and you'll be sorted.'

'Yeah, right. As easy as that.'

'But it has to be solid, so being at home watching the telly with the wife won't be enough.'

'I could say I was with you.'

'No, no way. I can't, mate. I've got enough shit going on in my head.'

Ian understood.

'I'd better get back to Beth. I just wanted to warn you.'

'Thanks. I appreciate it. Good luck with… you know.'

'We will get him back, you know. I know it.' He hit himself on the chest. 'I can *feel* it in here. And we'll get the bastard who did it.'

*

Ian's working day passed slowly. He found it difficult to concentrate. Soon after ten, Beth rang him. 'I thought you'd want to know, Ian,' she said. 'I–'

'I know. I saw Kris. I'm so sorry, Beth. If there's anything–'

'I lost the baby.'

'You what?'

'You heard. You're off the hook.'

He wasn't sure how to respond given her mental state but luckily he didn't have to – she rang off.

Come eleven o'clock, Manish asked to see him in his office. Manish closed the door behind him. He called it an office but frankly, it was little more than a broom cupboard, no ventilation, bare walls, a small desk with his computer on it, a single framed photo of his wife on his desk.

Manish ran his fingers through his hair. 'Look, Ian…'

'Yes?'

'This isn't easy. You can probably guess what this is about.'

Ian liked Manish so he resisted the temptation to lay into him about being a thief. 'About that memo you sent about us needing to be careful when using the till?'

Manish couldn't look at him. 'Yes, that. Look, it won't happen again. I promise you. I've been worried sick. I've learnt my lesson.'

'I won't say a thing.'

Manish's mouth dropped. 'You won't?'

'Nah. No one will hear it from me, mate.'

Manish let out a huge sigh of relief. 'Jeez, thanks, Ian. Thanks so much. I've been so worried I've not slept. Like I said–'

'But I need a favour in return.'

Manish hesitated, fearing, perhaps, that he was about to walk into a trap. 'What sort of favour?'

'Where were you on Wednesday night?'

'Wednesday night? I don't know. At home, I guess.'

'With your wife and kids?'

'Of course.'

'What were you doing?'

'I don't know. I can't remember.'

'Think.'

'Wednesday? Erm, oh yeah, I was watching the footie.'

'Good, good. So was I. I was with you. You invited me around and we watched it together.'

'We did?'

'We did. If anyone asks, and I mean *anyone*, as in the police, that's what we were doing.'

Manish looked distinctly uncomfortable. 'I'm not sure about this, Ian.'

'You want to keep your job, don't you? Cos if management find out, they'll bring in the police. You know that, don't you? No job, police record, no references. You'll be fucked.'

Manish considered him. Ian could see him thinking this through. 'You better know what happened then.'

'What?'

'Manchester City were at home to Liverpool. A bit of a dull game in the end. Man City won one-nil. Darius Vassell scored a penalty in the seventieth minute. We drank a few cans of Stella and shared a pepperoni pizza. That do you?'

'I arrived just before kick-off and afterwards, I stayed for a while and we talked about football and work. I left around eleven. I walked home.'

'Around eleven. OK. Can I ask why?'

'No.'

Manish thought about this.

'You'll need to get your wife on board. Maybe your kids, depending on what time they go to bed.'

'I can do that.'

'Good, so a favour for a favour.'

'Yeah. A favour for a favour.'

*

Ian returned home to find Juliet kneeling on the floor playing with Felix. She'd erected a baby play station with lots of brightly coloured mobiles hanging off it. Felix, delighted by this, was giggling. It was, thought Ian, a heartwarming sight. He kissed Juliet. 'Doesn't Felix get a kiss?' she asked.

'Of course he does.'

'Oh, Ian, he's lovely. Can't we keep him forever?'

'I wish,' he said. He wanted to say that that was the idea but he couldn't, not yet. It was too soon. He needed her to be so bonded with the baby that the thought of losing him would break her heart. He knew it wouldn't take long.

Part Two

June 2023

Chapter 16: Alan
2023

Alan Milner exited Pentonville prison via the main entrance without a backward glance and walked briskly up Caledonian Road, his small suitcase in hand, his mind blank. He knew he had to catch the tube to get back to his mother's place but, after eighteen years inside, he'd forgotten where the underground station was. He'd been walking a good five minutes when he allowed the emotion of being free to catch up with his brain and stopped.

He found himself opposite a small park called Market Road Gardens. Slowing up, he wandered in and found a vacant bench. He sat and, crossing his legs, allowed himself to catch his breath. The sun was shining although a brisk breeze kept the temperature down. He gazed at his surroundings – joggers, mums with pushchairs, a child with an ice cream and of course lots of dog walkers. He smiled and realised he hadn't smiled for a long time. This was freedom. He had expected to be overcome with joy but in truth, he found it all rather underwhelming. He looked at all the boring people doing their boring things and resented them all.

Alan knew he had a difficult road ahead of him, that he was having to start from zero and slowly build his life up again. In fact, he wasn't even at zero, he was starting several places behind because he had a criminal record. No one would ever give him a job but it didn't matter; he had other means. It's amazing what sort of contacts you gather inside. There was always someone on the outside looking for help in some form or other, a bit of muscle here, an accessory there.

He'd stay with his mother. She wouldn't like it but tough. He wasn't going to give the old sow the option. It wasn't as if he could afford rent. The probation services said they'd helped but on account he told his probation to fuck off several times, he didn't fancy his chances. As it is, they had to give him his discharge grant, a travel warrant and a small amount of money to help with immediate living expenses.

In the distance, he spied a man and boy attempting to fly a kite. He remembered doing that once with his old man; about the only happy memory he had of the old bastard, the only time he remembered the man sober. The man was a waste of space who'd drunk himself into an early grave. Oh, how his mother and he lauded that day! Got riddance to old rubbish, as the saying went.

'Can you take a photo of us?'

'What?'

Two young girls, about fifteen or so, stood before him, one black, one white, the white girl offering her phone. 'Please.'

He took the girl's phone. 'What is this?'

They looked as if they didn't understand the question.

'You what?'

'What sort of phone is this?'

'It's an iPhone, mate.'

'Oh? I've heard of these.'

'Actually, it don't matter.' Before he had a chance to look at this strange, new device, the girl had snatched it back. They walked off, arms linked, calling him a weirdo.

Alan had been inside for eighteen whole years. He knew he'd missed out on a lot of things. The iPhone hadn't been invented back then. He'd never seen one – until today. Back then, anyone who was anyone had a Blackberry.

He felt the first spots of rain. Time, he decided, to make his way home.

*

'Oh, God, you're back.'

'Hello, Mother, lovely to see you too.' She looked frightened of him, and so she should.

'You don't expect–'

He pushed past her. 'I do actually, yes.' He walked into the living room. Nothing had changed; it was still exactly the same as when he last saw it – the scuffed black leather three-piece suite, the claustrophobic flowery wallpaper, the swirly-patterned carpet, her display of decorative thimbles, a tiny television in the corner, and all so dingy and stinking of fag smoke. It was, he thought, as horrible as he remembered it. Next to the window were a few piles of old newspapers bound by string.

'You didn't say you were coming.'

'Didn't you get my card?' he lied. 'Put the kettle on, would you?'

'You can't stay here.'

'You've got a spare bedroom–'

'I use it for storage.'

He went upstairs to the bedroom, and sure enough, he could barely push the door open. 'Christ, what have you got in here?' he called down. The room was stacked floor to ceiling with cardboard boxes, so much so, he had difficulty seeing the bed. Returning downstairs, he said, 'It's disgusting. I'm not hearing the kettle.'

His mother swore but, doing as she was told, went through to the tiny kitchen.

'And make it strong. Not like the stuff we had inside. I'm desperate for a proper cuppa. Two sugars, in case you forgot.'

He sat in one of the squashy settees and wrinkled his nose. Old woman smell. Horrible.

She came through with a mug of hot tea. He took it without thanks.

'You can't stay here, Alan,' she repeated, looking terrified of him.

'You think I want to stay in this shithole? I don't have no choice.'

'Didn't your probation–'

'No. They're as useless as Anne Frank's drum kit. Hey, thanks for visiting me inside all those times. I really appreciated it. You know, made me feel loved and not forgotten.'

She looked away. She hadn't been once, not a letter, not even a Christmas card.

'What are you going to do now?'

'Now? I'm gonna drink this tea while you beat a pathway to my bed, Mother. Nice tea, by the way,' he added, lifting his mug.

'Me? You can't expect me to lug all that stuff around.'

'You put it in there, you can bleeding well take it out.'

'Alan, please, I'm not as young as I was and my hands are ever so arthritic now.'

'Stop your bleating and get on with it, will you?' His mother always had the propensity for self-pity, it was, perhaps, her most annoying trait. His father never had any truck with it and that, at least, was one thing they agreed upon.

'What I mean is what you're going to do now that you're out?'

He drank his tea and sighed. 'I've got a few people I want to see. I've got a few old scores to settle…'

Chapter 17: Alan

Mid-evening and the sun had finally melted away for the day. Alan was wandering down the middle of Caversham Avenue, one of Highgate's most salubrious streets, eating his way through a pack of cheese and onion crisps. He was avoiding the pavements, didn't want to be caught on any of those new doorbell cameras he'd heard about.

One could almost smell the money here. He paused to admire the occasional car parked up in the driveways, nice cars all of them. Gorgeous houses too. Imagine being brought up here, he thought, being born with a silver spoon in your mouth, never having to worry about money, always having Daddy to call on whenever you ran out of your Saville Row suits or cocaine. How the other half live.

Finishing his crisps, Alan dropped the packet. He saw an elderly woman walking towards him with two miniature poodles on leads. She had money written all over her but even Alan Milner wouldn't stoop to mugging an old woman on the street. 'Are you going to pick that up?' she snapped at him.

'You what?'

'Your litter. I saw you drop it. Pick it up this instant.'

She didn't realise who she was talking to. If she did, she wouldn't dare. But still, he retreated a few steps and picked up his litter.

'That's better,' she said, as one of her mutts sniffed at his trouser leg. 'There's a bin on the corner. You can dispose of it there.'

'Yes, Ma'am.' He almost bowed. Silly old bat.

Alan needed money. The pittance that the probation people had given him was nowhere near enough. At first, he thought he might be OK until he started living in the free world and realised just how much everything cost these days. He was going to start smoking again until he clocked how much a packet of twenty would put him back. He needed one of these new smartphones and he needed a car, even an old banger. He knew a bit about cars, knew how to patch an engine up so it didn't have to be anything special. As long as it worked and as long as it was a bargain. These were his priorities. But what hope did he have of obtaining money at short notice? His probation guy, a weedy ginger wimp, had said he'd help Alan apply for some jobs, help him build up a CV. Like hell. He hadn't done an honest day's work since he worked with his paedo uncle in Walthamstow market. No one in their right mind would employ him. Unless that is, he could get a job as a bouncer. He quite fancied that.

Anyway, that was all for the future. Right now, he needed cash straight away and he was convinced that with a bit of persuasion, someone on this millionaires' row would grant him a little charity.

He saw a car pulling out from a driveway about twenty yards ahead, a copper-coloured Bentley Continental GT.

Bloody nice cars those, cost a fortune. The man behind the wheel indicated right and eased away. Alan picked up his pace, keen to know which house he lived in. Number twelve, similar to its neighbours, a detached Georgian affair with two Doric columns on either side of the front door. He saw a woman appear at the window, closing the curtains, a middle-aged woman with red, bouffant hair. Now, this was perfect. He checked the coast was clear, then acting quickly, pulled on his balaclava and gloves and checked his rucksack for his claw hammer. He marched up to the door of number twelve and rang the bell and knocked loudly. A moment later, the woman he saw at the window answered. She tried to scream but he gripped her by the neck and slammed her against the hallway wall. Her eyes popped. 'Do as I say, and you won't get hurt. One squeak though and I won't hesitate. Do you understand?' She nodded through her tears.

He could see the kitchen at the end of the hallway. Yanking her by the hair, he dragged her through, her feet scuffing against the wooden floor. There was another woman in the kitchen, younger. He pointed at her. 'You, put your hands against that… that island or whatever you call it.'

She rushed to the island. 'Don't hurt us, please. Let my mother go.' She had a hint of an Irish accent.

The kitchen was huge, bigger than his mother's entire downstairs. And then he saw the ring binders on the island and the familiar logo – Greene Haulage. 'Christ, is your old man Niall Greene?'

The mother nodded.

He almost laughed. Addressing the daughter, he said, 'Is your name Amy?'

'Yes.'

'Oh my God.' He stopped himself from saying that he and

his mates almost kidnapped her eighteen years ago. Pushing the mother onto a wicker chair, he nabbed Amy by the wrist.

'Let go of me,' she yelled.

'Keep your mouth shut.'

Still holding her by the wrist, he slammed her hand onto the marble surface of the island before producing the hammer from his rucksack. He held it high as if about to bring it down on her hand.

'Don't hurt her,' screeched her mother. 'I beg you, please, anything, just–'

'Leave your phone here, Mrs Greene.'

The woman was shaking so much, she could barely stand but she took her phone and placed it on the island.

He glanced up at the kitchen clock. 'Right, Mrs Greene. I'll give you two minutes to find me any cash you have in the house, debit and credit cards and all your jewellery, and I mean *all* of it. Don't short-change me now. If you're not back in two minutes, I'll smash your daughter's hands to smithereens.'

She didn't move, just stared at him, the mascara running down her cheeks. He lifted the hammer. 'One minute, fifty.'

This time, she galvanised herself and rushed off. He could hear her rushing and tumbling up the stairs.

'Amy Greene,' said Alan. 'Who'd have thought it?'

'How do you know me?'

'Never you mind.'

'Why are you doing this?'

'Because you can afford it. I'm like Robin Hood, me. Steal from the rich to give to the poor. And I'm the poor. See it as an act of charity.'

'You don't deserve any fucking charity. You should be locked up, you maniac.'

'Ha! Funny you should say that.' He checked the clock. 'Thirty seconds, Mrs Greene.'

Amy tried to slap him with her free hand but Alan dodged and she missed. He waved the hammer in front of her as if reminding her of it. 'Do that again and I'll smash your knuckles.'

Seconds later, a flustered Mrs Green returned with a black wallet and a jewellery box. 'That's all the cash we've got at the moment. Please, *please*, let her go.'

'How much is there?'

'I didn't c-count it but it must be about three hundred. But the jewellery, it's worth… I d-don't know but a lot, I imagine.'

'Fine. You see, it wasn't that difficult.' He let Amy go. She ran to her mother, the two sobbing women hugging each other. He winked at them. 'Nice to see you again, Amy. I'll see myself out, no need to trouble yourself.' Before he left, he swung his hammer and smashed Mrs Greene's smartphone. 'Good day to you both.'

Chapter 18: Benedict

Detective Inspector Benedict Paige was at home watching a Korean crime drama on Netflix. His wife, Sonia, came down from upstairs. 'Don't forget it's Abigail and Tom's party Saturday night,' she said.

Benedict tried to stifle the groan. 'Oh yes, of course,' he said as breezily as he could manage.

'You'd forgotten, hadn't you?'

'No, no, I'm looking forward to it. So, are they, er…'

'Yes?'

'Still together.'

'Yes.' Benedict sensed her impatience. 'You know this, Ben. They've had counselling and they're trying to make a go of it. This party is part of that process so it's important that we're there for them.'

For them? thought Benedict. It made it sound as if they were the best of friends although, to be fair, Sonia was certainly friendly enough with Abigail.

'Try and show a little more enthusiasm, Ben.'

'No, really, I am looking forward to it.'

Sonia shook her head in exasperation.

Benedict received a call on his mobile from his detective sergeant. 'Jessica, how can I help?'

'We've got orders to go to the scene of a house robbery, boss. Mum and adult daughter at home earlier this evening when this fella barges in, scares the living daylights out of them, steals cash and jewellery and leaves them in a right state. I'll message you over the address. I'm on my way now.'

'OK, thanks, DS Gardiner. See you shortly.'

'Oh, you're not,' said Sonia.

'Sorry, love. Duty calls. What can I do?'

'Get a normal job perhaps?'

'At my age? Huh. Fat chance.'

'Go on then. Be off with you.'

Benedict drove the three miles from his house to Cavendish Avenue, a road known locally as Millionaires' Row. The houses here were certainly impressive and all worth an absolute fortune, even for such a wealthy area as Highgate. Highgate Cemetery, where Karl Marx was buried, was just a stone's throw away. He approached number twelve and rang the bell. The door was answered by a young policewoman he only vaguely recognised. 'DS Gardiner is waiting for you, sir. She's making the family a round of tea.'

Indeed, Benedict found Jessica passing around the cups of tea. 'Ah,' she said. 'This is my boss, DI Paige. Boss, this is Mr and Mrs Greene and their daughter, Amy.'

Benedict shook their hands and, on being invited, took a seat in an armchair opposite the family. Mrs Greene had been crying. Her daughter held her hand. Mr Greene sat jiggling his leg, his phone in his hand which he kept glancing at.

'Firstly, I'm very sorry to hear about your ordeal. It

must've been horrific.'

'All very well,' said Mr Greene. 'But the question is will you find the bastard who did this?'

'We will certainly endeavour to do that, sir. I know this is going to be difficult but can one of you tell me what exactly happened?'

'I wasn't here,' snapped Mr Greene. 'I'd gone out. I reckon he saw me because by all accounts it happened within a minute or two of me driving off. I reckoned we were targeted.'

'Who, apart from your family, knew you were going out, sir?' asked Benedict.

'Erm, well, no one. Apart from the person I was meeting and I've known him for years so you can count him out. The man was Amy's godfather.'

'OK, you drove off in your car, Mr Greene, then what happened?'

Mrs Greene cleared her throat. 'You tell him, Amy.'

Amy, a woman in her late thirties, Benedict reckoned, had near-black hair which she wore long. 'Yeah, Dadda had just left when we heard the rather urgent knock on the door. We thought Dadda must've forgotten something and couldn't find his key. Mum answered it.'

Mrs Greene took up the story, describing how she opened the door to a bulky man dressed in a grey hoodie, black gloves and a balaclava. He pinned her to the hallway wall by her neck before dragging her through to the kitchen.

'Did you notice a logo or any writing on the hoodie, Mrs Greene?'

'I did,' said Amy. 'It was a Lacoste.'

'That's good to know,' said Benedict. 'Can we go through to the kitchen?'

It was a large Shaker-styled space, everything gleaming, a large, marble-topped island dominating the space. Amy described how the man held her hand by the wrist, forcing it onto the island top, and threatened to break her fingers with his hammer if her mother didn't hand over whatever cash was in the house and all her jewellery. She had difficulty finishing the story, such was her upset. Jessica got her a glass of water.

'Would you remember exactly what he took?' asked Jessica gently. 'We'll need as accurate an itinerary as possible.'

'Oh yes,' said Mrs Greene. 'I took snaps of all my jewellery a few years ago for insurance purposes. I never thought I'd need to act on it.'

'He also took Mum's credit cards,' said Amy. 'We cancelled them straight away.'

'Good' said Benedict. 'We'll take the details. If he uses one, we might catch him out.'

'Don't forget the cash he stole,' said Mr Greene.

'How much are we talking about?' asked Benedict.

'About three hundred,' said Mrs Greene.

'Three hundred and thirty, to be precise,' said Mr Greene.

'So,' said Benedict. 'I assume you have no idea what he looks like.'

'No,' said Mrs Greene. 'I'm so sorry.' She looked close to tears again.

'Hey, no,' said Jessica. 'Don't apologise. You have nothing to apologise about.'

'He knew us though,' said Amy.

'Of course he did,' said Mr Greene, pacing the kitchen. 'That's why he targeted us.'

'No, Dadda, I told you, I don't think so.'

'Why do you say that, Amy?' asked Jessica.

'Because at one point, he said, "Christ, is your old man Niall Greene?" as if he knew Dad but it was a surprise, a coincidence.'

'I am quite famous in these parts,' said Mr Greene.

'And then he said my name as if it rang a bell,' said Amy.

'What do you mean?' asked Jessica.

'He said, "Amy Greene, who'd have thought it?" I asked him whether he knew me and he said, "Never you mind".'

'Interesting,' said Benedict. 'It does sound like he recognised you.'

'You didn't recognise his voice?' asked Jessica.

'No.'

'What sort of accent was it?'

'Proper London. East End, you know?'

'Cockney?'

'No, not quite Cockney but a hard London accent. There's something else. I think he may have recently been released from prison.'

'Really?' said Jessica. 'Why would you think that, Amy?'

'I said he should be locked up–'

'Very brave of you.'

'I know. I can't believe I said it but I was so angry.'

'And what did he say?'

'He laughed and said, "Funny you should say that".'

'Funny you should say that?' said Benedict. 'Did he finish the sentence?'

Amy shook her head.

'Still, that's good to know. We'll check that out. We'll also be checking your doorbell CCTV and asking your neighbours for theirs too. I doubt he walked down the street still wearing his balaclava so hopefully, we'll catch sight of him.'

'We'll also check with local jewellers,' said Jessica. 'And

pawnbrokers–'

'Huh,' said Mr Greene. 'He probably stole it to order and is shifting it through the dark web as we speak, or something.'

'Things we'll be checking, Mr Greene,' said Benedict.

Benedict thanked the Greenes for their time and promised to keep them updated on any progress.

Chapter 19: Daniel

Daniel Whitehead stood at the door of his flat, checking his pockets, making sure he had everything.

'I know this is important to you,' said Helene, his Danish girlfriend. 'But you will keep your phone on, won't you?'

'Of course I will.'

'I mean, I won't phone unless…'

'I know, babes. But if you have to, you have to. It's fine.'

'You won't mind?'

'I said, it's fine.' She looked so vulnerable standing there, her hands supporting the weight of her belly. 'Come here.' He engulfed her in a hug.

'I just want it over now,' said Helene.

'I know.'

'I feel like I've been pregnant for half my life.'

'It'll soon be over.'

'Equally as terrifying.'

'I know.' He kissed her on the side of her head.

'Good luck today. How are you feeling?'

He sighed. 'It'll be fine. Don't worry.'

Helene smiled. She knew he was putting a brave face on it and that he was dreading it.

'How do I look?' he asked.

'Like a man about to be led to the gallows. Apart from that, you look fine, very handsome.' She stroked his hair.

'Thanks.' He checked the time on his phone. 'I'd better go. Don't want to be late for my first session.'

'I'll be thinking of you.'

He kissed her again. 'I'll see you about half six.'

'I'll have dinner ready.'

*

Thomas Herreboudt worked from the second floor in an Edwardian townhouse in Hampstead. He'd welcomed Daniel in with a hearty handshake. He'd arranged the two armchairs so that they were angled and not directly opposite each other. Daniel liked it, the place felt comforting, everything was immaculate and clean. The walls were painted a soothing dull green colour, a couple of landscape paintings, and a few framed certificates proclaiming Mr Herreboudt's credentials and several potted plants. There was, he thought, a distinctly Scandinavian feel to it. Helene would love it.

Mr Herreboudt invited Daniel to sit down and then spent a good five minutes explaining how this and future sessions would work. He was, Daniel guessed, in his mid-forties with sleek almost grey hair, smooth skin, a green jacket and a loose tie – just the right side of smart-casual, professional but not intimidating. 'So, to you, Daniel… Do you mind if I call you Daniel?'

'No, no, that's fine.'

'And you must call me Thomas. We don't want to stand on ceremony here. So, tell me, Daniel, what do you hope to get out of these sessions?'

Daniel had expected this question and indeed had prepared an answer but now, sitting here in this comfortable chair, he found it surprisingly difficult to express himself. 'I suppose to try and make sense of what happened that night. I know that's probably not specific enough–'

'No, that's OK, I get that, and it's a good place to start. Now, I know you told me over the phone what happened, but would you mind telling me again, from the start?'

'OK.'

'I want you, if you can, to describe what happened in as much detail as you can face. For now, just focus on the night in question. If at any point, it becomes too difficult, then you must stop. You're under no obligation to tell me everything in one sitting. Then, once we've established what happened, we can go back through step by step and tease it all out. We can explore further back, for example, your upbringing and your relationship with your parents, both before and after, their relationship with your brother and their relationship with each other. But let's begin, as I say, with the night in question. So, as a starting point, are you comfortable with that?'

'Yes.'

'Good. Sounds like a plan. But first, a specific question… How old were you at the time?'

'Ten.'

'And how old are you now?'

'Twenty-eight.'

'So, why now, Daniel?'

'Oh. Erm, because…'

'Because?'

'I suppose because my girlfriend is expecting a baby. It's

due any moment. I know I'm a bit young to be a dad but it just happened and we're good together, Helene and me. It was an accident but we never once thought about, you know, *not* having it. So, as I'm about to become a parent, it's made me think more about my parents and how they brought me up and how they treated me after it happened.'

'OK, perfectly understandable. So, the night in question. Take me through it as best as you can. We have the best part of an hour. Help yourself to water.'

Daniel noticed the box of tissues. He'd be needing a few at some point, he was sure.

'OK, Daniel, whenever you're ready...'

Daniel swallowed. He'd been waiting for this. He'd thought about it a lot over the years; hardly a day passed when he didn't relay the incidents of that night and the subsequent fallout and he had talked about it with Helene but only in snatches. He'd never spoken about it in a logical sequence, had never had the strength to do so.

'We lived on a barge at the time. To be honest, there's not much to say but...'

And so Daniel began. He described the day Harry was born, or 'Prince Harry' as his parents often called him. How cramped it was on the barge with the four of them, and how surprised he was that one so small should take up so much space in their lives, so much living space and emotional space. But his mother changed after Harry came along. He hadn't been planned, after all, Daniel was already ten and Harry wasn't meant to be. His mother had a difficult pregnancy and now, looking back on it, she probably suffered post-natal depression. Had she ever really bonded with the baby? It was a question he'd asked himself many times since Helene became pregnant.

'So, that night, back in April 2005, Mum went out. Dad wasn't keen, in fact, he was really hostile about it. Looking back on it, he was rather controlling.'

'We can come back to that. But that night, your mother did go out.'

'Yes. She was meeting a friend at a pub in King's Cross, not far from where we were moored on the canal. Dad said she had to be back by ten or half ten. They argued about it. I went to bed at my usual time. But I couldn't sleep and I could hear Dad watching TV. Around ten thirty-ish, I heard him go out.'

'As in leave the boat?'

'Yes.'

'Did he tell you he was going out?'

'Yeah, he said he was going to meet Mum from the pub but I know he didn't. Afterwards, he told Mum he went out for a quick walk but it felt like ages at the time.'

'How did you feel about it?'

Daniel stared out of the window, his memory taking him back to that moment when he heard his father closing the barge door behind him. 'I didn't like it at all.'

'You didn't say anything?'

Daniel shook his head. 'I wish I had. So, now I was wide awake. I knew I wouldn't get back to sleep until Mum and Dad were back. I was frightened, I mean, I really was. And then…' OK, he thought, compose yourself, deep breaths, deep breaths. 'I heard a knock. I thought perhaps Dad had forgotten his key or something. But the thing is, it wasn't him…'

'You know this?'

'Hmm. Whoever it was, came inside. His… his footsteps were different. It wasn't Dad. There was a…'

'Go on, Daniel, you're doing fine.'

Daniel puffed out his cheeks. 'There was a stranger on the boat. And, Christ, I was petrified. I was ten but I thought I was going to wet myself. I hated him for putting me in that situation.'

'The stranger or your father?'

'Actually, both of them but I mean my dad. I never forgave him. I still haven't. I heard this… this person creep into Harry's room and a few seconds later, I heard him creep out. And then I heard him leave. And I was so relieved. But, and here's the thing, I never thought for a second he was stealing the baby. It never occurred to me. I was just a kid, I never thought people would do stuff like that.'

'It must have been awful for you.'

Daniel had to stifle a laugh at the man's understatement. His fingers gripped his thigh. 'You could say that. Everything changed in that moment. My life changed to shit. I never saw my brother again.'

Chapter 20: Alan

The first person Alan Milner decided to visit now that he was a free man was his girlfriend, Lana. Not that she was his girlfriend on account she only visited him in prison once, and that was when he was on remand before his case came to trial. And that was to tell him she wasn't his girlfriend any more. He swore at her and called her a few choice names while she calmly stood, gathered her handbag and with a satisfied smirk, walked out on him. Alan didn't like people turning their backs on him, it showed a lack of respect. So, he was going to call on her, demand an apology and demand recompense. She'll say it was eighteen years ago but people on the outside don't experience time as someone inside does. For a prisoner, something that happened years back can still feel as if it happened yesterday.

He called on Lana's now elderly mother. It was obvious straight away she didn't recognise him, and that was good. 'Good morning, Mrs Kozlowski.'

'Who are you?' she barked at him from the doorstep.

'I'm looking for Lana. I owe her some money from a while

back and I want to pay her back but, you see, the thing is, I've lost her address. Silly of me, I know.' Alan knew how to turn the charm on when he needed to. 'I like to pay off my debts.'

'Should think so too. Wait here a minute.'

'No hurry, Mrs Kozlowski.'

And so, Alan had the address of his former girlfriend. She still lived in Camden, in a sixties flat in Kilburn. As it was, no one was in. Perhaps she was at work. He was just walking away, thinking he'd come back later when she opened her door.

'Lana!'

'Oh, Christ.' She went to close the door but Alan, as quick as a flash, wedged his foot in the door. 'Go away, Alan.'

'Just a few moments of your time, Lana. That's all I want.'

She relented. Alan walked through to her living room, a squalid little place, cluttered and unclean but still somehow nicer than his mother's hovel.

'When did you get out?' she asked. The years had been kind to Lana. She still had her wild red hair that refused to settle into any sort of style, she wore a denim skirt which she was now trying to tug down a little, and a tight white tee shirt that drew Alan short. OK, there was a bit of the 'mutton dressed as lamb' about her but he liked it.

'A couple of days ago. They let me out a couple of years early for good behaviour.'

'Good behaviour? You? Pull the other one.'

'I kept me nose clean. I was a good boy. They reckon I'm good enough now to be allowed back into society.'

'God help us.'

He laughed, despite himself. 'So, tell me, do you still keep in touch with your old mate, Juliet?'

She hesitated. 'No.' She was lying.

He stepped up to her. 'You look good, Lana. You've still got it, baby.' He lifted her chin with his fingers. She stood her ground although he could tell she was itching to step away from him. 'What's her address, Lana?'

'I told you, didn't I? I don't know, right?'

'Stop lying to me, Lana. You didn't visit me.'

'So?'

'Why was that? You're as bad as me old mum. Both of you happy to see me rot away in that place. No compassion.'

'Compassion? You talk about compassion. My God, I've heard it all now.'

He felt like slapping her. If she didn't start talking to him with a bit more respect, he'd bloody do so. 'So, it's been a long time, girl, and I don't mind saying, it's been a long, long time since I... you know. So, how about you see me right, hey?'

'Get out of here, Alan.'

'Come on now, for old time's sake.'

'What do you take me for?'

He slammed her against the wall, dislodging a picture which clattered to the floor. 'My mates always reckoned you'd be buried in a Y-shaped coffin, so don't come all prissy on me, darling.' His left hand cupped her breast. 'Come on, I'm gagging here. Eighteen years Lana, too long for any man.'

'Get off me, Alan,' she said, slapping his hand away. 'I've got a fella now.'

'Oh, have you now?' He loosened his grip. 'What difference does that make?'

'Please, Alan.'

'You know if I want to, I will.'

'Don't.' He could hear the catch in her voice. For all her bravado, she was scared of him. Good, he thought, let her be scared.

'And what's his name, this fella?'

'Never you mind.'

He swung his hand back, ready to slap the bitch.

'Mark. Right? His name is Mark. Happy now?'

'So, you've got yourself a fella. I'm only asking for a one-off, something to remember you by.'

'Get yourself a whore then.'

'That's why I'm asking you.' That stung, he could tell. 'Where is he then, this Mark?'

'He'll be back any minute. He's been at work. You know, doing a decent day's work for money. You ought to try it one day. You might even find it rewarding.'

He laughed again. 'You always made me laugh, Lana. I liked that about you. So, if Mark is working, what's he doing coming home this time of day?'

'He works shifts.'

'I'll sit down and wait for him then.' He sat and crossed his legs, scooping up a TV listings magazine from her coffee table.

'Suit yourself.'

'Meanwhile, I'm still waiting for that address. Ian and Juliet. Are they still together?'

He could see her mulling this over as she looked out through the side of the net curtain.

'Looking out for Mark?'

'Listen, if I tell you, will you leave? I'm mean for good and never come back.'

'You're upsetting me, Lana. But OK, deal.'

'You promise?'

'Am I not a man of my word?'

'Yeah, right.' She sat at the table, scrolling through her phone. She wrote the address down on the back of an envelope. 'Here you are,' she said, passing it to him. 'They live down in Kent. Near Sevenoaks.'

'Posh.'

'I wouldn't know. Not seen her in years.'

He pocketed the envelope. 'Thanks, darling. So, you see, it wasn't all that difficult.' He got up, ready to leave. 'That's all I wanted. Well, that and erm… Anyway, nice seeing you again, Lana babes. I'll see myself out.'

He went to open the front door when, hearing a key in the door, it opened ahead of him and there, before him, was a broad-shouldered, hard-looking bugger with a huge neck tattoo. 'You must be Mark,' said Alan.

'Who the fuck are you?'

'Just an old friend of Lana's.' He was aware of Lana behind him. He turned around. 'We've been catching up, haven't we, Lana?' he asked with a wink which, he knew, the man would have seen. 'We go back a long way, your girlfriend and me. A long, long way. Thanks for… everything, babes. It's been great. We must do it again sometime.' Turning to Mark, he said, 'Look after her.' And with that, he was gone.

Chapter 21: Benedict

Benedict set both his detective sergeants, DSs Andrew Prowse and Jamie Kelly, a task, namely to make a list of men recently released from Pentonville Prison. 'The problem is,' he said to Jessica, 'just because the robber implied he'd been inside, doesn't mean he's been recently released. It could have been years ago.'

'Yes, and he could have served his time anywhere, not necessarily Pentonville.'

The forensics team had gone to Greene's house on Cavendish Avenue with little expectation of finding anything of use. Uniformed officers were interviewing all the neighbours and asking to see their doorbell cameras. Here, at least, Benedict was feeling a little more hopeful. Meanwhile, PC Stevens was phoning around the local jewellers and pawnbrokers and sending them the scanned photos of Mrs Greene's jewellery.

As it was, Benedict didn't have to wait long for the first useful bit of information. Soon after midday, he received a phone call from a woman called Hilda Sykes who, she said, might be able to help the police with their investigation.

Mrs Sykes arrived at the station within the hour looking gleeful. She was much older than she sounded on the phone, a woman in her seventies, perhaps eighties, she wore a bright red cardigan and a silk green scarf. Sitting in Interview Room 1, Benedict took notes as she relayed her tale. 'So, you see, Inspector, I live three doors down from the Greenes. They've not long been there.'

'No?'

'No, no, they're new to the road. They only moved in twenty years ago.'

'Relative newcomers then?'

'Nice couple although…' She lowered her voice. '*He's* Irish, you know.'

'Right.'

'Amy Greene told me of their ordeal. She was just leaving her parents. What an awful thing to have happened. If you can't be safe in your own home, where can you be safe?'

'Amy doesn't live with her parents?'

'No, Inspector. The woman's in her thirties, of course she doesn't live with them. Anyway, last night I was taking Minty and Beatrice for a constitutional when–'

'Sorry to interrupt. Constitutional?'

'Their walk, Inspector,' she said in an exasperated tone.

'Of course. Sorry. Do carry on.'

'I take them out three times a day. Firstly…' She rattled off her walking times while Benedict stifled a yawn.

'So, this last walk, you're saying it was at nine o'clock.'

'Yes. These days of course it's still light. Anyway, I saw this man ahead of me and I noticed he dropped his litter. A chocolate bar or a bag of crisps, I don't know. And I remonstrated with him.'

'That was brave of you, Mrs Sykes.'

'Not at all. It's what any good upstanding citizen would do. Wouldn't you?'

'Yes, yes, naturally, Mrs Sykes. So, you spoke to him.'

'Yes.'

'Face to face?'

'Well, I was hardly going to speak to the back of his head.'

'No. My apologies. And did he pick up his litter?'

'He did, Inspector. You call me brave but it takes a brave man to mess with me, I'll tell you that much.'

He didn't doubt it for a moment. 'Did you recognise him? Had you met him before?'

'No to both of your questions.'

'Can you describe him?'

'Oh yes. He was what you'd call a *meshuggener*.'

'I'm sorry, a what?'

'*Meshuggener*, Inspector. A mad person.' She proceeded to describe the man in astonishing detail – his bald head, his squinty, blue eyes, his fair eyebrows, his 'prominent' nose and what he was wearing – dark blue jeans and a grey hoodie.

'Ah.'

'Ah?'

'Yes, the Greenes said the man who broke into their home was wearing a grey hoodie. Did you notice the logo by any chance?'

'I did, not that it meant anything to me. It was an alligator or crocodile.'

'Give me a moment, if you will.' Using his phone, Benedict found the Lacoste logo on his phone and showed it to Mrs Sykes.

'Yes, that was it.'

'Well, Mrs Sykes, you've been incredibly helpful. But I'm

going to ask for more. We employ an artist on an ad hoc basis. If I gave him a call, would you be able to help us build a sketch of this man?'

She almost clapped her hands with glee. 'Oh yes, I would love to.'

'Excellent. His name is Dave Turner. I'll give him a ring and see if he's free at the moment. He usually is.' These days, photofitting could be done digitally but Benedict still preferred the human touch.

An hour later, Dave Turner and Mrs Sykes came through looking pleased with themselves.

'How did it go?' asked Benedict.

'Dave is a very talented man,' said Mrs Sykes.

'Oh, no, I wouldn't go that far.'

She slapped his arm. 'Oh, don't go all modest on me, I won't have it.'

'Anyway?' said Benedict.

Turner handed over his artwork. It showed a man exactly as Mrs Sykes had described, and he wasn't the sort of man one would want to meet down a dark alleyway.

'Can I see that?' asked PC Stevens. He looked at the picture closely, his eyes narrowing. 'I be damned.'

'What is it, Stevens?'

'I know this man. Oh yes, I know him very well. His name, sir, is Alan Milner.'

Chapter 22: Daniel

Daniel Whitehead didn't want to go back to the therapist but he knew he would, he had to. After that first time, he experienced a strange medley of emotions. The first was a strange and intense affection for Thomas Herreboudt, the psychotherapist. He wanted to hug the man and tell him how grateful he was; he felt as if he'd found a friend for life. Is this how torture victims feel about their torturers once the torture's over? He left Mr Herreboudt's house and walking down the street he had to hold himself back from doing a happy jig; he was on cloud nine. He felt as if a tremendous burden had been lifted off his shoulders. He knew what people meant by that now. But, by the time he got to work, he was emotionally shattered. He drank coffee and, pacing around outside puffing on his vape, tried to clear his head. He phoned Helene but found he couldn't talk to her over the phone, promising he'd tell her all about it when he got home. He spent the rest of the day in a haze, getting through his work on autopilot, not really caring. By the time he did get home, Daniel experienced a slump and really didn't want to talk about it at all. He drank several beers which, on reflection, was a mistake; it had left him feeling maudlin and on the brink of tears.

Thomas Herreboudt greeted him back like an old friend. He asked Daniel how he'd felt after his first session and then, consulting his notes, he recapped what Daniel had said as if Daniel might have forgotten. 'Did you tell anyone about the footsteps you heard that night?'

'No. You see, afterwards, I wasn't even sure I had heard something. I thought maybe those footsteps were my dad's and me, being sleepy, got confused. I just wasn't sure so I didn't feel as if I could say anything. And then, the other thing, those footsteps scared me. You know, as kids we all worry about the monster under the bed – well, for most of us, it's just our imagination. But not me, I really did have a monster and I heard him just outside my bedroom and I heard him steal my baby brother, and I never said anything to anyone. I've not even told my girlfriend. You're the first, Mr Herreboudt.' Dan looked down at his hands, playing with a ring on his right hand. 'You're the first. It's messed with my head. I should have said something but I didn't because I wasn't sure what I heard, and I was frightened that they might say that if I heard something, I should have done something about it. So, I didn't say anything and I've had to live with that decision ever since, and it hurts. It hurts like hell.'

'It's a big thing for you.'

Dan nodded, unable to speak.

'But even if you had said something, you didn't see the man, assuming it was a man, so it wouldn't really have helped.'

'I know, but everyone kept asking me all the time, the

police, Dad and Mum, especially Mum. She was still asking months later. She kept saying, *You must've heard something.* It was as if she knew.'

'So, I assume the police never found Harry.'

'No. I never saw him again, none of us did.'

'It must have been terrible for all of you.'

Daniel had to nod, unable to speak for a while. Finally, taking a deep breath, he started. 'Mum hated us, both Dad and me. They argued all the bloody time. She blamed us but I was only a kid. I blamed Dad. It was awful. It was never easy with all of us on that barge but after Harry disappeared, it became impossible. We all wanted to be as far away from each other as possible. I mean, this was the time we needed each other the most but the opposite happened. Dad thought he knew who it was.'

'Really? Do you want to tell me about that? You don't if–'

'He knew a man, this bloke called Alan. Horrible bloke. I met him a couple of times and he frightened me. He was massive and looked hard. He's in prison now but not for stealing Harry. He beat up an old bloke in a shop during a robbery. The police questioned him about Harry but, for whatever reason, they weren't able to pin it on him. But Dad was convinced.' Daniel looked at Herreboudt. 'And so am I. I didn't think so at the time, but the more I've thought about it over the years, the more I'm convinced Dad was right.'

'But if this man went to prison, what happened to the baby?'

Daniel shrugged. 'I don't know. But, I mean, he wouldn't have stolen a baby to keep him as his own, he'd have sold him.'

'Do you think of Harry often?'

'God yes. I think of him all the time. He'd be eighteen

now. A man. I wonder all the time, what's he doing now, what does he look like, what is he doing with his life? Where does he live? Is he happy? Did his new parents give him a decent life? You know, every time I walk down the street, I'm looking out for him. I'm convinced I'd recognise him if I saw him. Someone called out my name at the train station the other day. I almost had a heart attack, thinking this was it, Harry had found me. And I turned around and it was just someone from work and I felt like…'

'You were upset.'

'Yes.'

'How's your relationship now with your parents?'

'God.' Daniel sat back, sweeping his hair. 'I haven't seen Dad for a couple of years. He lives in Islington somewhere. He and Mum split up soon after Harry went. Mum couldn't bear to look at him so he upped and left. I wanted him to take me with him but he refused. We don't keep in touch.'

'And your mother?'

'We tend to avoid each other. She still lives locally. She had a new fella for a while but it didn't last. But, actually, I've got to admit, things have been a little better since I told her about becoming a dad. I think she likes the idea of becoming a grandmother.'

'Has she met your girlfriend?'

'Helene. Yes. They get on OK. You see, I keep hoping the baby will fill this huge hole in my heart. And that's what it's like – a gaping hole that's messed me up all these years. And the hole's been there since that bastard came on our boat and for whatever reason stole my baby brother…'

Chapter 23: Alan

It was a super-hot day in London and Alan was pleased to take his seat in an air-conditioned train. It took thirty-five minutes by train to go from London's Charing Cross to Sevenoaks in Kent. Alan enjoyed the short journey, settling back in his seat and closing his eyes. Everyone around him was engrossed in their phones. Didn't people make conversation any more? They seemed obsessed. He enjoyed seeing Lana again. She looked bloody good in that tight tee shirt of hers. Got him all hot under the collar. Shame she wasn't up for it but his time would come. He'd go see her again and next time, he wouldn't let her off the hook quite so easily. She owed him for deserting him like that.

Once in Sevenoaks, he had to ask several people for directions to Ian's address in a village called Heaverham. No one knew. Someone, a smart alec of a young woman, suggested he look the address up on his phone. Finally, someone behind the counter in the post office told him Heaverham was out in the country, a good four and a half miles away, and if he didn't have a car the only way to get there would be by Uber.

'A what?' he asked.

'Uber, mate.'

'I don't know what that is.'

The man looked at him as if he was mad. 'A taxi. You been living under a rock or something?'

Alan cursed. A taxi would cost and despite the Greene's donation, he was having to mind the pennies here. The train fare was expensive enough. But needs must, so he walked back to the station and found the taxi rank.

The driver, an Asian guy, drew up somewhere on the edge of a woodland and pointing vaguely ahead told Alan he'd have to walk from here, about four, five minutes straight on. He suggested Alan used his phone. Alan swore.

Ten minutes later, out of breath and sweating, Alan found himself looking at a large cabin-like construction with a steep apex slate roof, lots of glass and surrounded by a picket fence, the sun filtering through the trees forming dancing shadows on the wooden house. If this was it, then Ian and Juliet had done well for themselves. He could hear the sound of what sounded like someone chopping wood. He followed the path, disturbing a few chickens along the way and alerting a dozy dog who couldn't be bothered to get up. Not much of a guard dog, thought Alan.

Circling around to the back of the house, he found Ian who was indeed chopping wood. Alan stood and watched Ian hard at work. The man had aged. He was thinner, almost gaunt, his hair, what was left of it, had turned grey. He didn't look in the best of health. He wore a chequered shirt and scruffy jeans. Perhaps aware that he wasn't alone, Ian stopped and looked over.

'Shit!' His face, thought Alan, was a picture.

Alan stepped forward. 'Hello, Ian. Long time no see.'

Ian looked around as if hoping to be rescued. 'What are you doing here?'

'It's good to see you too, mate.'

'How long have you been out?'

'Not long. So, you see I'm here already, that's how keen I am to see you.'

'How did you find us?'

'Us? So, you're still together then, you and Jools?'

'How did you find us?' he repeated, gripping his axe.

'It wasn't difficult.' He motioned the house. 'Lovely place you have here. How did you afford this?' He stepped up to him. 'And before you tell me it's none of my business, remember we're old mates so you can tell me.' He punched Ian playfully on the arm.

'Dead parents, if you must know.' He wiped the sweat from his brow. 'And a decent price on the London house.'

Alan nodded. 'That figures. Better than that place you had in Camden, eh? Can I have a glass of water? This is too hot for me. I'm not used to it.'

Ian hesitated. 'All right but stay here.' He placed his axe against the pile of logs. 'I don't want you in the house.'

'Suit yourself.' Alan sat and leaned against the trunk of a tree, please to take the weight off. He could hear the rhythmic tapping of a woodpecker somewhere high up, nearby. He saw an upstairs curtain twitch. Was that Juliet there? She quickly withdrew. He doubted she'd come out to say hello. It was lovely here, he thought, with the sun slanting through the trees and the chickens and all this greenery and the fresh smells. Idyllic even. Ian returned bearing a glass of water.

'Where's Jools?'

'Out at work.'

He glanced back up at the upstairs window. 'Oh, so it's just you and me then. Tell me, don't you get lonesome out here?'

'Look, Alan, tell me what you want then go.'

'You know, no one seems happy to see me. Funny that. I mean, if I didn't have the skin of a rhinoceros, I might be hurt. Do you keep in touch with Kris and Beth?'

'No. Haven't seen them for years.'

'So you wouldn't know where they live now?'

'No idea.'

'OK.' A flock of starlings flew by. Alan looked up and smiled as they passed. 'I just want to know how you did it, Ian.'

'Did what?'

'You know what I mean. Don't play games with me. Eighteen years inside has taught me the virtue of patience but even I have my limits so don't push it. But OK, let me give you a bit of a steer. Eighteen years ago, we robbed a supermarket, you and me. A silly man tried to play the hero and got himself hurt. I got caught out because I was stupid.'

'They found your fingerprints on those packs of cigarettes.'

'Yeah. Like I said – stupid. I thought I was cleverer than that. More fool me. I was sent down but you were not. And why was that, Ian? Because despite being with me…' he said, jabbing himself in the chest, 'You had a cast-iron alibi. And all because you managed to persuade your boss.'

'You what?'

'Oh, Ian, your face. Manish, wasn't it? Manish Patel.'

'How in the hell do you know that?'

'I had some amazing mates inside. Men who knew people,

had contacts on the outside, like, er, the odd bent copper, that sort of thing. So, it wasn't difficult. How did you manage it, Ian? Hmm? Offered him money? Bent over for him?'

'It was a favour for a favour.'

Alan laughed. 'That's what you call it. Quite some favour. I'm impressed. Now, I want a favour in return. A bit of money to keep me going.'

'We're not exactly well off here.'

'And I'm not asking for much. In fact, I'm not even asking you to give it to me, just to lend it to me until I do the next job.'

'How much?'

'Three hundred would do it. Cash.'

'I can spare you two hundred.'

'That's fine. Thank you. I don't care what people say about you, Ian, you're a good man at heart. What's that noise?'

Both men turned. 'My sons coming back on the quad.'

'Sons? You've been busy. Right…' He stepped right up to him, their noses almost touching. 'This is what we're going to do. With your loan, I'm going to get myself a little temporary phone – in cash. Then I shall write to you the old-fashioned way with the number. You will then buy your own phone, also in cash, and put my number in it. Got it?'

'And why would I do any of that?'

'Well, it's obvious, ain't it? So that we can keep in touch before our next job.'

Ian stepped back, almost falling over his feet. 'No, no way, Alan, no. I don't do that sort of thing no more.'

The quad bike came into view, slowing up, two young lads on it.

'I'll find him, you know. Manish Patel. Someone was telling me about that thing, what's it called? Linked Up or something. Tells you where people work, doesn't it? And I'll go and see him and I'll persuade him to do the right thing, to tell the police that he lied for you that night. Now, Ian, I can cope with prison because people don't give me any shit but you…' He shook his head despairingly. 'You wouldn't stand a chance, mate. They'll eat you alive.'

'Hi, Dad,' came a cheery voice.

'Oh, hi, boys,' said Ian with a stutter.

Both boys came over, young, tall men, good-looking, one dark, one blonde, both wearing tee shirts and shorts. They both looked quizzically at Alan.

'Oh, boys, this is an old mate of mine. Alan.'

'Hello, lads. Nice to meet you.'

'This is Kelvin,' said Ian, pointing out the slightly shorter, blonde boy. 'And this is Felix. Did you get what you wanted, Kel?'

'Nah, they said come back tomorrow.'

'Good looking lads, aren't they?' said Alan. 'Tall too.'

'I'll just go and…' said Ian, heading to the house.

'How old are you, son?' asked Alan.

'Me?' asked Kelvin. 'I'm seventeen.'

'Ah, what I'd give to be seventeen again. Boys, I'm going to be a bit cheeky here but could one of you run me back to the station?'

The boys looked at each other. Both shrugged. 'Yeah, I'll do it,' said Felix. Kelvin handed Alan his helmet.

'Thanks, mate. I appreciate it.'

They stood in awkward silence until Ian returned and passed Alan a brown envelope.

'Thanks, mate. Well, Ian, it's been good to see you again.' He slapped Ian on the arm. 'If I speak to Manish, shall I send him your regards? No? OK, I'll be in touch,' he said with a wink. Turning to Felix, he said, 'Thanks, son. I'm ready when you are.'

Alan followed Felix to the quad bike. It was only then Alan saw the backs of Felix's legs. He stopped short. There, on the back of Felix's right leg, a large, dark, rather unsightly birthmark.

Chapter 24: Patricia

'Come on, Dad, you need to take this. You heard what the doctor said.'

Her father groaned but he did as she asked and swallowed down yet another couple of pills.

'Well done. You know it'll help you sleep.'

He nodded.

'Good night, Dad.' She took his hand and squeezed it. 'I'll see you in the morning. Sleep tight, don't let the bedbugs bite.'

He smiled at that, he always did. She turned his bedroom light off and made her way downstairs where she collapsed on her armchair and, using the remote, turned on the TV. The end of another long day, a bit of time to herself. There was a new mystery drama on ITVX she fancied watching. She'd seen the trailer several times and it looked good.

Patricia Godwin's life was not an easy one. She was a full-time carer and had been for eighteen years, and she did it all by herself. Yes, she belonged to a couple of carer groups on Facebook and the nice woman from social services popped around every now and then but essentially she did this solo. Once a month, she and Dad went to a diners' club not too far away where she met other carers and their dependents. Patricia had never been the sort of person to attend social clubs but now, it was always the highlight of her month. And she had God. God looked after them both. She'd always had faith but the older she got, the more she relied on Him.

Looking after Dad wasn't necessarily a thankless task because she knew her father appreciated it but nonetheless, it was a solitary and exhausting existence, always looking after someone, making sure they didn't get into difficulty, were never in a position where they could harm themselves. Today panned out exactly the same as yesterday, and yesterday the same as the day before and so it went on, eighteen years the same. Dad had paralysis of his right side and aphasia which left him with limited speech.

Tomorrow, she and Dad would get up at eight, like they did every day. She'd help him into the shower. Once a week, he washed his hair and she'd have to do it for him. He could dry himself but Patricia always had to dry his back. She'd dress him, brush his hair and clean his teeth.

When they went out, Dad had to use his mobility scooter. He'd learned how to cross the road and recognise the red and green men and what they meant. Patricia enjoyed shopping as it meant she could talk to the checkout person which was usually the only conversation she had during the day – besides her father.

*

The following morning, Patricia got up as usual at seven-thirty. She liked to have half an hour to herself before she went to see her father and start the day. She made her morning tea, sat down in her favourite armchair and scrolled through her phone, catching up on the morning's news. She heard the post arrive, much earlier than normal. Still in her slippers and dressing gown, she padded over. Picking up the post, she stopped short on seeing an envelope franked by the probation service. A sense of dread pricked her. This was bound to be bad news. Sitting down again, she read the letter, her eyes quickly scanning the short note. She swore and re-read the letter, this time more slowly. She leaned back, the letter slipping from her grasp. She knew it had to happen one day and she knew it'd be soon. But it still left her reeling.

Her father was upstairs. Soon, he'd be awake. But there was no release date for him, was there? There was no specific day on which God declared, *OK, Bernard Godwin, you've served your time as a victim, you can be released now. You're free to get on with your life and put these last eighteen years behind you.* No. Her father's sentence, and by extension her own, had no end date. They were here for the long haul – until the day he died. Life was unfair but ultimately, God would see them right.

She didn't often think back to that day, the day that changed everything, but having received this letter, she couldn't prevent her mind from wandering back. Dad was fifty-five at the time. It was late, almost eleven, when Dad suddenly got up from watching the telly and declared he had a craving for chocolate. The local convenience store couldn't have been more convenient – it was just a hop and a skip away. Patricia, about to go to bed, needed a pack of tampons which she was going to get on her way to work the following morning. But if Dad was going to the shop… But she couldn't ask him, feeling too embarrassed. So, instead, she went with him.

Dad wore his new baseball cap with the words 'God's Favorite' on the front, spelt the American way. She remembered the security man asking them to be quick as he was about to lock up. But he said it nicely, with a smile. Dad promised him they wouldn't be long. It all started a minute later – the men barging in wielding their guns, dressed head to toe in black, balaclavas, shouting at the security man and the young man behind the counter, demanding cash.

Patricia felt her bowels loosen; this was terrifying. The man at the counter, a brute of a man, was shouting. 'You press any buttons, mate, you're dead. Open the till. Now!'

She felt her father tense up. She gripped his arm. He'd do something, he always did. He was incapable of standing aside. 'No, Daddy, leave it. Please.'

He nodded but she didn't let go of his arm, fearing the worst.

The brute was demanding cigarettes now, the poor lad behind the counter was shaking with fear. This, thought Patricia, was a nightmare but it was about to get a whole lot worse. Dad, shaking her hand off, marched up to the front of the store. 'Daddy, no.'

She heard him yelling at the man. 'Put it back. All of it. Give this lad his money back. It's not yours to take.'

Rooted to the spot, Patricia started shaking. Dad went to grab the man's canvas bag. But the brute pushed him back, pushed him hard. But Dad tried again. The security guy took a step forward. 'Don't move,' said the second, smaller, thug.

The brute slammed his gun onto the side of Dad's face. Patricia knew she'd never forget the sound of it. Dad staggered back. The brute punched him. Dad collapsed, cracking his head. The cowards ran out, leaving Dad on the linoleum floor, the blood pouring from his head. Patricia screamed. The security man called for an ambulance. The young lad behind the counter rushed off and returned with a towel to stem the blood.

Eighteen years ago. The day that changed everything. Dad spent almost a month in hospital. The doctors told Patricia that he was now paralysed down the right side. He'd live but both his mental and physical capabilities would forever be compromised. She would need to care for him, day in, day out, for the rest of his life.

The police found one of the two men who did it, the main one, the big one. He'd left his fingerprints on those cigarette packs. His name was Alan Milner. He was found guilty and sent down. The guns they brandished turned out to be fake. But they weren't to know at the time.

Today, Patricia found out that Alan Milner had, apparently, served his time. He was due to be released. Alan Milner would soon be back in society, walking the streets as a free man.

It was eight o'clock. Time to wake Dad, time to start another day.

Chapter 25: Alan

It took Alan a few seconds to recognise the significance of that large birthmark on the back of the boy's right leg. He put his helmet on and took his place on the back of the quad bike, holding onto a bar behind him. Felix revved up the quad. 'All set?'

'All set,' said Alan.

Ian and Kelvin watched as Felix turned the quad around. Alan waved goodbye. Neither responded.

Five minutes later, Felix dropped Alan off at the train station. 'Thanks, mate,' said Alan, getting off and handing Felix his brother's helmet. 'So, tell me, have you always lived here?'

Felix lifted his helmet up, perching it at the top of his head. 'We moved about a lot when I was a kid but yeah, we've been here for years. I'll be off in September.'

'University?'

'Yeah.'

'What about your brother?'

'What about him?'

'Will he be going to uni too when his time comes?'

'Don't know. Probably.'

'Were you born in Kent?'

'Nah, I was born in London.'

'Last time I saw you, you were still a baby. How old are you now?'

'Just turned eighteen.'

'Nice age. Your brother looks like your dad but you… you look totally different. You don't look like either of your parents.'

'Don't I? Suppose. You're not the first to say it. I'd better get back.'

'Sure. Thanks for the lift. I appreciate it.'

'No worries. Seeya.'

Now, this was interesting. Felix had a port wine mark on the back of his leg in the shape of the island of Cyprus. Kris and Beth had a baby eighteen years ago, a baby with a birthmark. He'd remembered seeing it all those years ago, remembered at the time thinking it was shaped like Cyprus. And then that baby went missing. There'd been huge media interest at the time, with Beth and Kris on TV pleading with the kidnappers to bring back their precious, beautiful baby. But he was never found.

But he'd found him. Eighteen years on, Alan Milner had done what the police and everyone else had failed to do – he'd found the missing baby.

So, Alan concluded as he waited for his London-bound train, that was two items ticked off his 'to do' list: he'd seen Lana and he'd visited Ian Turner. Next, he'd go visit Kris. He wondered whether he was still married to Beth. He doubted it somehow. And he'd tell Kris that he knew where his son was. He deserved to know.

*

Thanks to Ian Turner and Mrs Greene, Alan now had a decent amount of cash and, the following day, he bought himself a cheap little pay-as-you-go mobile. He jotted down his new number and posted it to Ian. Next, he borrowed his mother's library card and went to Swiss Cottage library and there, asked a member of staff to help him on the computer. He explained he knew nothing about computers and didn't know how the internet worked but he was looking for a register that could tell him about a specific canal boat, narrowboat or barge. 'I'm looking for a boat called *The Purple Mermaid*, and also the name of the person who owns it.'

He had, in truth, used the internet but hadn't done so in almost two decades. He was impressed with the librarian – in a matter of a few minutes, she said, 'There is an official register, you're right, and I found your boat.'

'Brilliant!'

'And it tells us where it currently is but it doesn't tell you who owns it. That information's private. So, at the moment, it's moored on Regent's Canal, not too far from Islington.'

'Excellent. Thank you. Next thing, have you heard of something called Linked Thing? It tells you what jobs people have.'

'Oh, you mean LinkedIn. Yes. Why? Who are you looking for?'

Twenty minutes later, Alan thanked the helpful librarian and left the library. That, he decided, had been a very good use of his time. Now, it was time to catch the tube to King's Cross and pay *The Purple Mermaid* a visit.

It was a bright and warm June day as Alan walked along the canal, hoping to find *The Purple Mermaid*. Seeing a man sitting in a deckchair on the top of his boat, he asked and was told it was just a hundred yards or so further along. And so Alan found it. *The Purple Mermaid*. He knocked and called out hello. A woman with, appropriately enough, purple hair popped her head up from the back of the barge. He asked whether she knew where Kris or Beth Whitehead lived. She didn't but told him to try a canal boat further down. This continued for a while – being told to ask someone else or a different boat until he was directed back to where he'd started from, the woman with the purple hair. She apologised for his wasted journey but said after he'd gone she remembered. There was a woman called Beth, she didn't know her surname, who rented a boat called *Lazy Suzan* which, if memory served, was currently moored in the Islington direction. No one called Kris though. Alan thanked her.

Finally, Alan found *Lazy Suzan*, moored up, as the purple-haired woman had said, not too far from Islington. He saw Beth as he approached. She clocked him but didn't recognise him. Truth was, he wasn't sure if it was Beth. If it was, she too had changed, the years had not been kind to her but, he supposed, she'd lost a child, it was bound to take its toll on a person. He called out her name. She looked up and squinted, shielding her eyes from the sun. 'Alan?'

'Yes. Hello, Beth.'

'If you're looking for Kris, I don't know where he is. And I don't care.'

'Can I have a word?'

'No.' She dipped down and disappeared inside the boat.

But you haven't heard what I've got to say, he thought. I've got news for you, something that will change your life…

He stepped onto the boat and knocked on the door. He

could hear the radio on inside. Opening the door, he stepped down the short step ladder into the boat's kitchen. Beth, coming through carrying a washing basket, stopped on seeing him.

'I didn't invite you in. How dare you come in?'

'No, Beth, listen–'

'So, they've finally let you out.'

'I've served my time, Beth. Been a good boy.'

She put the washing basket down. 'If it was down to me, I'd have thrown away the key.'

'Well–'

'To think you paralysed that poor man, you worthless piece of shit.'

That hurt. 'You've got some big words for a small woman.'

'Dan's due in a minute.'

'Dan? Oh, your son. Last time, I saw–'

'I don't care. Now, get off my boat. You were always bad news, leading Kris astray with your stupid plans. He was weak and you exploited that, so if you think I'm going to give you the time of day, you can think again.'

'So you're not with Kris any more?'

'No, I told you. I've not seen him for years. He could be dead for all I care. So, now that you know, get out.'

'Just shut up for a minute.'

'Oh? Are you threatening me now?' She reached for her mobile.

'What are you doing?'

'Phoning the police, that's what I'm doing.'

He was getting fed up with the woman. 'Bloody hell, Beth, all I want…' Alan heard a voice coming from outside.

'Hello? Mum?'

'In here, Dan.' He could see her relief, the fact she'd been rescued.

Alan turned around to see a pair of legs descending the steps – and then, in front of him, Beth's grown-up son.

Dan's eyes widened on seeing him. 'Sorry, I didn't know you had–'

'Alan's just going. Aren't you, Alan?'

'You Alan?' asked Daniel, stepping back a little.

'Yeah. You won't remember me.'

'I remember you.' There was something in the way the lad said it that Alan didn't like, an edge to his tone. Alan looked at Beth. Despite her attitude, he could see she was frightened of him. He swung around towards the boy. 'Boo!'

Dan jumped back. Yes, as he thought, the lad was scared too, scared shitless, they both were.

'I want you to go now,' said Beth, tilting her chin up.

Alan put his hands up. 'OK, OK, I give in. I just wanted to tell you something…' One last chance, he thought. One last chance…

'And I don't want to hear it.'

Stupid woman. 'OK, if that's what you want, I'll go.'

He glared at Dan before heading out. The boy winced as if Alan had raised his arm to strike him.

He stepped off the barge onto the towpath. He looked up at the sky. A beautiful blue sky. Such a lovely day. A shame it had been such a frustrating one.

He made his way back to King's Cross tube station.

To think he'd come here to help her, to tell her where her missing son was. It would have changed her life. She had no idea that she'd been seconds away from knowing. But fuck it, she didn't deserve it. The woman was a total bitch.

By the time Alan got to the tube, he had an idea. A

monstrous idea perhaps but an idea that could earn him a fair bit of money. He stopped outside the tube station and admired a girl in a pink straw hat. Such a simple idea. But yes, he could do it, he could make it work. He smiled to himself and, turning, went down into the tube station.

Chapter 26: Kris

Kris Whitehead almost dropped his mobile when he saw the name of his ex-wife appear on the screen. He hadn't heard from her for a year or more. He was tempted not to answer it – even the sound of Beth's voice caused him anxiety. But no, she wouldn't be phoning for a chat or a catch-up, she wouldn't contact him unless it was important, namely the fact that Dan's girlfriend was about to have a baby. So, reluctantly, Kris answered it.

'Have you heard?' she asked without preamble.

'Heard what? Has she had it?'

'Not that. The other.'

'What?'

'He's out.' It took Kris a few seconds to realise what she was talking about. 'You mean Alan?'

'Who else?'

'Shit. When?'

'Just recently I think.'

'How do you know?'

'He came to see me, here, on the barge.'

'He came to see you? Why? What did he want?'

'I don't know. He didn't get a chance to speak. I threw

him off. Dan saw him too.'

Kris tried to absorb this. This was not good news. 'Did he ask after me?'

'Yes, but I told him I've not seen you for the longest time.'

'Did you give him my number?'

'No, Kris, don't you worry your pretty head, I did not do that. Give me some credit. Anyway, I thought I better let you know. Oh, and the other minor detail – I'll be seeing you later today.'

'You what? What for?'

'You're about to become a grandfather.'

'How do you know? I mean, I know but why this afternoon specifically?'

'Dan told me – Helene is having a caesarean as we speak. Right now, we could already be grandparents. We can go visit from four this afternoon.'

He finished the call. A grandfather? Hell, how frightening, how exciting! Beth's call had woken him up from his afternoon nap. He worked as a postman now which meant very early starts but it also meant he was finished by early afternoon. So, each day he'd come home to his bedsit, have a kip and then face the rest of the day. He lit a cigarette. He never used to be a smoker; it was all that stress over losing Harry that had driven him to it.

He hated speaking to Beth because it always brought everything back to those horrendous days following the abduction. Beth never stopped blaming him. It drove him insane. Yes, it had been his fault, he should never have left the barge that night. He knew that and he'd acknowledged it a hundred times but it made no difference – Beth hit him with it day and night, day and night. It got to the point, and very rapidly, where they couldn't bear to be in each other's company. She hated him with a vengeance. And poor Dan didn't fare much better; she continually laid into him too. But he was just a kid; it hadn't been his fault.

Once, a few months after, when they were alone, Kris asked Dan the same question Beth had asked so many times – had he heard anything? But while Beth screamed the question at him, reducing the boy to tears, Kris asked him quietly in, he hoped, a sort of man-to-man way. And for a moment, the briefest moment, Kris thought Dan was going to say something. He urged him to say it, to spit it out. But Dan dried up, he couldn't bring himself to say it. 'Please, Dan,' he'd said. 'You heard something or saw someone, didn't you?'

Dan shook his head fervently. 'I didn't, Dad, I didn't, honest.'

'OK, Dan. OK.' He patted his son's knee. 'I believe you. Don't cry now, it's fine.'

Kris didn't believe him then; he didn't believe him now.

Kris was convinced then and he was convinced to this day still that Alan Milner had something to do with Harry's disappearance. He may not have stolen the baby himself but he'd been involved somewhere along the way. And he'd told the police and although they acted on it, they never got anywhere. But they did get him for that robbery and for making a near-vegetable out of the bloke he lamped. And he was sent to prison for eighteen years. Did that provide solace? The fact that the man Kris reckoned had taken Harry was behind bars? No, it did not. He and Beth wanted *their* justice, not someone else's.

And now Alan was out. This didn't bode well. He had effectively shopped Alan that night when he told the police about the robbery. Thank God he hadn't been involved.

He'd even volunteered himself but Alan said no, it was a two-man job, and obviously, he preferred Ian's company.

Ian had managed to get away with the robbery, had some solid alibi by all accounts, someone who was able to vouch for him. Like hell. Again, Kris had been tempted to snitch on him but he held back. After all, his hands weren't exactly lily-white back in those days. He still woke up at night sometimes remembering how close they'd come to kidnapping that girl. Thank God, he'd left those days behind.

Stubbing out his cigarette, Kris decided to ring Ian – he had to know Alan was free. Ian was someone else he hadn't spoken to for years. He might have changed his number. But he tried it nonetheless and to his surprise, Ian answered straight away.

'Ian. Kris here.'

The silence at the other end stretched. 'What do you want?'

'I thought you'd want to know, Alan's out.' No response. 'Ian? Can you hear me?'

'Yeah, I hear you. So, he's out, you say.'

'You didn't know?'

'No,' came the immediate response.

'So, anyway, how are you? Where are you living these days–'

The line went dead.

'Ian? Are you there? Ian?' He'd rung off, the ungrateful bastard. 'Sod you then.'

*

A few hours later, Kris arrived at St Cuthbert's hospital and quickly made his way to the Mary Keats Maternity ward. He saw them ahead – Beth and Dan sitting around Helene's bed.

Slowing up, he approached. Had she had the baby? Yes, she had! 'Hello,' he said, cheerfully. Helene smiled up at him. 'Hello, Helene.'

'Hello, Kris,' she said in her Scandinavian accent. 'Meet Erik.'

'Erik?'

'Spelt with a K at the end.'

Kris peered down at the little bundle in Helene's arms. His heart lurched on seeing the little one at his mother's breast. It took his breath away. He remembered twenty-eight years ago seeing Dan like this and ten years later, Harry. He glanced over at Beth. She smiled at him. He asked Helene how she was. He hugged his son. 'Congratulations, son. I'm so happy for you.'

'Thanks, Dad.'

'You'll make a far better father than I ever did.'

'Don't say that, Dad.'

He turned to Beth. 'He's got Dan's nose, don't you think?'

'Isn't it marvellous?' she said.

Dan sat with Helene and Erik, whispering to her and making her laugh.

'We're grandparents, Beth. Who would have thought it?'

She didn't answer and Kris realised she was crying. He didn't know whether to put his arm around her. He couldn't remember the last time he'd touched her with any affection.

'I'm sorry,' she said. 'I'm so happy but I just keep thinking…'

Kris knew what she was about to say.

'Harry should know about this, Kris. It's so unfair. He should be here with us now. He should know he's an uncle now.'

Chapter 27: Ian

Ian put the phone down on Kris. He had no interest in doing small talk with the man. He'd asked where he was living these days. As if he was going to tell him. It felt as if his past was catching up on him – first Alan turns up and now Kris rings him out of the blue. Ian had felt dazed by Alan's visit; he found it difficult to concentrate on anything and had difficulty sleeping. Alan was right – he wouldn't stand a chance in prison. There was no way he could 'do another job' with Alan. He wouldn't have the nerves for it now. But how to stop him? He dreaded the post arriving, dreaded receiving Alan's letter with his new mobile number.

The moment Alan had left the day before on the back of Felix's quad bike, Juliet had come charging out in a panic. 'Felix is wearing shorts, Ian.'

'I know.'

'He would have seen, wouldn't he? The birthmark, he'd have seen it, you can't miss it–'

'I know, Juliet. Calm down, will you?' Lowering his voice, he added, 'Kelvin will hear.'

'Where is he?'

'I don't know. Listen, Jools, you're right. Alan will have seen the birthmark, but so what? He's probably never seen it before, you know, when Felix was a baby.'

'You don't know that for sure.'

He had to concede he couldn't know for certain.

'I can't believe this is happening,' said Juliet, running her hand through her hair. 'Felix has been ours all this time and now we're going to be found out by that bastard, of all people.'

'It might not come to that.'

Ian had told Juliet the truth within a couple of months of taking Felix. Initially, he kept to his original script about his friend's wife being ill. He ran with it – saying the woman had died and her husband was too grief-stricken to take back the baby. A person of normal mind would never have fallen for it but Juliet's mind was still too fuzzy and emotional following the miscarriage or, as she called it, the death of Toby. But after a while, Juliet began asking more questions and Ian hated lying to her. Plus, the burden of guilt began to take its toll; he knew through the grapevine and the media that Beth and Kris were suffering, so he told Juliet the truth and fully expected her to order him to return the baby. But she said not a word. Instead, she effectively retired to the bedroom for three days and refused to come out, talk to him or allow him to share the bed. Ian slept on the sofa and had to call in sick for three days running. He fed Felix on his wife's supply of expressed milk and when that ran out, he reverted to formula. Finally, on the fourth morning, Juliet came downstairs, took Felix from Ian's arms and placed the baby at her breast. She never mentioned it. And she never did – until this very day.

'So, what did he want?'

'Alan? Nothing. He said he was just passing so he thought he'd pop in and say hello.'

'Bullshit, Ian. What did he really want?'

'Nothing. Honest to God, Jools, that was it. No demands. No hidden agendas, nothing.'

'How did he know where we live?'

'I asked but he didn't say.' That at least was true.

She looked hard at him. 'You better be telling me the truth, Ian.'

He couldn't tell her what Alan had really said, he just couldn't. He heard Felix coming back on his quad bike, a welcome distraction. Felix drew up and jumped off, removing his helmet.

'You alright, Felix?' said Juliet.

'Yeah.'

'You dropped Alan off OK?' asked Ian.

'Yeah. No probs.'

'Was he all right? Did he speak to you?'

'No, not really.' He began walking back to the house but stopped. 'Actually…'

'Yes?'

'He said he thought Kelvin looks like you, Dad, but that I looked nothing like either of you.'

Ian sensed Juliet tensing up beside him. 'He said that?' she whispered.

'Yes. He asked if I was born here.'

'Right.'

'Any lunch on the go, Mum?'

'Hmm. Yes, erm, yes. I'd better make a start.'

She followed Felix back to the house leaving Ian feeling nauseous. He picked up the axe and swung it down on a length of wood, splitting it into two in one hit.

The following morning, the post duly arrived. Ian ran to collect it, wanting to beat Juliet to it. Sure enough, among the junk mail and takeaway offers, was an envelope with his address handwritten in the scruffiest writing. It was like a toddler had written it. The letter inside was blank save from an eleven-digit number. That was it. Ian felt sick. He scrunched the sheet of paper and threw it in the outside bin. He was *not* going to buy a crappy little phone just so that Alan could have a direct line to him. He was determined to expunge Alan Milner from his mind.

It didn't last long. Three days after his first visit, Alan turned up again. It was another fine day, Juliet, especially, seemed buoyed by the sun. But her face crumpled on seeing Alan at their door. He walked into the lounge as if he owned the place, his bald head shining with sweat. 'You really have got a lovely place here,' he said, walking around admiring the decor and picking things up. 'It's like one of those… what do you call them? Those chalet things they have in Switzerland.' To be fair to the man, that was the look Ian and Juliet had gone for – wooden floor, wooden beams, colourful rugs, a large fireplace stocked up with wood ready for the winter.

'Make us a cup of tea, will you, Jools? I'm parched.'

Juliet went to the kitchen. Ian knew she'd be listening but as soon as Alan thought she was out of earshot, he stepped right up to Ian. 'Where's your phone? Your burner?'

'I haven't got one.'

'No? I'd advise you to do so pronto, mate. I went to the library in Swiss Cottage and one of the nice librarians there helped me with that LinkedIn thing. There're quite a few Manish Patels. But I'll find him,' he said, tapping his temple. 'Mark my words, I'll go back to the library and find our man.

Our Manish.' He chortled to himself.

'Look, Alan, why? I can't help you. I'm fifty now, for God's sake. I can't go around kidnapping people or robbing shops or whatever you have in mind. I'm too old, I'm not as fit as I used to be.'

'You live in the country, mate. You look fit as a fiddle.'

They were interrupted by the sudden appearance of Kelvin. 'Oh, hello again.'

'Hello, son,' said Alan. 'You're off out? It's a lovely day out there.'

'Yes, in a bit. Dad, have you seen my trainers?'

'Which one of the eighty-eight pairs of trainers you own are you referring to?'

'Black ones, the Pumas.'

'No idea.'

'Right. Thanks.'

Juliet came in bearing a single mug of tea. She passed it to Alan. He thanked her and sat down in an armchair. Kelvin nodded goodbye and left. Ian and Juliet sat together on the sofa.

'Nice lad,' said Alan. 'Well brought up.' He smiled. 'And your other lad… Felix, isn't it? A credit to you both, I have to say. Although that's quite an unfortunate birthmark on the back of his leg.'

Ian and Juliet exchanged a panicked look.

Alan laughed. 'I remember Kris and Beth's baby. Had a similar birthmark. I remember thinking at the time it was shaped like that island, Cyprus, you know? Anyone would think it was the same birthmark.'

Ian feared his heart was going to give out. 'Alan, please–'

Alan turned to Juliet. 'Jools, haven't you got some washing or something to be getting on with? I'd like to have a word with Ian alone. A man-to-man chat.'

'Whatever you say to Ian you can say to me.'

He thought about this. 'Really? As you wish.' He sipped his tea noisily. 'OK, Jools, your funeral.' He placed the mug on the floor. Leaning forward, he said, 'Now, you listen and you listen hard. You see, none of us are getting any younger and I need to think about my future. I need to plan for my retirement.' He turned to Juliet again. 'Jools, do you know the name Manish Patel?'

She shook her head.

'Mr Patel has the potential to put your husband in prison for a very long time.'

'What did you say? You bastard. How dare you come into my home and threaten my husband–'

'Hear me out, woman. It gets better. I thought Mr Patel was the ace up my sleeve. But no, I discover I have an even better one. Your son Felix. Or should I say... Harry. Prince Harry, indeed.'

Juliet shot up from the sofa. 'Get out of my house.'

'Jools–'

'I swear I'll phone the police.'

Alan laughed. 'I really wouldn't do that. One word from me and it won't just be Ian going to prison. You both will. And for a very long time. Eighteen years you've denied that poor couple their child. A judge and jury would throw the book at you.'

Ian bit his hand, convinced he was going to sob any moment.

'But,' said Alan. 'I'm going to give you a choice, both of you. Ian, like I said the other day, I have a job in mind but I'll need your help. I'll give you the details when I'm ready but suffice to say it'll be worth near enough a hundred thousand.

I'll give you thirty-three per cent. That leaves me with sixty-seven thousand pounds. Or…'

'Or what?' asked Juliet.

'You *give* me sixty-seven thousand.'

It was Juliet's turn to laugh. 'How in the hell do you expect us to come up with that sort of money?'

Ian could feel his heart thumping. 'She's right though,' he said. 'We don't have that much.'

'Oh, but you do,' said Alan. 'You own this house.'

'What?'

'Sell this house, move to somewhere smaller. You won't need all this space. Felix told me he and Kelvin will be going to university.' He smiled.

'You're mad as well as ugly,' shrieked Juliet.

That took the smile off his face. He bounded over to her, waving his fist in her face. 'You call me ugly again and I'll make you ugly too, you hear?'

Juliet shrunk back.

'Talk about it. Decide what you're going to do.' He checked his watch. 'I'm going to go now. Buy yourself that phone, Ian, and then let me know. I give you exactly forty-eight hours.'

And with that, he was gone.

Chapter 28: Ian / Patricia

After Alan had left, Ian and Juliet stood staring at each other, unable to speak. Ian was shaking, whether from stress, fear, anger or all three, he didn't know. Kelvin chose that moment to come into the living room, whistling to himself as he always did when happy. He stopped on seeing his parents standing silently, their faces white. 'What's up?' he said, looking worried.

'Hmm?' said Juliet. 'Oh, nothing, darling.'

'You sure?'

'Yeah.'

'Right. OK. I hope you don't mind me saying but you look like shit, both of you. Was it that man?'

'No, no. We're fine. Aren't we, Ian?'

'Yes, yes. Fine, absolutely fine.'

'Right. Just to say, I, er, I found my trainers.'

'Trainers?'

'I was looking for them, remember, Dad? My black Pumas'

'Oh, yes, yes. Black Pumas. That's good then. All good.'

'OK, I'm off out. Won't be long. Are you… are you sure you're OK? That man, who was he?'

'Oh, no one,' said Ian. 'An old mate of mine.'

'Some mate. Looked hard as hell. Anyway, catch ya later.'

'Yeah, yeah, mind how you go, son.'

'What in the hell do we do?' asked Juliet once Kelvin had left.

Ian realised he was shaking again. 'I don't know. I don't bloody know.'

'We're fucked. Either way, we're fucked.'

'I know, Jools. I know. We either end up in prison or we sell the house and hand over… how much?'

'Sixty-seven grand, Ian,' she said flatly. 'You heard him.'

Ian fell onto the settee. 'We can't go to the police, that's for sure.'

'And he knows that.

They heard the back door closing. They looked at each other. 'I thought Kelvin had already gone.'

'Me too.'

'Do you think he heard?'

Juliet shook her head. 'No, we were virtually whispering.' She sat beside him and took his hand. 'We have to do something.'

'But *what?*'

'I don't know. We'll think of something. We've got forty-eight hours. We'll think of something.'

Ian stood and reached for his coat from the back of a chair.

'Where are you going?'

'Into town.' He shrugged. 'I need to buy that phone.'

*

It was that time of the month when Patricia Godwin took her father to the diners' club for the impaired and their carers, always a jolly occasion, usually the highlight of Patricia's month. And her father's. But today, she wasn't planning on staying. She had things to do. She was worried about it but God would give her the strength. She put her father in her dark blue Fiat Panda and secured his seatbelt. But the bloody car wouldn't start. It was fifteen years old; it was ancient. But she couldn't afford to do anything about it. She offered a silent prayer, pressed down on the accelerator, and finally, it sputtered into life.

Patricia settled Dad at the long, Formica dining table and tucked his bib in. There was already a good crowd and lots of noise. She approached one of the staff and asked if she could leave Dad with them for forty-five minutes. Carers weren't obliged to stay, the staff were fully qualified and capable, so yes, it was fine.

Patricia knew where Alan Milner's mother lived. She'd done her research soon after Milner's incarceration. She knew he lived in the Camden Town area and consulting the electoral roll, found a Shirley Milner and her address. She stalked it occasionally in those early days although she was never sure why, and she saw Shirley Milner and yes, there was a definite resemblance between mother and son. Milner was like a bald-headed version of his mother. But she hadn't been back for years – until today. She still didn't know why she was doing this but she wanted to catch a glimpse of the man, the man that ruined her and her father's life that night eighteen years ago.

She drove the two miles south to Camden Town and, passing a small post office, parked up on the other side of the street and not too far away from the small, terraced house belonging to Milner's mother. She sat in her car knowing this was a waste of time and that she could be enjoying herself with her fellow carers, having a chat and a much-needed laugh and de-stress. But here she was, feeling distinctly nervous, desperate to see him and desperate *not* to see him. Not too many people passed and no one, as far as she could tell, noticed the fifty-year-old, grey-haired woman in a blue cardigan sitting by herself in her fifteen-year-old Fiat Panda.

Almost half an hour had passed and Patricia decided she had had enough and that it was time to go back to the diners' club. Just another five minutes – and that's when she saw him, coming out of his mother's house. And he was walking on the pavement in her direction. Shaking, Patricia got out of the car, locking the door behind her. He hadn't changed much in the intervening years, a bit fatter perhaps, fuller around the face, but otherwise still the same, ugly brute he was before – and still healthy. They were close now. Would he recognise her? She'd sat through every day of his trial and given testimony against him. Surely, he would.

He had his eyes on the ground, humming to himself. How dare he hum without a care in the world?

'Excuse me,' she said, aware of the tremor in her voice.

He stopped, clocking her. 'Yes?'

'Sorry to bother you. Is there a post office nearby?'

'Yeah, you just passed it, love.' He pointed down the road. 'Two-minute walk. You can't miss it.'

'Thank you. Thank you very much.'

'No worries.'

He walked on, his hands in his pockets, humming again. He hadn't recognised her.

Patricia quickly returned to her car and sat, gripping her

car keys in her hand. 'Oh my God,' she said aloud, her breath coming short. She'd done it; she'd spoken to the man. She hadn't achieved anything but somehow it was important to her.

She looked up into the rearview mirror. He'd stopped and turned around. He was looking at her car, at her, a puzzled expression on his face. And then the moment of realisation. He *did* recognise her.

'Oh, shit.' She locked the car door and with trembling fingers inserted the key into the ignition. 'Please start, please start…' It didn't. Foot on the accelerator, she tried again. And again.

The knock on the driver's side window made her jump out of her skin. 'Hey, I know you, don't I?' he shouted from outside.

'No, no, I don't think so.' She tried the ignition again. She couldn't think.

'I recognise you.'

'No, you've got me mixed up.'

'Hang on…'

Finally, the engine roared into life. 'Oh, thank the Lord.'

'Wait a minute,' he said louder, rapping his knuckles against the car window. 'I know who you are. You gave evidence.'

She slammed her foot on the accelerator and the car kangaroo jumped. 'No, leave me alone, please.'

'Christ almighty, you're *his* daughter, Bernard Godwin's daughter. What are you doing following me, you stupid bitch?'

Back into neutral, then first gear, and she was off.

Checking her mirror, she could see him standing in the middle of the road yelling obscenities at her.

Ten minutes later, still shaking, Patricia was back at the diners' club. She rushed inside and found her father tucking into a rhubarb crumble, his bib splattered with food, custard smeared over his grey moustache. Dad was here in body, his broken body, but his mind could have been anywhere. Meanwhile, that bastard walked around, healthy as anything, humming to himself. Why was life so unfair?

Here, in the diners' club, surrounded by people, Patricia stood with her head in her hands and wept.

Chapter 29: Benedict

DS Kelly soon provided Benedict with everything he needed to know about Alan Milner, the man they suspected of having so violently robbed the Greenes. The man had just a few days before been released from prison following an eighteen-year sentence. So, Amy Greene was right – the man was an ex-convict. DS Kelly was told by Milner's probation officer that he'd given his mother's address as his first place of residence. So, it was to Sheila Milner that Benedict and Jessica now headed.

Benedict and Jessica drove the short distance to Sheila Milner's house, a rather dilapidated terraced house fronted by overgrown weeds. A couple of boys were leaning against the garden wall smoking. On seeing Benedict and Jessica approach, they hot-footed it away. The detectives sniffed the air and exchanged a knowing look. Jessica knocked on the door.

A woman answered, wearing a sort of off-white kaftan, long, scraggy grey hair. 'Mrs Milner?' asked Jessica.

'Who are you?' she asked, narrowing her eyes.

Jessica and Benedict showed Mrs Milner their identification.

Her shoulders slumped. 'What's he done now?'

'Can we come in?'

She hesitated a moment but knew she had no choice. The detectives followed her through to the living room. Benedict took in the scuffed black leather three-piece suite, the claustrophobic flowery wallpaper, the swirly-patterned carpet, her display of decorative thimbles, a tiny television in the corner, and all so dingy and smelling strongly of smoke. Mrs Milner sat in an armchair.

'Mrs Milner,' said Jessica. 'We understand your son's living with you.'

'He ain't, no.'

'Oh. We were under the impression–'

'He was for a few days but I chucked him out. I couldn't bear him being around.'

'Just to confirm, Alan returned here following his release from prison?'

'Yeah.'

'But he's moved out already?' asked Jessica. 'Where to?'

She hesitated a moment. Reaching for a pack of cigarettes from the small table next to her armchair, she lit one. 'Don't know, love. Don't care.'

'He didn't mention where he was going?' asked Benedict.

She shook her head and drew on her cigarette. 'No surprise there. Alan never tells me nothing. He never speaks to me unless he wants something.'

'No?' Somehow, Benedict didn't believe her.

'So, what's he done now?'

'We can't tell you, Mrs Milner,' said Benedict. 'But we do need to speak to him as a matter of urgency.'

'How was he following his release?' asked Jessica.

'Cocky. But he always is.'

'Did he mention any plans about what he's going to do now?'

'Huh, I'd be the last to know, love. Like I said, he doesn't tell me stuff.'

'Can you tell us about him?'

She pulled a face as if the question was too difficult. 'What's to say? He was a right handful from the moment he could walk. His dad buggered off when he was a toddler and I reckon it's true what they say – a lad needs a man about the house, someone to knock him into shape. God knows I couldn't.'

'Was he an only child?'

'What do you think? I wasn't gonna make that mistake twice.' She stubbed out her cigarette, half-smoked. 'Alan was bad enough on his own. Always getting into trouble, always on the wrong side of the bleeding law. And he was forever getting into fights. He got off on it, he liked the violence. Got it off his dad.'

'It must've been difficult though,' said Jessica. 'The day he was sent down for so long.'

Mrs Milner looked at her as if Jessica had just sprouted a third eye. 'You're joking, right? Bloody happiest day of my life that. I'd finally got shot of him.'

'OK,' said Benedict. 'Thanks for your time, Mrs Milner.' He handed her his business card. 'If he should call or should he mention where he's staying, could you let me know?'

She took the card and stuffed it in a pocket without looking at it.

Benedict and Jessica left Mrs Milner lighting a second cigarette and returned to the station.

An hour later, PC Stevens received a phone call which he now related to Benedict. 'Now, that, sir, was a jeweller called Equinox in Kentish Town. Our man's been in there trying to fob off Mrs Greene's jewellery.'

'Marvellous. What did the jeweller say?'

'He told our man to sling his hook.'

'CCTV?'

'Not good, I'm afraid. He's already sent me the file and it's probably our man on account of his size but he's wearing a baseball cap pulled down.'

'He knew he'd be on film.'

'Exactly, sir.'

Benedict would have thought a man who knew what he was doing wouldn't be hawking his ill-gotten gains to local jewellers. Like Mr Greene said, there'd be safer means via the dark web. But maybe the man was not tech-savvy and if he had, indeed, spent some time in prison, that might explain it.

He was catching up on his emails when PC Stevens returned. 'He's tried Cash Converters too now. They sent him packing too but I'm afraid the CCTV footage is just as useless.'

Two hours later, Mrs Milner rang.

'Mrs Milner, how can I help?'

'He's upstairs,' she whispered. 'He came back for some of his clothes and stuff.'

'Right, thank you. We're on our way. Can you keep him there?'

'Me? Fat chance of that.'

'Can't you offer him something to eat?'

She laughed. 'I don't cook. He knows that. Oh, shitting hell…'

Benedict could hear a man's voice, swearing followed by a

commotion of some sort. 'Mrs Milner? Mrs Milner, are you OK?'

The phone went dead.

Benedict couldn't find Jessica so called on DS Prowse. 'DS Prowse, we need to be somewhere.'

Using the blue light, DS Prowse drove like the clappers through the streets of Camden. They quickly reached Sheila Milner's house, DS Prowse screeching to a halt. DS Prowse sprinted to the front door, knocking hard, Benedict following.

Mrs Milner answered, holding a packet of frozen peas to the side of her face, and Benedict knew straight away that Milner had gone. Mrs Milner ambled back inside. The detectives followed her through to the lounge. She'd been crying. 'What happened, Mrs Milner?'

'He bloody hit me, that's what happened.' She put down the frozen peas to reveal a red cheek. Nasty, thought Benedict, but nothing severe. She reached for her cigarettes but unable to coordinate her hands, gave up.

'He hit you?'

'Yeah, he heard me on the phone talking to you. He called me some choice names and then slapped me.' She began crying again. 'Then he scarpered. And no, I don't know where he went.'

'We should go, boss,' said DS Prowse. 'He wouldn't have got far. We could try and find him.'

He was right, of course, but it seemed a little heartless to leave this woman in such distress. 'I'm so sorry this has happened to you, Mrs Milner.'

'What sort of bastard does that? Me? His own mother. What sort of man hits his own mother?'

Chapter 30: Alan / Dan

'Hello? Could you tell me if Manish Patel is working today, please?'

The woman at the other end of the line said that yes, Mr Patel was working today. If he needed to make an appointment to see Mr Patel, it'd have to wait for three days, he was fully booked. Alan thanked her.

Alan caught a tube to Brent and from the tube station walked down the busy high street until he found the Barclays Bank Manish Patel worked in. He was still shaking a little after seeing that woman. How in the hell did she find him and, more pertinently, what was she doing? He hadn't recognised her at first and then, walking on, he realised he'd seen her before. And then it hit him, she was the old bloke's daughter that night in the supermarket, the one who screamed the place down. She stood up in court and testified against him. What was the bitch doing following him around? If he ever saw her again, she'd regret it.

Alan took his place in the queue. He told the woman on the reception desk behind a perspex screen that he'd come to see Mr Patel.

'Have you got an appointment?'

'No. I don't need one.'

'I'm afraid you do, sir. He's fully booked until–'

'He'll see me. Tell him it's about Ian Turner. That'll be enough.'

The woman, Belinda, according to her name badge, made the call, lowering her voice. Alan smiled at a boy in a wheelchair waiting in the queue behind him. 'He'll see you now,' said Belinda. 'You see that office there,' she said pointing behind him. 'His name's on the door.'

He thanked her.

Manish Patel stood as Alan entered without knocking. 'Who are you?' he asked straight away. He was tall, his hair sleek, his suit sharp, the very image of a bank manager.

'An associate of your old friend, Ian Turner. Mind if I sit down?' They both sat. 'Nice office you have here.' In truth, it was a sterile space, clean and efficient but devoid of any character except for a couple of framed photos on Patel's desk. 'You're the manager here according to your LinkedUp profile.'

'I think you mean LinkedIn.'

'That's the one. I had a look at your company website. I see you have a vacancy for a manager in your Enfield branch. You're not tempted?'

'There'd be no point. It's the same job, just further to travel.'

'Sixty thousand a year. Not bad.'

'What do you want, Mr... I'm sorry, you haven't told me your name.'

'Milner. Alan Milner.'

'Tell me what you want, Mr Milner, then get out of here.'

'Blimey, is that how you greet all your customers?'

'How do you know Ian Turner?'

Alan leaned back in his chair and clicked his knuckles. 'This is the story. Eighteen years ago, I did something stupid. Very stupid. I got caught and they threw the book at me.' He put his hands up. 'I deserved it. No complaints. So, they sent me down and I served me time. And now, as you can see, I'm out. I have officially paid my debt to society. But when I did this stupid thing, I didn't act alone. I had an accomplice. Ian Turner. You worked with him?'

'I… I don't remember.'

'I think you do. You provided him with an alibi for that night.'

He hesitated but didn't answer.

Alan leaned forward in his chair. 'I said you provided him with an alibi for that night. Yes or no?'

'I… I c-can't remember.'

'No? I think you do. Try harder, Manish.'

'He…'

'Yes?'

Patel seemed to slump in his chair. 'He forced me into it.'

'Forced?'

'As in he blackmailed me. I too did something stupid back then and Turner knew, and he said if I didn't provide him with an alibi, he'd tell on me. I would've lost my job, my career, everything. I had no choice.'

'I see. Nonetheless, Manish, perjury is a serious matter.'

'Please, don't go to the police. It was a long time ago.'

'But do you see where I'm coming from, Manish? I spent eighteen years behind bars while my accomplice roamed free, getting on with his life. I believe I deserve compensation, don't you? And yet, to get that, I'd have to go to the police.

And I don't want to do that because you seem like a nice bloke, Manish. You've got your career here and I see by those photos you have a lovely family. It'd be a shame to lose all that and find yourself in prison. Tragic, even.'

Patel looked exhausted. 'How much?'

'I'm not a greedy man, Manish. The maximum you can withdraw from your bank's cash machine per day is five hundred quid. I want five hundred now. I'll come back every day for a week for another five hundred per day–'

'No, wait a minute–'

'This is not up for negotiation, Manish, my dear man. You do earn sixty thousand a year. We've established that. That's a hefty salary. Leave it in an envelope every day and we need not meet again. After one week, we'll call it quits and you need never hear from me again.'

'How do I know you won't come back in six months' time or–'

'You won't know. But I'll give you my word. Honour among thieves and all that. Do we have a deal, Manish?'

The man looked as if he might start crying. 'Yes.'

'Excellent, Mr Patel. It's been a pleasure doing business with you. I'll wait outside while you use your cash dispenser.'

*

Little Erik (with a K at the end) had barely stopped crying from the moment he was born. Helene was exhausted from the caesarean and the constant breastfeeding, and Daniel, although he would never admit it, was finding everything a little overwhelming. Ideally, he really wanted to go see Thomas Herreboudt, his therapist, and have some time to dissect his confused feelings but Helene needed him at home on constant call. He knew that having a newborn at home would change things but he hadn't anticipated just how huge a change it would be. The little chap seemed to dominate the flat and Daniel's whole life. He was on paternity leave and, again, he would never dare voice this, but frankly, he couldn't wait to return to work, to see his colleagues and ground himself with a bit of normality.

On the day after Helene's return home from the hospital, Beth, Daniel's mother, came for a visit. Naturally, she spent most of the time helping Helene and making all the right noises. After a while, Beth joined Daniel in the kitchen. 'Mum and baby are asleep,' she announced.

'Good, thanks.'

'How are things with you?'

'Yeah, great.'

His mother, he knew, could see through the falsehood. 'It will get easier. Trust me.'

There was something he wanted to ask his mother and he knew it wasn't going to be easy so without asking he filled the kettle and started making a cup of tea simply so that he wouldn't have to sit opposite her and look her in the eye.

'Mum, why was that man on the boat the other day?'

'What man?'

He sighed. 'You know who I mean. Alan Milner.'

'He wanted to see your dad. He'd been in prison for a while so he didn't know we'd split up.'

'I remember him from when I was a kid. I didn't like him then either.'

'No, he's not a nice man.'

He took a deep breath and then said it, the question that had been burning inside him for so many years. 'Why did you keep blaming me, Mum?'

She didn't answer. He turned to look at her and she was

pulling a loose thread on the end of her cardigan sleeve. 'Don't, Daniel.'

'It wasn't my fault, you know.'

'I know. I'm sorry.'

The kettle boiled. He poured the water into the mug and stirred the teabag around. With his back to her, he said, 'It really hurt me, thinking that you thought I was to blame.'

'I shouldn't have said it. I was in shock for so long, I just lashed out at you and your dad. He deserved it; he should never have left Harry and you on the barge. But I should never have taken it out on you. I'm so sorry, Dan.'

He passed her her tea. 'Why did Dad leave the boat that night?'

She shook her head. 'I still don't know.' She reached over the table and squeezed his hand. 'I am sorry, you know? It was unfair of me to lay the blame at your door. Totally unfair.'

Dan tried to smile. 'Dad thought it was Alan who took Harry.'

'Yes, but we know he didn't. He was with friends in the pub. The police saw him there on CCTV.'

'I still think of him. Every day.'

'I know, love. So do I. So do I.'

'I wonder what he's doing now, whether he's happy. Whether he even knows that this family that brought him up isn't his.'

'I still think we'll find him, you know.'

'Mum, it's been eighteen years…'

'I still believe though. I can feel it here,' she said, her hand on her heart. 'One day, out of the blue, he'll come back to us with a big smile on his face.'

'I hope so, Mum.'

Chapter 31: Ian

Ian returned from Sevenoaks with a small pay-as-you-go mobile. He paid for it in cash. He was back at home in the living room unpacking it when his sons walked in. He tried to stuff the box beneath a cushion. 'What have you got there, Dad?' asked Felix.

'Oh, this.' He laughed. 'It's just a crappy little phone.'

The boys looked at each other. 'Why do you need that?' asked Kelvin.

'Well, as a... as a backup. My proper phone is so unreliable these days.'

'Is it hell, Dad?' said Felix. 'You've only had it a year. There's nothing wrong with it.'

'Well, in case I lose it or something.'

The boys were clearly unimpressed.

That evening, Felix went out to meet his friends at a local pub while Kelvin, as always, remained in his room playing on his PlayStation.

Ian and Juliet were half watching an old comedy on BBC iPlayer. 'I ought to phone him, you know.'

'Have you any bright ideas on how to deal with him?' asked Juliet.

'No.'

'We could try killing him. That'll shut him up.'

'Don't be daft.'

'There's no way we're selling this house, Ian. No way on God's earth.'

'I'll go and see him. See what this new job is about. It might not be so bad.'

'If it's worth a hundred thousand, it will be.'

'I know but…'

'What?'

'There's no harm in hearing him out.'

Later that evening, Felix returned from the pub. They asked after his evening. Ian loved his sons but he had a special fondness for Felix, the son who shouldn't have been. They'd have never got away with it now, now that everyone's details were kept in digital form. But back then, in 2005, yes, there were computer records, but doctors, surgeries, health care workers, took greater store by the Personal Child Health Record or, as it was known, the 'red book', the little book all new babies were given that recorded their early years – growth and development, measurements, injections, immunisations, etc. It was relatively easy to declare that they'd lost Felix's red book and receive a replacement. Luckily, Felix was a healthy baby and child and they rarely needed to come into contact with the authorities. They moved out of London soon after he became theirs and rented a place until they found this wonderful cabin-like house in the woods, isolated and away from society's prying eyes.

The following morning, Ian rang Alan on his new Nokia.

'You win,' said Ian. 'I'll do the job.'

'Ah, good man. I knew you'd see sense. I didn't want you to sell up so that's good. Are you free today?'

'Today. Well–'

'I'm living on a boat these days but meet me at my mum's house. Get here as soon as you can.' He hung up.

'What did he say?' asked Juliet.

'He wants me over there now.'

'OK. You'd better go then.' She hugged him. 'We'll get through this, Ian. One way or another, we'll get through it.'

'I know, love. I know.'

Two hours later, Ian was back in Camden Town. He'd not been here for years, he tried to avoid London these days – too many traumatic memories. He made his way to Alan's mother's house. Alan let him in. 'My mum's just gone out.'

Alan made Ian a cup of coffee. 'Right,' he said, sitting down. 'This is the plan. We're gonna rob a bank.'

'You what?' Ian choked. 'We can't rob a bank. Don't you realise how much technology they've got these days? We can't just walk in with stockings over our heads and say hand your cash over.'

'If you'd shut up a minute, you girl. *We* are not actually going to rob a bank.'

'You just said–'

'Manish Patel is.'

'Manish?' Ian bellowed. 'How do you work that out?'

Alan put his hand up. 'Step at a time, lad. I went to see him. Very accommodating he was. Nice bloke. He works in a bank in Brent. He's the manager there, the big cheese. He'll have the keys. Now, poor old Manish knows he's a phone call away from being locked up – and you, as well, mate. So, he'll do what we say.'

Ian looked at him, his mouth open. 'You've lost it. You've actually gone and lost it.' He stood up, placing the coffee mug to one side. 'I'm going home now. This has been a total waste of time.'

Alan sprang to his feet. 'You'll sit down and do as I say.'

'Alan, what you're planning is a one-way ticket back to prison.'

'Patel will have the keys. He'll know all the alarm codes, he'll know where to go and what to do. He'll know the security guys.'

'He'll never get past them, even if he does know them.'

'No, they'll listen to him. We'll do it Sunday late, Monday early hours. Banks hold the most on Sundays as all of the nightclubs and bars drop their takings off in the night safe. Also, Patel's branch has four cash points. The more ATMs, the more dosh. It's a big branch. By my reckoning, they could have anything up to a hundred grand there. And if it goes tits up, which it won't, it'll be Patel's neck on the line.'

'And he'll talk. He'll drop us right in it.'

'No because he won't want them knowing about providing you with your false alibi. That's a serious charge.'

'Why will you need me?'

'You'll keep his missus company. A bit of insurance, like.'

'You mean like a hostage?'

'If you like.'

'Christ, this gets better by the minute. Prison's frazzled your head, mate. Where do we keep the cash? We can't store it here.'

'I thought of that. We'd store it in my new boat. It's a barge near where Beth's moored. I saw it the other day. It's empty. I broke in and you can tell no one's been in for yonks. It's gonna be my new home for a while. I've already moved a few things in and made it secure.'

Alan spent the next ten minutes going into detail. He'd clearly thought it through, thought Ian, but his plan was still utterly bonkers. He returned home, his head in a daze.

'Well?' asked Juliet on seeing him.

Ian flung his phone on the coffee table. 'He's got a simple plan. He wants to rob a bank. And if we go through with it, I'll be heading straight to prison. The man is in cloud cuckoo land. He wants to do it on Sunday night. We have to do something, Jools. I can't go to prison.'

'You may have to.'

'What?'

'We can't risk losing Felix. You may have to sacrifice yourself for the sake of our son.'

Was she joking? He loved Felix, of course he did, but surely she wouldn't expect him to go to prison. 'No. No, I can't. I'd rather kill Milner first.'

'Are you serious?' she asked, narrowing her eyes.

He thought about this. 'What alternative is there?'

He'd robbed a supermarket, he'd blackmailed a man and he'd stolen a baby. Back in the day, he'd never believed he was capable of such acts. But could he kill a man? No. But like he said, what alternative was there?

Chapter 32: Benedict

Sonia and Benedict went to the party thrown by their friends Abigail and Tom. It was one of those middle-class, middle-aged affairs. They stood around with a glass of wine in their hands, discussing house prices and local schools. Benedict couldn't help but notice that Abigail had left a number of prospectuses for private schools lying around.

Lined up outside was a fleet of 4x4s belonging to Abigail and Tom's new friends, whose children were equipped with the newest trainers, mobiles and computer games. Each time Sonia and Benedict went there, they met new people but rarely met the same people twice as each new set of friends was superseded by someone richer or better acquainted with the in-crowd. Sonia seemed to be the only constant in their social life and so, by extension, Benedict as well. Benedict suspected they were only there to remind Abigail and Tom how far they'd gone, how much they had achieved and to remind them that if things turned for the worse they could never be as poorly off as the Paiges. Sonia and Benedict had more chance of sending their children to the moon than private school.

Benedict was horrified to see Abigail and Tom's friends Sandra and Charles arrive. Benedict thought they'd fallen off the Abigail and Tom radar but obviously not. Charles was a lovely, unassuming chap, all the harder to credit that he was the UK MD of some huge credit card company and had a salary twice as large as Luxembourg's Gross Domestic Product. But it was his wife Benedict was scared off. A large, over-made-up woman with huge, unruly hair and habitually dressed in voluminous flowery dresses, Sandra had no need to work, spending her day getting drunk, getting lost in their huge Kent manor house and occasionally buying her children obscenely expensive toys so that they didn't bother her. The Dr Jekyll and Mr Hyde of the Tunbridge Wells set, she was quite charming when sober. Problem was being staggeringly drunk was her preferred state of being. And then Benedict found her an alarming prospect, especially when she considered you rather attractive, as, for some maddening and strange reason, she did of Benedict.

It was a small gathering, a select few, said Abigail by means of justification, so it was hard to avoid Sandra who arrived half-cut and by ten o'clock was well on her way to being totally cut.

'Oo,' she said, swaying slightly. 'Benedict, you look so… so dashing tonight.'

'Really? Thank you.'

'And meee? Don't I look lovely?'

'Erm, yes, delightful.'

'Delightful he says. Oh, Benedict, you're so English. Aren't you drinking?'

Tom came to his rescue and Benedict managed to avoid Sandra for a while until Abigail suggested they all head for the living room for a game of Jenga, the game where you have a tower of small wooden blocks and you take turns removing one at a time without collapsing the whole thing. Steady hands and full concentration are needed. So when Sandra insisted on playing, brushing aside her husband's advice, Benedict knew the game was not destined to last.

'Sandra, love,' said Charles, hoping his tone of voice was enough to deter her.

'Oh, stop being such a stuck in the bog. Mud. Stick. Whatever.'

Charles may command a workforce of thousands with Stalinist authority but when it came to his wife, he was a mere pup.

Sure enough, Sandra brought the relatively sturdy tower of bricks down with her first go. 'Oh, silly me,' she giggled. A second game was also brought to a premature end by her shaky hand, and one by one, the others left, Sonia being the first to desert ship. Within a blink of an eye, Benedict found himself alone with Sandra, everyone having gone off to top up their drinks or to the loo or out for a smoke. Left alone together, Benedict could hear the nearby hubbub of animated conversation above the thud of music and the smell of freshly baked quiches wafting through to the living room. Sandra and Benedict sat on the floor, cross-legged; Sandra eyeing the detritus of wooden blocks as if surveying the aftermath of a car accident. Benedict felt moved to ask whether she was OK.

'It's all shit,' she said in a heavy, lost voice.

'It's only a game of Jenga,' Benedict said, thinking that perhaps he was missing the point.

'It's shit. Charles is so crap in bed.'

'Oh.' Benedict hadn't expected that. 'Right…'

'I need a man. A proper man.'

'I guess we all do. I mean not literally, I don't need a man, but in a… a…'

'Are you a man in bed, Benedict?'

Heck, what sort of question was that? 'Don't know, erm… not really, if truth be told.'

'That's not what I've heard.'

'What?!'

'I'm only teasing.'

'Oh, I see.' He forced out a nervous laugh. And just as he was wondering how to extricate himself, Sandra started coming towards him on all fours. He shuffled backwards on his backside as she lolloped towards him, ungainly with evil intent.

'Come 'ere, you.'

'No, Sandra, really.' And in no time, they'd done a complete lap of the living room, scattering pieces of Jenga in their wake.

Fortunately, Abigail came to Benedict's rescue, leaning against the doorframe, glass in one hand, cigarette in the other. 'You two having fun?' she asked, grinning.

'I want Benedict to f–'

'F-forget,' said Benedict, springing to his feet.

'Forget what?'

'Forget that I ever beat Sandra at Jenga. Anyway, I need to organise another game. I'll get the others.'

Sandra collapsed in an undignified heap in the middle of the room, muttering, 'Why's he so crap in bed, why, why?'

Abigail shot Benedict a questioning look. 'Not me; she doesn't mean me. I think I need a drink if you'll…'

Benedict spent the next hour in the kitchen safely by Sonia's side. The rumour went around that Sandra had locked herself in the bathroom, sobbing, with Charles at the door, trying to coax her out and receiving nothing but very personal abuse for his efforts. No one seemed particularly perturbed or surprised at Sandra's emotional meltdown; it was par for the course and most of the guests had witnessed it before. Several times. Benedict pitied poor Charles; he may apparently be crap in bed but he was a long-suffering soul accustomed but wearied by his wife's drunken rollercoaster of emotions. As midnight approached, Sandra re-emerged looking triumphant as if everything was well in her world and having re-applied rather clumsily her make-up. Charles hovered near her, looking drained and sheepish.

Soon after, Sonia and Benedict made to leave, saying protracted goodbyes and best wishes. Sandra clenched Benedict in a bear hug and actually nibbled his ear. Given her state of inebriation, Benedict was lucky to survive with his lobe intact. 'If you ever want a real woman…' she whispered into Benedict's chewed ear.

'That's most kind, Sandra, but–'

'Most kind!' she shrieked, deafening him. 'You're so funny.'

'Yes, isn't he?' said Sonia, prising them apart. 'But he won't be feeling so funny when Rosie wakes him up at seven o'clock tomorrow morning. Come on, lover boy, time to take you home.'

Chapter 33: Alan

Alan now had a decent amount of cash, thanks to Mrs Greene, Ian Turner and Manish Patel. He'd seen a decent-looking car in a second-hand dealer's showroom on sale for five hundred pounds, and now, at last, he could afford it. A short while back, the prison service had renewed his driving licence for him. In a rare moment of generosity, he'd even given his mother fifty pounds towards groceries and household bills. She wasn't as delighted as he expected her to be. 'I thought you were moving out,' she barked at him.

'Don't you like me being here? A bit of company for you in your dotage?'

'Do you want the honest answer? No, I don't. I want me house back to myself. Why do you have to take up so much space?'

'Do me a favour, Mother, and shut up. You're getting on my nerves. I had cellmates that have been easier to live with than you.'

'Sod off back to them then.'

'Be careful, Mum. You may be my mother but that doesn't

mean I won't slap you again if you get too mouthy. So, just watch it.'

'God, you're just like your father.'

'I'll go when I'm ready, all right? As it is...'

'What?'

'I've found myself a nice little boat near King's Cross to live on for a while. It's called *Crazy Lou* and it suits me just fine.'

Saturday night, Alan decided to visit a couple of old pubs he used to go to, see if there was anyone he knew from the old days. The first pub had turned into a trendy Greek restaurant so he made his way to the second, the King George. The place had changed since he'd last stepped through these doors, everything spruced up, carpets, loud music and packed with youngsters. He didn't like it one bit and not a single familiar face. Still, while he was here, he'd have a pint or two. The girl who served him his drink didn't look old enough, and when she asked him for five pounds for a pint, he couldn't stop himself from screeching, 'How much?' He couldn't see anywhere to sit so he decided to remain at the bar. He watched as various people came and went, ordering their drinks. At one point, a pretty white girl with a nose ring and a swirly tattoo on her left arm, about twenty, took her place in the queue. She caught his eye. Alan raised his glass. 'All right, love?' he asked.

She nodded and turned her back on him.

'Charming. You can join me if you want.'

'No, you're alright, thanks,' she said, over her shoulder.

'This is your local then?'

She ignored him, trying to catch the eye of one of the bar staff.

'Last time I was here was about eighteen years ago. You

were probably still at school then.'

Her turn came next and she asked for a white wine and a vodka and lime.

'Bring your mate over, let's have a chat.'

'I said, you're all right, no.'

'What? Not good enough for you?' He watched as she paid for her round by touching her card on a reader. This was another novelty to him. You couldn't do that eighteen years ago. 'Don't worry, love, it's not as if I wanna get into your knickers or nothing. You're a bit young even for me.'

'Well, that's just as well, ain't it, you twat?'

She made to walk off but incensed by her, Alan reached out and caught her by her upper arm. She screeched as she spilt her drink. 'Hey, what the fuck?'

'What did you call me?'

A tall, black guy with a goatee suddenly appeared at her side, his shirt bulging with gym muscle.

'Oh, look, the sodding cavalry's arrived.'

'What's going on?' said the man.

'This idiot's hassling me.'

'Only trying to be nice, you stuck-up little cow.'

'Don't you speak to her like that—'

'Why? What are you going to do about it, shit for brains?'

'Oh, piss off, you loser.' The man led his girlfriend away.

But Alan wasn't finished yet. 'Hey, wait up.'

The man stopped and turned to face him. Stepping up to him, Alan drew his head back, then tensing his neck muscles, slammed his head into the man's face. The girl shrieked, the man fell back, clutching his nose. People screamed. Alan heard someone urging the bar staff to call the police. Others brought their phones out to film the spectacle. The girl put her arms around her boyfriend. 'Oh my God, Jason, I think he's broken your nose.' Blood poured between his fingers. 'You maniac,' she screamed at Alan. 'You should be locked up.'

Alan finished the rest of his drink in one and, slamming the glass down on the bar, wiped his mouth and belched. 'That's me done,' he said to the girl who served him. And with that, he left the pub.

As much as he tried to play it cool and as much as he enjoyed hearing the man's nose snap, the altercation had riled him. He stormed down Camden High Street, barging past people, swearing to himself. People stepped aside not wanting to bump into the mad bloke with the bald head and attitude. Eventually, he slowed up and, catching his breath, calmed down. He felt hot. He realised he was feeling lightheaded; after all, that had been his first drink in almost two decades. He looked around and realised he wasn't too far away from Lana's place. Pretty, sexy, Lana. He'd go say hello, see how she was.

Five minutes later, he was there, knocking on her door. She answered, wearing a silk dressing gown. 'God, you look sexy, Lana. Have I caught you at a bad time?'

'You can't come in. Mark almost killed me that time he saw you here.'

He could see a shadow of darkness beneath one eye. 'I'd better be quick then.'

'I'm about to have a bath.'

'Great. I'll come in then. I can watch.'

'Piss off, will you?'

He pushed past her. 'We've got some unfinished business, Lana.'

'Mark could be back any minute.'

'You think I'm scared of him?'

'No but I am.'

'Oh, Lana, that's not good. Do you want me to deal with him? I could make sure he never—'

'No, Alan! I want you to leave and never come back.'

'But, Lana, you and me, we used to be so good together.'

'In your head, maybe,' she said, tapping her temple. 'You're deluded, always was.'

He pressed her against the hallway wall. 'Nice dressing gown, Lana. What if I told you I'm gonna be rich soon?'

'Bully for you. Now get off me.'

'Like I said, babes, unfinished business.'

'Please don't do this to me, Alan. Please don't…'

*

Twenty minutes later, Alan left Lana's. It was still a warm evening, the night sky clear of clouds. He made his way home but halfway there, he stopped and decided instead he'd sleep on his newly-acquired barge. He was happy, happier than he'd been in a long time. He had money in his pocket and tonight, for the first time in eighteen years, he'd had a drink, got into a fight and had sex.

What more did a man need?

And even better, tomorrow was Sunday, the day Manish Patel was going to make him a rich man.

Life, Alan Milner concluded, was sweet.

Chapter 34: Ian

Sunday and Ian Turner's mind was in turmoil expecting and fearing a phone call from Alan Milner at any moment. It was a beautiful day and both his boys were out, meeting friends, having fun and doing what teenagers do. How Ian envied them. Juliet too was full of anxiety. She hugged Felix before he headed out, embarrassing the boy. Ian wanted to hug him too but that would have set alarm bells ringing. He watched as his son got ready.

Felix had had a wonderful upbringing, showered with love, sent to a decent school. He'd never been in need of anything. They lived in this beautiful house in the woods surrounded by nature and fresh air, and Felix and his brother had grown up the epitome of the outdoor types. What sort of upbringing would Felix have had, had he been brought up by Beth? A single parent with no money, living on a barge? As parents, their only crime had been to spoil him. The thought of all this crashing down was too awful to contemplate. He had the feeling that this was to be Felix's last day of innocence, eighteen years coming to an end on this very day. As soon as Felix had gone, Ian broke down and cried.

Sure enough, come five o'clock, Ian's Nokia sounded. He saw Juliet stiffen. 'This is it,' he said. Twenty seconds later, Ian put the phone down. 'He wants me to head over there now.'

'Oh God. Ian.'

'What can I do, Jools? He's got me over a barrel. And there's no one who can help us. I actually want to be sick.'

'I know, love, me too.'

'I'd better go. See what hell awaits me.'

'Good luck. You will let me know.'

'No, I'm leaving my phone here. I don't want the cops to trace me.'

'Are you going to do it?'

He shook his head. 'What choice do I have?'

'I love you, Ian.'

'Yeah. I love you too.'

Before leaving the house, Ian sneaked into the shed behind the house and retrieved a claw hammer, stuffing it into his drawstring bag.

Ian caught the Sevenoaks train into London's Charing Cross and from there a tube up to King's Cross. From King's Cross, he made his way to the canal and walked along the towpath, passing beneath the arched bridge where, so many years ago, he'd thrown away his black Puma trainers. He shuddered at the memory. He rang Alan on the Nokia. 'Stay by the bridge,' he said. 'I'll come and meet you. I'll be there in five.'

Sure enough, Alan came lumbering up the path within a few minutes. Ian's stomach lurched on seeing him.

'Nice day for making lots of money,' said Alan, rubbing

his hands. They started walking. 'My new home's just up here. It was gonna be temporary but I'm thinking of staying there now. I need to get away from my mum. She's doing my head in. I can see why Beth and Kris liked living on a barge so much.'

'I think it was more a financial thing than choice.'

'And I'll have Beth nearby. I can pop in for a cup of tea every now and then.'

'Hmm.'

'What have you got in your bag?'

'Oh, erm, just a book for the train.'

'Here we are. She's called *Crazy Lou*. Come aboard.'

Ian followed Alan onto the barge. He had to make sure he didn't touch anything; he couldn't leave a single hint that he'd been here. 'Is the boat registered?'

'I don't know. I certainly haven't done it.'

Inside stank of mould. It was nowhere as nice as he remembered Beth and Kris' barge: dirty wooden panels, filthy plates piled high, stained cushions. Ian reached inside his bag and felt the wooden handle of the hammer but Alan was walking around too much, picking things up, putting them down again. Despite his bravado, the man was nervous.

'I've rung Manish. He's expecting me.'

'You've told him already?'

'Don't be daft. He's expecting us but he doesn't know why. He's probably bricking it. Come on, let's go.'

'Alan, I really don't think–'

'Oh, shut it, will you? I told you, I've planned it all out. You've got the easy bit; all you have to do is keep Mrs Patel company for an hour, an hour and a half. Make sure, she's frightened of you. Any hint of trouble, give her a slap. Manish needs to know we mean business.'

Ian followed Alan off the boat, his heart hammering. He had to do this. For the sake of keeping Felix, for the sake of his family, he *had* to do this.

He had to do it now, here, on the towpath. But there were too many people milling about, enjoying the late afternoon sun. They walked side by side, Alan talking; Ian needed to get behind him.

After five minutes, they reached the bridge, Alan's voice echoing beneath the arch. The path here was deserted, damp as always. Ian stopped and pretended to do his shoelace. Alan sauntered ahead. Now! Ian pulled the hammer from his bag. His arm behind his head, his hand gripping the hammer, three, four steps… Alan half twisted his head. His eyes flashed. Ian brought the hammer down. Alan moved. The hammer fell onto his left shoulder. He grunted as his right arm swung around, his fist catching Ian on the jaw before Ian had time to readjust and try again. It wasn't a powerful hit but the second one, to the stomach, was, taking Ian's breath away. Ian slouched as Alan's uppercut slammed into Ian's jaw. He still had the hammer. He lifted his arm but he knew already everything was lost. A third punch sent him sprawling across the grass verge on the lip of the canal. The hammer slipped into the water. Alan hoisted Ian up by his shirt and hit him again and again. Ian's mouth flooded with blood.

A voice! Somewhere distant, a voice shouting. A man's voice. Alan dropped Ian but, for good measure, kicked him hard in the ribs, twice, the bone cracking. Ian drifted in and out of consciousness as he heard Alan run away. Footsteps, several footsteps. 'Christ, are you alright, mate?' A man's voice.

'We need to call an ambulance.' A woman's voice.

'Look at his nose. Fuck.'

Ian tried opening his eyes. His right one wouldn't open. Gritting his broken teeth, he hauled himself over onto his front.

'You need to keep still, mate. We're going to call 999.'

From his front, he managed to hoist himself up on all fours and spat out large dollops of blood. His nose was hurting like hell, the blood pouring from it. One of his helpers was rubbing his back as he coughed and spat. 'No am-ambulance,' he managed to say.

'What did you say?'

'I'm OK.'

'You're not, mate. You're—'

'I'm fucking OK, right?' Christ, everything hurt. He had to get up, he had to get out of here. Gripping the woman's arm, he pulled himself up. He stood, his head swaying, his legs weak.

'Listen, mate,' said the man. 'God knows what injuries you have…' He had his phone in his hand, ready to use it. 'You have to get to a hospital.'

'Y-you t-touch that phone, I'll throw you in the canal.'

He saw them exchange glances. The man put his hands up. 'Alright, you win, you tosser. You can fuck off and die as far as I care. Sod you, you bastard. We were only trying to help.' With that, he grabbed his girlfriend by the arm and pulled her away. 'You ungrateful shit.'

Ian felt like hell – one tooth was missing, several others were loose, he had a broken nose and god knows how many broken or cracked ribs. But he'd stopped Alan from robbing the bank. At least for now. He knew it was only a temporary reprieve; Alan would soon be back…

Chapter 35: Patricia

Eight o'clock Monday morning. Time for Patricia to wake Dad up, the start of another day. The sun was out and the day was already warm. Dad didn't like it when it got too hot. Patricia finished her tea and made her way upstairs. As soon as she opened the bedroom door, she knew something was off. Dad was on the bed, his chest arched, his face white as a sheet but he was sweating profusely. 'Dad?' she rushed over. 'Dad, what's the matter?' He groaned, a spool of saliva down his chin, his eyes glazed over. His breathing seemed erratic and he was wheezing. She knew what was happening, she'd prepared for it – her father was having a heart attack. 'I'm going to call for an ambulance, Dad.'

She rushed back downstairs and, finding her phone, rang 999.

She returned to her father and, sitting on the bed, took his clammy hand. 'It's on its way, Dad.' She needed to compose herself for his sake. 'Hold on now, it won't be long.' She placed an aspirin tablet in his mouth. 'Chew this, Dad. It'll help.' But he couldn't do it; he didn't even have the strength to do that. He didn't look good. She had to remain calm but her heart was hammering. She willed the ambulance to hurry. 'You'll be OK, Dad. Just hold on. Don't leave me now.' She placed an extra pillow behind his head. Ideally, she needed to hoist him up into a sitting position but he was too heavy for her. Instead, she bent his knees up. These were the things she'd been advised to do. She tried again with the aspirin, massaging his jaw but it wasn't working. He groaned again, a horrible, rattling noise. He seemed so frail. She prayed but she knew now that he wasn't going to make it.

She heard the siren of the ambulance. 'They're here, Dad. Not long now and we'll get you to hospital. You'll be OK.'

She ran downstairs and unlocked the front door. The ambulance pulled up. The two paramedics approached. 'Hi, it's my dad. I think he's had a heart attack. He's upstairs.'

She followed them back upstairs. 'What's his name, love?'

'Bernard.'

'Bernard, we need to get you to the hospital now. Bernard? OK, we've got a situation here.'

'Is he all right?' said Patricia, conscious of the panic in her voice.

The woman didn't answer as she started CPR on him. Her colleague told her to stand back as he prepared the defibrillator. Patricia put her hand to her mouth. She felt so small, so useless. She prayed they'd save him. The second medic unbuttoned Dad's pyjama top and applied the pads to his chest while his colleague continued with the CPR. The defibrillator's automated voice guided the medic although it was obvious he knew what he was doing. Once ready, he told Patricia to stand further back. He pressed the shock button. Patricia had to leave the room for a minute. Her own heart felt as if it might collapse on her. She could hear the two medics talking in urgent whispers, she could hear the worry in their voices. Nothing was working, Dad was too far gone. Bracing herself, she returned to the bedroom. They persevered, the woman pressing down on Dad's chest, the man using the defibrillator to apply another shock. After a while, they swapped, the woman too exhausted to continue. 'Come on, Dad, come on. You can do it…'

The paramedics tried their best. But it wasn't enough. The woman held Patricia's hand as she delivered the bad news. Bernard Godwin, aged seventy-five, was with God now.

*

The rest of the day passed in a haze. The paramedics stayed until a doctor arrived to confirm and register that Patricia's father had died. He, in turn, stayed long enough for a local funeral director to arrange the removal of Dad's body to a funeral home. By midday, Dad was gone.

Patricia made herself a simple lunch, watched the lunchtime news, and went to the local shop to buy a few things she didn't need. She returned to a quiet house. To be fair, she always had. Dad barely said a word and when he did it was always a struggle to hear, but there was always his presence in the house. Now, there was nothing, just a strange, heavy silence.

That evening, Patricia braced herself and went into her father's room. The bed was still as it was at the point they'd removed him. She decided to leave it the following day; she couldn't face removing and washing the sheets now. She opened his wardrobe doors and, seeing his clothes hanging up, breathed in the familiar smell. And then she saw it on the upper shelf inside the wardrobe. She reached up and brought it down. God's Favorite. This was the baseball cap Dad used to insist on wearing despite or perhaps because of, the cheesy slogan.

She returned downstairs, taking the cap with her, and switched the television on. This was the baseball cap Dad was wearing when Alan Milner punched him so hard, it destroyed his life – and hers. She circled it around her hands, wondering what Milner was doing at this moment. Probably watching TV too, humming to himself, maybe drinking a can of beer, happily ignorant of the fact that he had, in effect, killed a man. Did he ever pause and think of Dad? Did he ever experience even a passing moment of guilt? She doubted it. The man was a thug, a heartless thug, who'd killed her father – for what? A pocketful of cash and a few packets of cigarettes.

She consoled herself with the thought that Dad was in a better place now, spared his daily torment. He was free now.

Come ten o'clock, Patricia went to bed. She turned the light off, offered her prayers and for the first time allowed the tears to come.

*

Seven thirty, Tuesday morning. Patricia got up at her normal time and had her routine cup of tea. Come eight o'clock, her heart tumbled within her – she didn't need to go wake her father, didn't need to guide him to the shower and help him get dressed. These things she'd diligently done for the last eighteen years were finished. God, she was going to miss him so much.

Her father had given her life a purpose, looking after him a sense of routine. And now that that was gone, how was she going to fill her day? She viewed her future with dread. She was going to have to find something to fill the void. But not now, not today. Today, she had a plan.

She considered her collection of kitchen knives and choosing the largest, sharpened it and, wrapping it in a tea towel, placed it in her handbag.

She drove the three miles to Camden Town and, like before, parked up on the street outside Mrs Milner's house. She knew what she was about to do was wrong and it was going to be by far *the* most difficult thing she'd ever have to do but she didn't have a choice. Alan Milner had served his pitiful sentence and he'd got off lightly. They had imprisoned him for the robbery and the assault, not for killing her father. Too much time had elapsed now; it had taken Dad eighteen years to die, the courts would not equate his death to the assault and Milner would remain a free man. But she knew and God knew that Dad's death was a direct consequence of Milner's punch all those years ago. If the justice system could not make him pay, then she, and God, would.

She walked up to the house, aware of the sweat drenching her blouse. She rang the doorbell and, putting her hand in her handbag, grasped the handle of her kitchen knife. Mrs Milner answered the door.

'Hello. I'm sorry to bother you but is Alan in?'

'No. Who are you?'

'Oh, I'm…' She should have prepared for this. 'I'm an old friend…'

'Friend? Alan? Who are you really?'

'No, I am. Before, you know… But before that. My name's… erm, J-Jane. Did he not mention me?'

'Jane? No.'

'Do you know when he's due back?'

'He'll be on his boat on the canal.'

'Oh yes, he used to talk about wanting to get a boat.'

'Did he?'

'Is it on the canal?'

'Yeah.' She went to close the door.

'Thank you so much.'

Maybe there was something in the way she said it but the woman paused a moment, her face softened. 'It's called *Crazy Lou*. It's near King's Cross.'

Patricia smiled. 'Thank you.' She returned to her car.

Patricia drove home. There was no point driving to King's Cross, there'd be nowhere to park. She made a cup of coffee, her mind telling her that what she had planned was mad, inhumane, cruel and a whole host of other adjectives telling her it was plain wrong. She needed to listen to these voices. And then she saw the baseball cap on her settee. The man didn't deserve to live.

She caught a bus and the tube to King's Cross and using her phone, found her way to the canal. There were so many boats moored up. She had no idea. She couldn't remember the last time she was here. She strolled along the path, looking at each boat, trying to find *Crazy Lou*. She walked under a low bridge, her shadow dancing on its stonework. People passed – joggers, dog walkers and cyclists. Many said hello to her, everyone buoyed by the sunny weather.

She must've walked a mile and she hadn't found it. The day was getting hotter and she'd forgotten to bring any water. She saw a young man stepping onto a boat called *Lazy Suzan* with a baby strapped to his chest. A woman came out to greet him. 'Dan,' she cried, kissing the man on the cheek. 'How's little Erik?'

Patricia walked on. She must have missed it. Seeing a woman with purple hair on a boat, she asked if she knew where *Crazy Lou* was. She didn't. Maybe this was God's way of telling her not to do this. She could feel her determination draining away. She was almost back at the bridge when she saw it – *Crazy Lou*. How did she miss it the first time?

She put her hand to her chest. This was it. She offered a silent prayer, beseeching God to give her the strength to do this, to mete out His justice and avenge her father. It had to be now; she knew if she didn't do it now, she'd never come back.

Carefully, she stepped onto the boat. It creaked in the water. She knocked on the door. No answer. No sound. She knocked again. 'Hello? Mr Milner?'

She eased the door open. He hadn't locked it. She stepped inside. 'Hello?' Her eyes adjusted to the gloom. The place stank of dampness and decay. 'Is anyone home?' She crept forward. There were plates in the sink, an empty baked bean tin and half a bottle of whiskey on the draining board. She recognised a Degas print on the wall. The carpet was stained, the furniture even more so. The place gave her the creeps. How could someone live in such filth? She saw ahead a door ajar swinging slightly with the sway of the boat. She inched forward, every nerve on end. She fingered her crucifix necklace, pushed open the door and flapped away the flies that appeared. The room was dark, the curtains drawn. She found a light switch and flicked it on.

'Oh, Lord!' she screamed. There, lying on the floor crammed beside a single bed in front of her, was Alan Milner. She stepped forward. 'Mr Milner?' His eyes were wide open, his mouth too. He was dead, she knew that. Peering down at him, she saw the pool of congealed blood beneath his head. Someone had done this to him. The bile rose up within her. She had to clamp her mouth shut. She reached out and steadied herself against the wall.

Someone had been here and killed Alan Milner. Someone, some bastard, had stolen her moment.

Part Three

July 2023

Chapter 36: Benedict

Benedict viewed the bucolic scene in front of him. The canal stretched into the distance, the water reflecting the sun, a couple of ducks floating by, dipping their heads in the murky water. It was the sort of place he and his wife might wander along on a Sunday afternoon before heading to a canalside pub. A number of canal boats, or were they barges, were lined up, although the one he'd come to visit was moored a small distance from its neighbours. A police tape surrounded it and various officers in white forensic suits milled about, coming and going. And this barge, *Crazy Lou*, stood out from the others. While the other boats were obviously well cared for, freshly painted and sporting buckets of flowers, this one looked battered and old. He could see a couple of uniformed officers asking questions of nearby boat residents. He spotted Jessica on the towpath talking to the usual crime scene manager, Adrian Collins. Benedict joined them.

'Ah, sir,' said Collins. 'Too nice a day to be investigating a murder.'

'It is indeed. So, what do we have?'

'One white male by the name of...' He consulted his notes. 'Alan Milner, aged fifty-three.'

'Oh? Alan Milner? We've been looking for him.'

'Well, I'm afraid someone beat you to it.'

'Who found him?'

'An anonymous phone call from a payphone near Kings Cross tube station.'

'Anonymous?' said Jessica.

'Yep. A woman. Said she didn't want to leave her name, apparently. Shall we climb aboard?'

The boat's interior smelled musty, everything looked dirty, the lounge floor was littered with beer cans. Benedict noticed the framed painting of ballet dancers.

'He's in the bedroom,' said DS Collins, leading the way. Pushing the bedroom door open, Collins bumped into the station's pathologist Dick Evans, coming out. They did a little dance while a photographer squeezed between them, apologising, his huge camera clunking against the door frame.

'Not enough room to swing a cat,' said Evans. 'Ben, we've been expecting you. Hello there, DS Gardiner. Haven't shot back to Glasgow yet?'

'Manchester, sir. No, not at all.'

Collins hung back to allow Jessica and Benedict to squeeze in beside the pathologist. There, on the floor, crammed between the tiny bed and the wooden wall, was Alan Milner lying on his back, his eyes still open. He wore a pair of dark jeans and a grey Lacoste hoodie. There was a sleeping bag on the bed and a dressing gown on a wardrobe hook.

'Lacoste, boss. Just as Amy Greene described.'

'Indeed.'

'You can see the blood on the carpet,' said Collins. 'We haven't been able to move him yet so take everything I say with a pinch of salt at this juncture. But I think it's safe to say he was hit on the back of the head. How many times, I don't know yet.'

'Any sign of–'

'No. Sorry to interrupt, DS Gardiner. But no, no sign of the murder weapon. And, anticipating your next question, he's not been here long. Ask me again after the postmortem, but I'm guessing this happened within the last twenty-four hours.'

'Any other injuries?'

'Actually yes but it's got nothing to do with the killing. Mr Milner has been in a fight recently. He's got bruising on the knuckles. Furthermore, to add to the mix, one of the lads found a tea towel in the kitchen smeared with blood and the blood is dry. It's older.'

'How much blood are we talking about?' asked Jessica.

'Not a lot.'

'He got into a fight,' said Benedict. 'Got himself hurt and wiped the blood on the towel.'

'Yes, or it could be the other person's blood.'

'Hmm.'

Benedict thanked Evans and, heading out, he and Jessica rejoined DS Collins in the tiny kitchen, watching an officer dusting the surfaces for fingerprints. 'Shall we go outside?' said Collins.

Back on the towpath, Benedict asked, 'Any damage to the boat, Adrian?'

'We've not found anything yet. The lock on the door's OK and nothing seems out of place. But it's early days yet.'

'Could be a robbery gone wrong?' said Jessica.

'Ah, well, now you're talking because had it been a robbery, the perpetrator missed out on the grand prize.'

'Meaning?' asked Benedict.

'Nigh-on two and a half thousand quid in fifty-pound notes stuffed in a tin marked tea. Yes, there're a couple of tea bags in there but also this wad of cash in batches of five hundred pounds with elastic bands.'

'Whoa,' said Jessica. 'Two and a half grand?'

'Yep, and pristine. So pristine I reckon it's not long left a bank.'

'We'll check that out,' said Benedict.

'There's more,' said Collins. 'We found a jewellery box under his bed stuffed with rings and necklaces and so forth.'

'Which I reckon belongs to Mrs Greene, Jessica.'

'Undoubtedly.'

'Mrs Greene gave us pictures so we'll check.'

'But the perpetrator couldn't have known about the money or the jewellery otherwise the boat would have been ransacked,' said Jessica.

'Good point,' said Benedict.

'We found his wallet. It had one of those fifty-pound notes in it. And a fiver and some change. We also found another £205 stuffed beneath his mattress plus an interesting collection of jewellery.'

'So,' said Jessica. 'We've found Alan Milner. I'll let the Greenes know. Mrs Greene will be delighted to get her jewellery back, assuming it's hers.'

'Yes,' said Benedict. 'And check to see who this boat belongs to. Was it Milner's or did he rent it? I assume there must be a register for these boats or whatever they're called. Hopefully, uniform might find something interesting from one of the neighbours. Right, Adrian, thanks for everything. We've got a lot to work on.'

'My pleasure, sir.'

Benedict and Jessica walked back along the towpath. 'Have you ever been on a canal boat holiday, boss?' asked Jessica.

'Me? Once. I was just a kid, can't remember much about it, to be honest.'

That wasn't true – he remembered it very well. He was fifteen and booked to go on a half-term school trip on the Leeds – Liverpool canal. Just three weeks before, his father died unexpectedly. A heart attack. It shook Benedict's world to the core. His mother's too. He didn't want to go on the trip now. Somehow, as the eldest son, he felt it was his responsibility to stay at home and help his mother, especially in the days and weeks after his father's funeral when all the mourners had gone home. At least, that was the story he told himself. In reality, he needed his mother more than she needed him during those dark days. But Mum insisted. They argued about it. In the end, with tears in his eyes, Benedict went. He sat on the train by himself, ignoring his friends and the teachers who knew about his father, who tried to cajole him into joining the others. But once on the boat, he couldn't avoid them and so, he got stuck in.

It ended up being the best week of his childhood.

Chapter 37: Benedict

Having gathered his thoughts, Benedict stood before his team and summarised: 'So, Alan Milner, aged fifty-three, had recently been released from prison following an eighteen-year stretch for armed robbery and aggravated assault. This robbery took place in a small Turkish-run supermarket in Kentish Town in 2005. He was not alone and he named his accomplice, one Ian Turner, another local man. But Turner had an alibi for the night in question, he was watching football with a friend and work colleague, his manager, in fact. They worked in a furniture store. During the robbery, Milner hit a man, a shopper, who fell and hit his head so hard that it damaged him for life. The only witnesses to this were the young man who worked in the shop, the security man and the daughter of the man who was hit. None of them could identify either robber. Milner was only caught through his DNA. So the investigating officers at the time had no idea whether Milner's accomplice was or was not Ian Turner.' He paused. 'I think that summarises everything.'

'Do we know the name of the daughter, boss?' asked

Jessica.

'Erm…' He consulted his notes. 'Yes, Patricia Godwin. Lives, or lived, locally.'

'Do you think it's worth visiting her? Assuming she's still around.'

'For sure.'

*

But first, Benedict and Jessica revisited Sheila Milner. She invited them in. Her cheek showed no sign of the slap she received at the hands of her son a few days before.

Jessica began. 'Mrs Milner, I'm afraid we've got some terrible news for you.' Benedict could sense her stiffen as she waited. 'This morning, we found a body on a canal boat on Regent's canal. It is Alan.'

Mrs Milner sighed. 'Oh God.'

Jessica paused, allowing Mrs Milner to absorb the news. She stared out of the window, twisting a ring around her finger. She got up and, going to a sideboard, lit a cigarette. 'What happened?'

'We're not totally sure yet but we believe he was killed.'

She shook her head. 'Killed? Bloody hell. The idiot. Doesn't surprise me. You live by the sword, you…' She didn't finish the sentence. 'I can't believe this. Killed, you say? I can look after me-self. That's what he always used to say.'

'He was living on a boat called–'

'*Crazy Lou*, I know.'

'Oh? Last time we spoke, you said you didn't know where he was.'

'Yeah, I know. Sorry about that. I couldn't tell you. How could I? You know what he was capable of.'

'Mrs Milner,' said Benedict. 'Your son named someone as an accomplice the night of the supermarket robbery. A man called Ian Turner. Do you think there was any truth in that?'

Mrs Milner stubbed out her cigarette. 'Aye, I do, actually. Alan was many things but there was no way he'd have grassed up someone for the sake of it. If he said this bloke was involved, then he was.'

'Turner had a solid alibi for that night though.'

'Are you asking me to do your job now? You work it out for yourself, chum. Don't ask me. But, like I says, if Alan said Turner was there, then Turner was there. You should grill him again, see if he'll crack.'

'We will, Mrs Milner,' said Benedict.

'Can you think of someone who might wish your son harm, Mrs Milner?' asked Jessica.

She laughed. 'In a word – no. But I reckon once you start asking around, you'll have a list longer than your arm.'

'He didn't mention anyone since his return?'

'No.' She scratched her arm. 'The only person he mentioned was his old bird, Lana.'

'His girlfriend?' asked Jessica.

'I wouldn't go that far, but yeah, he liked to think so.'

'Do you remember her surname?'

She gazed into the distance. 'Lana… something Polish although she was as London as me. I can't remember. Sorry.'

'Not to worry,' said Benedict. 'You've got my card so if the name comes to you, perhaps you could give me a ring? Did Alan have a computer?'

'Alan? He wouldn't know a computer if it bit him the arse. Nor me, to be fair.'

'OK. Well, I think–'

'Oh, but hang on, he did borrow me library card a couple

of times.'

'He was into reading?' asked Jessica.

She laughed again. 'Hardly. The only thing I ever saw Alan read was *The Sun*, and he stopped that after they got rid of the girls with the boobs. No, he wanted to use the computers there. He said he got one of the librarians to help him.'

'What library was this?'

'The big one up at Swiss Cottage. You know it?'

'I do,' said Benedict. 'I spent many an hour there when I was a student.'

'You can borrow me library card if you want. You could go and see what he was up to.'

'Not a bad idea. Thank you.'

Rummaging around in her purse, she found her library card.

'One last thing, Mrs Milner. Can we ask you to come to identify Alan's body?'

'You what? Do I have to?'

'It would help.'

She closed her eyes. 'If I must.'

Chapter 38: Benedict

Benedict and Jessica were driving to Swiss Cottage library, the windscreen wipers fighting against the rain, when Benedict received a call on his mobile from DC Kelly. 'Jamie, how can I help?'

'Boss, a couple of updates but nothing useful, I'm afraid.'

'Fire away.'

'The canal boat is littered with several unidentified fingerprints—'

'No surprise there. It's an old boat, after all. Anything else?'

'You're right about it being an old boat. It's been around since 1985 so *really* old.'

'Not so old, actually.'

'What? Anyway, the boat's registered to the name of Miriam Abbott. I've got an address. Do you want me to go speak to her?'

'Yes, do. Good idea.'

Benedict rang off as Jessica parked up near the library. 'I've got an umbrella in the boot,' said Jessica.

Swiss Cottage library, opened in 1964, was architecturally ahead of its time, Scandinavian in influence and boasting an exterior consisting of a series of concrete 'fins' designed to resemble the leaves of a book.

Inside, Benedict and Jessica were greeted by a resounding rendition of *The Wheels on the Bus* ringing out. Sure enough, peeking in the children's section, they saw a number of young parents and carers jiggling their babies and singing away, conducted by a young librarian who didn't look old enough to be out of school. Benedict and Jessica approached the enquiry desk pausing briefly at a display of books celebrating Windrush. 'Of course,' said Jessica. 'We're celebrating seventy-five years, aren't we?'

They showed their ID to the librarian sitting at the enquiry desk and asked to see the manager. A phone call later, a woman with braids and wearing a long purple dress appeared. 'Hi, I'm Carole. How can I help?'

Jessica explained the purpose of their visit – namely to view any Internet history for the library card belonging to Sheila Milner but used by her son, Alan Milner. They provided Mrs Milner's library card. Benedict could see Carol's reluctance. 'We can come back with a warrant if you prefer, and that's totally understandable, but we are investigating a suspicious death and time is of the essence. We don't know whether it's a one-off or whether others may be at risk.'

'I think I should check with my manager. She's not based in this building. Can you wait?'

'Of course,' said Benedict with a bow.

He and Jessica perused the shelves while they waited. Benedict flipped through a guidebook to Regent's Canal. The canal, according to the blurb, opened in 1820, was eight and a half miles long, much shorter than the 127 miles of the Leeds and Liverpool Canal he remembered from the month his father died. It cost the tidy sum of £772,000, about £60 million in today's money. 'What have you got there?' he asked Jessica.

'*The Bell Jar*. I've always meant to read this.'

'Ah, Sylvia Plath. A tragic woman. Committed suicide in 1964.'

'Yeah, driven to her death by her cheating husband.'

'Ted Hughes? We can't know that for sure, Jessica.'

'Yeah but it couldn't have helped, could it?'

'No, you're probably right.'

'Sixty-three.'

'What?'

'1963, not 1964. That's what it says here.'

'I stand corrected.'

Carol returned. 'I'm sorry to keep you waiting but my manager is fine with it. Do you want to come through to my office?'

The three of them settled around Carol's computer. Benedict and Jessica waited for quite a while as the librarian tapped away on the keyboard. Benedict noticed a book on the Mediterranean diet on her desk. Sonia and he were very partial to a bit of Italian. Although, on the whole, they avoided Italian restaurants. Why pay all that money for a bit of pasta or a pizza? But they loved tapas and being presented with lots of small and rich dishes.

Eventually, Carol leaned back and said, 'So, it appears Mrs Milner's card has only been used twice to access our computers but both times within the same week and both recently. Do you want me to write down the dates?'

'Please. And what was her son searching for?'

'Looks like he was looking for a boat, a canal boat called… called *Purple Mermaid*. There's an official boat register by the looks of it.'

Benedict made a note of the name – *Purple Mermaid*.

'Next, your friend joined LinkedIn.'

'LinkedIn?' That came as a surprise. Benedict always tried not to assume things about people but given what Milner's mother had said about the man, that did come as a surprise.

'Maybe he was looking for a job,' said Carol. 'Most people around here looking for jobs use Indeed or Total Jobs, one of those. Was he a professional?'

'He was certainly professional at something but not necessarily white-collared in nature.'

'I don't have his login details, of course, but if we search for him, we could see his profile.' The detectives waited while Carol did her work. 'According to the search history, he was keen on finding someone called Manish Patel.'

'I've got the LinkedIn app on my phone,' said Jessica. 'I can look up the name.'

'You've got LinkedIn on your phone?' asked Benedict, before he could stop himself. Why did Jessica have the LinkedIn app? She hadn't long been with the team; surely she couldn't be looking for another job?

'In fact,' said Carol. 'That's it, he looked at the profiles of dozens of men called Manish Patel. And there's quite a few of them.'

'There's quite a few Alan Milners as well,' said Jessica, her eyes focused on her mobile.

'I wonder if he found what he was looking for,' said Benedict.

Carol remained silent while she continued to peer at her computer screen. 'Hmm, he spent some time looking at two

Manish Patels based in Camden, but one of them was Camden in Nova Scotia. Maybe he got confused. Give me a minute.' A few seconds later, she said, 'It appears we have a Manish Patel who works for Barclays Bank in Brent, so not far from Camden. It seems your man focused on this particular gentleman. In fact, he's the branch manager there.'

'Interesting. Thank you. Anything else?'

'Yes, he googled how to invest cash. He looked at a couple of articles on *The Times* and a site called Money Farm. Oh, and second-hand cars. That's about it.'

'Fascinating. Well, Carol, thank you for your time. That's been most helpful.'

They left the library at the same time as all the young parents with their babies and got caught in a veritable tsunami of buggies and pushchairs. Benedict held the main door for several to the point of embarrassment while Jessica waited outside under her umbrella. 'No hurry, boss,' she called.

Having finally made it back to the car, Benedict said, 'So, the question is – why was Alan Milner so interested in a man called Manish Patel?'

A moment later, Benedict's mobile rang. 'Inspector? It's Shirley Milner here. I've just remembered that girl's name, you know, the one with the Polish name. Her name is Lana Kozlowski.'

Chapter 39: Benedict

The following morning, DC Prowse managed to find an address for Lana Kozlowski. For his next task, Benedict asked the detective constable to find out what he could on Manish Patel, the man Alan Milner was so keen on finding. He worked in a bank, so he suggested that the detective constable apply for a warrant in order to check his financial records.

Meanwhile, DC Kelly was expecting Sheila Milner, his job was to accompany her to the morgue where her son lay on a slab.

Sitting at his computer, Benedict was catching up on his email and sighing that he, along with the whole CID team, were obliged to complete an online course about money laundering – how to spot it, how to report it, etc. These courses were compulsory. They didn't take long but they still took long enough to be considered irritating. He was at the start of a murder enquiry, for Pete's sake, he didn't have time for this.

DC Prowse came bumbling in, a doughnut in his hand and

his mouth full. On seeing Benedict, he rushed over to his desk and held up a sheet of paper as if waving a flag. 'Miriam Abbott, boss,' he said with his mouth still full.

'Did your mother not ever tell you not to talk with your mouth full, DC Prowse?'

DC Prowse swallowed, his Adam's apple popping up and down. 'Sorry, sir. Custard doughnut. Delicious. This is about Miriam Abbott.'

'Remind me.'

'The woman who owns *Crazy Lou*. She says that although the boat is registered under her name, it was her husband's project but he died a couple of years ago and she's not been back since. She keeps meaning to put it on the market but hasn't got around to it yet.'

'Did she realise that Alan Milner was squatting it?'

'She had no clue.'

'Boss,' said DC Kelly, staring at his computer. 'We've found the telephone box. The telephone used to call in the discovery of Milner's body.'

'And?'

'On York Way opposite the entrance to King's Cross tube station.'

'Hmm. Any CCTV around there?'

'There's a McDonald's and a Five Guys there. They might have a camera over their entrance.'

'We know the exact time that call was made so it's probably worth asking. Will you see to it, DC Kelly?'

'Of course. Leave it with me, boss.'

'Good man. Thank you.'

*

Lana Kozlowski lived alone in a small flat at the top of a

terraced house in Queen's Crescent. A woman in her late forties with unruly red hair answered the door in her dressing gown and a pair of Minnie Mouse slippers. She didn't seem particularly surprised to see two detectives turn up at her door. 'I'd offer you coffee or something but I've no milk. Well, I have but it's gone off. Smells like puke. Anyway, what do you want?'

'Can we sit down?' asked Jessica.

She shrugged. The detectives sat. Benedict noticed a painting of a skeletal figure on her wall. Lana saw him looking at it. 'That's a Beksiński. Good, isn't it? Polish artist. It reminds me of home.'

'You're Polish?'

'Yeah, but I've been in this shit country since I was a kid.'

'OK.'

'And I know what you're thinking… if this country is so shit why don't I go home? Cos Poland is even more shit. Sorry. I didn't mean that. I'm not in a good place at the moment.'

Jessica leaned forward. 'Is there anything you want to share with us, Lana?'

Lana stared at her as if deliberating her offer. 'OK, as you're here, yeah, I want to report a crime.'

'Go on.'

Lana puffed out her cheeks. 'There's this bloke I know. Well, I used to know him years ago, we used to hang around a bit. I never actually liked him; he was too rough for me. But he got me drugs, so… you know. So, then he gets sent down, and I think thank the Lord for that. And then, the other day he turns up like a bad penny. He'd been released. I've got a fella now, another loser. But he's my loser. And he's a hundred per cent better than the first bloke. So, he comes around and thinks he can take me to bed like it's his right. I told him where to go. Luckily, Mark came back. That's my new fella.' She stopped talking and pulled on a loose strand of hair.

'And was that the last you saw of him?' asked Jessica.

'I wish.'

'He came back?'

'Yeah, late Saturday night. He came back alright. Mark didn't rescue me this time. And er, well, he er…'

'Did he hurt you, Lana?'

'Yes.'

'Sexually.'

She nodded.

'OK. I'm sorry to hear that.' Jessica waited a few moments. Benedict knew that telling her story, albeit briefly, was a strain on the poor woman. After a while, Jessica asked, 'Have you been to the doctor?'

She shook her head. 'I'm fine. After he… he did it, he gave me fifty quid. Made me feel like a right whore. That's what he called me, so that's how he treated me. I wanted to throw it back at him but, you know, beggars can't be choosers so I kept it.'

'This fifty quid, Lana,' said Benedict. 'Was it a fifty-pound note, perchance?'

'Yes. Yes, it was.'

'Can I see it? Or have you spent it?'

'No, I've still got it. Why do you want to see it? It's just a normal note. Oh God, it's fake, isn't it?'

'No, but we would like to see it, please.'

'OK, hang on a minute.' She rushed off.

Benedict leaned towards Jessica. 'It's Milner, don't you think?' he whispered.

'Definitely.'

Lana returned and handed the note to Benedict. 'It's new,' he said. 'Pristine even. I'm afraid we'll have to keep hold of this as—'

'No, hang on. You can't take that. It's fifty quid, I need it.'

'Don't worry,' said Jessica. 'We'll get someone to bring you a replacement.'

'Do you want to tell us his name?'

'No. I c-can't. I can't face it. What if you don't believe me; he'll kill me.'

Benedict spoke. 'Lana, I think my colleague and I know who this man was.'

That got her attention. 'How can you?'

'Was his name Alan Milner?'

She jumped up from her chair and swore in Polish. 'How did you know that? Is that why you're here?'

'I'll tell you,' said Benedict. 'Sit down, Lana. It might be for the best.'

She did, sitting on the edge of the chair, pulling on her thumb. 'What's happened?'

'Alan Milner was found dead on Tuesday morning on a canal boat on Regent's Canal. We spoke to Mr Milner's mother and she is, as we speak, identifying the body.'

She stood again and paced to the window. 'How did he die?'

'Someone killed him.'

She laughed at that. 'Really? Someone actually killed him. I can't believe it.'

'You OK, Lana?' asked Jessica.

'I don't know what to think.' She sat again, then immediately sprung back to her feet. 'Oh my God. Alan's dead? Who killed him?'

'We don't know that yet,' said Benedict.

'Yet?'

'We will. Can we ask you some questions?'

'I can't believe it.' She laughed again. 'Good God, the bastard's dead.'

'Lana, we need to ask you a few questions.'

'Yeah, yeah, sure.'

'How was he the two times you saw him?'

'His usual arrogant self. He'd been in prison for several years. I sorta thought that would change a man, you know, but it didn't.'

'How do you mean?' asked Jessica.

'He was the same. He hadn't changed. Arrogant, knew what he wanted. Threatening.'

'And when he came to see you,' said Jessica. 'Was it just because he wanted to… to have sex with you or was there anything else?'

'He was angry because I didn't visit him in prison. I mean, that's how arrogant he was. As if I would. He said I lacked compassion. *Compassion*! As if he knew the meaning of the word, the bastard.'

'Did he mention any names?'

'No.'

'Did he talk about what he planned to do now that he was a free man?'

'No. Actually, yes, he did mention wanting to see someone. A friend of ours from back in the day called Juliet.'

'Juliet who?'

She scratched her chin. 'You know, I can't remember. But I reckon he wasn't looking for her, he was looking for her husband, Ian.'

'Ian Turner?

'Turner, that was it. I think he and Ian used to do stuff together.'

'Stuff?'

'Dodgy stuff, drugs, theft, that sort of thing. I had an address for them. No idea if they still live there but I gave it to him anyway, just to get shot of him.'

'Could we have the address?'

'Sure.'

'Will you be OK, Lana?' asked Jessica.

'I don't know. I wasn't going to tell you, the police, about what he did but then you turned up and I thought perhaps you knew. That's why I told you. It's a shame he's dead because he should have been made to pay for what he did to me, but at the same time I'm happy because, believe me, this world is a better place without Alan Milner in it.'

Chapter 40: Benedict

DC Prowse confirmed that Manish Patel did work as a branch manager at Brent's Barclays Bank. Benedict phoned Mr Patel and arranged a time to meet him. It was only after he'd spoken to the bank manager that DC Prowse found something of interest. 'Hey, boss, you remember that Alan Milner named his accomplice for that robbery he did?'

'Ian Turner. He's on my list of people to speak to. What about him?'

'You remember he had an alibi?'

'Yes, as in he was watching football with a friend.'

'Yes, and that friend's name? Only Manish Patel.'

Benedict stared at him; he hadn't expected that. 'Seriously? So, in the days before his death, Milner was googling the name of the man who gave his alleged accomplice an alibi for the night of the robbery. Well, that's made our conversation with Mr Patel that much more interesting. Well done, DC Prowse. Thanks for that.'

'Sure thing, boss.'

'So, next job, please. Dig around for anything you can find

on both these men – Patel and Ian Turner.'

'On it, boss.'

*

Patricia Godwin lived in a small, pebble-dashed terraced house north of Kentish Town underground station. A small, neat woman in her fifties, she offered Benedict and Jessica a coffee which they accepted. 'Have you lived here long?' asked Jessica.

'Thirty years almost,' she called through from the kitchen. Patricia Godwin liked her books, thought Benedict, several shelves packed with novels, books on Christianity, cookery books and birdwatching. He wouldn't have her as a twitcher. She was religious, that was obvious from the framed pictures of Jesus on her walls and a metallic crucifix above the marble fireplace, not to mention she wore a crucifix around her neck. She came through to the lounge bearing two mugs of coffee. 'I'm thinking of selling up now, maybe move to the country. I was born in Sussex and I feel the pull to go back there but the prospect of buying and selling houses is so daunting. My father died a few days ago.'

The detectives offered their condolences as she sat down, clasping a handkerchief. 'I'm sure you know this,' she said. 'My father was the victim of a horrible assault many years ago. He hit his head and it damaged his brain. He was never the same.'

'You looked after him?' asked Jessica.

She nodded. 'I had to give up work. I used to work as a secretary for a company that dealt with stationery. It was a good job but after the incident, I became a full-time carer. Dad needed constant care. I was an only child and my mother died when I was young, there was no one else.'

'It must've been difficult,' said Jessica.

'I was happy to do so but it wasn't easy. I had to learn a lot of new things. But we adapt, don't we?'

'Needs must.'

'Exactly. Dad had a heart attack. He'd had one before and I'd be warned that he could have another. So, I knew the day would come and I tried to prepare myself but it didn't work. It still came as a shock. I'm still processing it.'

'It's early days, Pat.'

'Yes. Sorry, I don't mean to sound rude but I prefer Patricia.'

'Patricia. I'm sorry.'

She smiled. 'So now I'm free to do whatever I want. I should get myself a job. But, you know, I'm terrified. Dad gave my life a routine and without it, without him, I feel rather…' She searched for the word. 'Rudderless. How can I get a job now after all this time? And I'm fifty-one now–'

'That's no age,' said Benedict.

'Very kind, Inspector, but it is when you haven't worked for eighteen years. I have my faith and that always sees me through. I'm in the midst of arranging Dad's cremation. It's going to be a rather drab affair, I'm afraid. He had no friends. He did, back then, but they've all drifted away or died. Everything is…'

'Is?'

'Oh, I don't know. It's only now that Dad's gone, I realise how much I'd cut myself off from the outside world. I had an excuse, Dad was my excuse, but now I need to face it and it's rather daunting. I'm sorry.'

'No, don't be,' said Jessica. 'There's bound to be a period of adjustment.'

'Anyway,' said Patricia, sitting up and taking a deep breath.

'If you're not here about my father, what brings you here?'

'Patricia, the man who was responsible for your father's injury has died in suspicious circumstances–'

'Oh?' She gripped her handkerchief. 'Alan Milner.'

'Yes.'

'I'd been told he'd been released only a few days ago. How did he die?'

'He was found on a canal boat on Regent's Canal. He'd been murdered. Any more than that, we can't say at this stage.'

'Right. I see.' She leaned back in her armchair. 'I'm a Christian, Detective Sergeant, but right now I'm thinking some very un-Christian thoughts.'

Benedict suppressed a smile. 'Understandable,' he said. 'Patricia, we wanted to ask about the second man at the robbery that night your father was hurt.'

'I told the police at the time everything I saw.'

'I know. We've read your statement but it's always worth following things up. Sometimes–'

'I have nothing to add, Inspector. I wish I did but…' She shook her head. 'I'm sorry to interrupt you. Is your coffee OK?'

'Oh yes, thank you. Lovely. You said he was wearing a balaclava. You said he was a lean man and you saw his wrist under his sleeve so you knew he was white but otherwise…'

'Exactly. He could have been anyone. Anyone at all.'

'But it was Mr Milner who hit your father.'

'Yes.'

'You were under the impression that Milner was very much the one in charge of this operation?'

'Operation? You make it sound legitimate, Inspector.'

'I'm sorry, that wasn't my intention.'

'But you're right. The second man didn't speak, at least I didn't hear him. The police thought they knew who it was but I couldn't confirm it for them and the man had an alibi so they let him go.'

Jessica leaned forward. 'Did Mr Milner contact you at all since his release, Patricia?'

'No,' she snapped. 'Why should he?'

Benedict stiffened. Was she lying? She was quick to answer, he thought, too quick and her face flushed. 'You didn't see him?' he asked.

She shot him an irritated look. 'I just said, no, I didn't see him.'

'We have to ask, Patricia.'

'Is there anything else? I have a funeral to arrange.'

'No,' said Benedict. 'That's it for now. Thank you for your time, Patricia.'

*

Jessica and Benedict sat in the car. A man with dyed blond hair, his roots showing, stopped on seeing the police car, then walked on quickly. Jessica laughed. 'How not to look guilty. Was it my imagination, boss, but did Patricia Godwin go all frosty on us?'

'Didn't she just?'

'Do you think Milner made contact with her?'

'But like she said, why would he? And how would he find her address?'

'True but something went on.'

'Yes. The question rattled her. But why?' Benedict's phone rang. 'DC Kelly, how can I help?'

'Hi, Boss. Just to let you know Mrs Milner has identified the body.'

'And?'

'It's definitely Alan Milner.'

Chapter 41: Benedict

Back at the station, Benedict had just sat down at his desk when he was approached by the station's pathologist, Diana Evans. 'Ben, you OK? You look hot and flustered.'

He laughed. 'Busy day catching criminals.'

She winked. 'You wouldn't have it any other way.'

'That I can't deny.'

'Well, quite a lot has happened while you were out gallivanting.'

'Well, I wouldn't call it–'

'Firstly, uniform have found a blood-stained mallet.'

'Have they indeed?' He swung his chair around in order to face her. 'As in the murder weapon? Don't tell me, too soon to tell.'

'Too right it is. I've only just come into possession of it. But it seems likely, let's be honest.'

'Where was it found?'

'In the undergrowth within a hundred yards of the canal boat. Now, I've done Mr Milner's post-mortem. I'll email you the full report but for the headlines, Milner was killed at some point on Monday. As we know, he was killed by one single blow to the back of the head. I found a tiny trace of beechwood which, indeed, could easily have come from something like a mallet.'

'Beechwood?'

'Yes, it's, er, a medium-density wood that won't damage workpieces but, if wielded with enough force, can do damage to a person's head.'

'To the point of killing them.'

'Yes but…'

'But?'

She ran her fingers through her hair. 'Fact is, Ben, if you wanted to kill someone, I mean, seriously planned it ahead of time, would you use a wooden mallet? Yes, you can do some serious damage with a mallet but you'd need a bit of luck.'

'In what way luck?'

'To hit them in a way that causes an artery or vein to burst and leads to bleeding in the victim's brain. And of course that's not a given. Now, use a metal-headed hammer and we're talking. Can't go wrong with a hammer. You know, images of teaspoons and boiled eggs come to mind.'

'Yes, thank you, Diana.'

'He's also got, or had, a very nasty bruise on his left shoulder. I mean, it's vivid. Not the sort of bruise you get by bumping into something.'

'The mallet again?'

'No. The impact wound is a lot smaller. Now, here, we could indeed be talking about a hammer. But, again, let's put ourselves in the killer's shoes… you wouldn't take a hammer to someone's shoulder.'

'Unless he misaimed. Or she.'

'Exactly. Or maybe Milner moved at the last moment.' She

illustrated this by jerking her upper body to one side.

'So, are you saying both wounds were part of the same attack?'

'I don't know, Ben. The timing fits. The shoulder wound was inflicted, if not exactly at the same time, then very close to it. If it was our killer, then he had quite an arsenal on him – a hammer and a mallet. We'll be testing the mallet for fingerprints and DNA. Now, more news if you can take it. That towel we found in the victim's canal boat…'

'Ah, yes.'

'So, two sets of blood on the towel. The first belongs to Alan Milner. No surprise there. The second, we don't know. No matches.'

'Pity.'

'Now, we've analysed the blood and it's clear that the towel was used to remove blood from someone's hands, probably Milner's. In other words, it wasn't used to mop up blood from, say, the kitchen surfaces or the floor.'

'So, who else's blood is on that towel?'

'Indeed, Ben. I'll leave you to puzzle that one out.'

*

DC Kelly and DC Prowse came strolling into the office, both flushed from their morning exertions, each munching their way through a packet of crisps. 'Do you want one, boss?' offered DC Kelly.

'I'm fine, thanks.'

A moment later, PC Stevens returned also. 'Too hot to be outdoors all day.'

'So, how did it go?' asked Benedict.

'I reckon we spoke to someone on every single boat within half a mile on either side of *Crazy Lou*,' said PC

Stevens.

'And?'

'DC Kelly spoke to someone.'

'Yeah,' said DC Kelly, wiping his greasy fingers on his trouser legs. 'Only one point of interest but I spoke to one boat owner, this woman with dyed purple hair, who said Alan Milner asked her for someone called Beth.'

'Really? Interesting. How did she know it was Milner?'

DC Kelly looked momentarily puzzled by the question. 'Because I showed her a photo of him, boss.'

'Oh yes, of course. Silly me. So, who's this Beth?'

'She said Beth lives on a boat called *Lazy Suzan*. I can check it out if you want, boss.'

'Yes, do that. Thanks, DC Kelly.'

*

Benedict followed Jessica into Barclays Bank on Brent High Street. Having introduced themselves to the receptionist, they were shown through to a glass-fronted office. They could hear an irate customer complaining to a clerk. Peering over the frosted part of the glass door, Benedict could see a woman speaking to an Asian man in a suit who was trying his best to placate the woman. If this individual was indeed the manager, then that was Manish Patel. Three minutes later, Patel entered the office. A short, lean individual, he was obviously nervous. 'Sorry about that. It's part of the job. Hardly a day passes when someone doesn't call for the manager.'

'Must get stressful,' said Jessica.

'Can be but it's how you treat them that's the most important. You have to listen and be empathetic. Anyway, what is it you want to speak to me about?' he asked, his eyes darting between the two detectives.

'Mr Patel,' said Benedict. 'Thank you for your time. Does the name Alan Milner mean anything to you?'

'Erm, I think so. I can't remember.' He crossed his legs and Benedict wondered whether Patel realised he was wearing odd socks.

'Try harder, Mr Patel.'

'Wasn't he... Yes, I remember, he was that bloke who... who...'

'Yes?'

'He tried to implicate a friend of mine in a crime he committed.'

'That's right. Well done. That friend, what was his name?'

'Ian. Ian Turner.'

'Are you still in touch?'

He shook his head vigorously. 'No. Not seen him in years.'

'Do you know where he lives?'

'No.'

'Do you know where Alan Milner lived?'

'No! Why are you asking me about this? This was dealt with years ago.'

'Alan Milner was found dead on a canal boat the day before yesterday. He'd been murdered. He'd only just been released from prison. Had you had any contact with Milner, Mr Patel?'

'God, no.'

'And yet, he seemed very keen to track you down.'

'D-did he? How do you know?'

Jessica spoke. 'He looked you up on LinkedIn, Mr Patel. He found your profile which clearly states where you work. So, what you're saying, he never came to see you or didn't contact you in any way?'

'No.'

'Would you have any idea of why he was so keen to find you? Were you friends?'

'No,' he screeched. 'I've never spoken to him.'

'Really?' said Jessica. 'I mean, he'd only be out of prison for a few days and he didn't have a computer but one of the first things he did as a free man was to go to a library and hire a PC. The first thing he did was look up your name. Why was that?'

Patel glanced at Benedict. 'I've not got a clue. Honest.'

'Perhaps it was to do with that robbery eighteen years ago?'

'Like I said, I don't know.'

'Because it's the only thing we know of that ties the two of you together.'

'Doesn't mean anything. Look, this is getting a little hairy for my liking. You're talking to me as if I've done something wrong–'

'Do you remember the score?'

'What? What score?'

'The game you watched that night with your friend Ian Turner.'

'Oh, this is ridiculous. It was twenty years ago–'

'Eighteen.'

'Whatever.'

'Did you provide Mr Turner with a false alibi, Mr Patel?'

'No. I did not. I've been through this.'

'Your wife backed you up. We should speak to her again–'

'She'll tell you the same story.'

'Why did you provide Turner with a false alibi?'

'It was the bloody truth–'

'Did you owe him one, perhaps? Was it out of some misplaced loyalty?'

'No!' He checked himself and, lowering his voice, said, 'No. Look, Ian and I weren't the best of mates or anything but we worked together and we got on. So, one day, I invited him around to watch the footie.'

'That's the story you told the investigating team at the time.'

'Yeah, it was, because that's what happened, right?'

'Tell us about your relationship with Turner. So were you friends first, or colleagues?'

Patel told the detectives he was Turner's boss at the furniture store, that they occasionally had lunch together but the football match was a one-off.

'Manchester City are doing much better these days, aren't they?'

'They won the league.'

'You still follow the football?'

'Sort of.'

'So where were you Monday, Mr Patel? The day Alan Milner was killed.'

'Here. Working. You can check, you can—'

'Until?'

'What?'

'Until what time were you working, Mr Patel?'

'Half five, as always.'

'And then?'

He shrugged. 'I went home.'

'Your wife can vouch for that?'

'Of course.'

'Can anyone vouch for your movements Monday after work?'

'I don't think so.' He sounded flustered. 'No. But…'

'But what, Mr Patel?' asked Jessica.

'I didn't kill anyone,' he said in a gentle voice. 'Look, I don't know why Milner was looking for me. I didn't speak to him. I've never met him.'

Benedict leaned forward. 'Mr Patel, I hope for your sake that you're being honest with us. About both Milner's murder and providing a man with an alibi in 2005. Perjury is a serious offence.' Benedict swung his arm about. 'You'll be saying goodbye to all this. Your career will be over. You do appreciate this, don't you?'

The man seemed to shrink in his chair.

'Speak now, Mr Patel. Better to spill it now because I think you're lying about something and when, not if, but *when* we come back, the consequences will be dire.'

'I've got an appointment now.'

Benedict stared at the man. OK, so he was going to hold out. It wouldn't last. He didn't have the strength for it. 'OK, fair enough. But you are a suspect in the death of Alan Milner. As such, we have to ask you for your fingerprints.'

The man nodded. He looked half-broken already. But was Manish Patel capable of murdering a person? Maybe, probably not. But somehow Manish Patel was central to his investigation into the death of Alan Milner.

Chapter 42: Benedict

Benedict was sitting at his desk when he received a phone call from DC Prowse. 'Boss, we've got an address for Ian Turner. He lives in Sevenoaks down in Kent.'

DC Kelly, sitting at his desk, also had some news for Benedict. 'Boss, you remember the woman who said Alan Milner was looking for a woman called Beth on a barge called *Lazy Suzan*?'

'Ah yes. How did you get on?'

'I found her. *Lazy Suzan* is registered to a woman called Beth Whitehead.'

'Good, good.'

'There's more, boss.'

'Oh? Go on.'

'Beth is or was married to a man called Kris, Kris with a K. Back in 2005, police interviewed him about that robbery Milner did but they released him without charge. Also, at the same time, the Whiteheads had a baby called Harry. And someone stole that baby.'

'Oh, how awful.'

'They accused Alan Milner of stealing their baby boy.'

'Alan Milner? Really?'

'Huhuh. Why they thought Milner nicked their kid, I don't know.'

'Presumably, Milner had nothing to do with it otherwise we'd know about it.'

'Yeah. But they never found the baby.'

'To this day?' said Benedict. 'Heck, so that baby must be eighteen or so now.'

'If he's still alive.'

'Yes. OK, that's most useful. Beth and Kris Whitehead, you say? I'll add their names to my list. Thanks, DC Kelly. Good work.'

*

Jessica drove and Benedict could tell she was dying to put her foot down and felt contained by the speed limit. Like a dog on a leash. It took them an hour and a quarter to drive the 35 miles from Camden to Sevenoaks in Kent. From Sevenoaks, they followed a number of narrow roads to a forest to the south of a small village called Heaverham. Jessica parked up. 'I think it's a short walk from here,' she said, checking her phone.

'Lucky it's not raining,' said Benedict. 'Shall we go? I'll follow.'

Indeed, it was a lovely afternoon, the sun shining through the trees but an earlier downpour had left a fresh smell, the only sound was the constant singing of the birds. 'Must be lovely living out here,' said Jessica. 'It's so peaceful. Listen to those birds.'

'Lovely but a bit isolated. Imagine this in the middle of the winter.'

'I think I'd still like it. I've always wanted to live in the country.'

'You? That surprises me.'

She laughed. 'Oh, I think this is it.'

Sure enough, ahead of them, a beautiful timbered house on an incline, an old stone wall to one side, a wooden annexe at the back, a narrow patio at the front. One couldn't deny that it looked idyllic. About twenty yards off, a quad bike parked on a gravelled drive. To the side of the drive, a pile of logs, part-covered by a tarpaulin. 'Keep an eye out for the big, bad wolf,' said Jessica. She knocked and a tall, grey-haired man with a wispy beard answered. But the thing that stood out were the cuts and bruises on his face. 'Ian Turner?'

'Yeah. Who are you?' said Turner, glancing at Benedict.

The detectives showed the man their IDs. 'You've come all the way down from Camden?'

'Yep. We have a few questions we'd like to ask you.'

'What about?'

'Can we come in?'

'We can sit out here if you want.' He pointed to a wooden table, a bench on either side of it. 'It's a nice day.'

'Sure. Thanks.'

'Gorgeous place you have here,' said Benedict. 'How long have you been here?'

'A while now.'

Benedict hoped the man might offer them a drink but he didn't. 'What happened to your face?'

'What? Oh, I fell into a ditch.' He forced a laugh. 'Serves me right for walking through the forest with my head in my phone.'

'You look like you've been in a fight,' said Jessica.

He laughed again. 'That's what my wife said. I still don't

think she believes me.'

'You live here with your wife?'

He nodded.

'Anyone else?'

'Yeah, my two sons. So, what is it that's so important you've come all this way to seek me out?'

'We wanted to ask you about your friend, Alan Milner,' said Benedict.

He jerked up. 'Christ. He's still in prison, isn't he?'

'Not any more,' said Jessica. She explained that Milner had been found dead on a canal boat he was squatting on Regent's Canal. He didn't respond nor show any emotion or surprise whatsoever.

'Why are you here? I couldn't give a toss about Milner. You can hardly suspect me, can you?'

'Well, we're not sure at this point.'

That worried him. 'What do you mean?'

'Mr Turner,' said Jessica. 'Why did Mr Milner say you were his partner for the supermarket robbery in 2005?'

'I don't know. But I wasn't involved. I told the police at the time. You'd have to ask him but you can't, can you?'

'We've been speaking to a friend of yours – Manish Patel.'

'Manish? I haven't…' He ran his fingers through his hair.

'Alan Milner went online searching for Mr Patel.'

'I didn't know that.'

'Do you keep in touch with Manish?'

'God, no. I was about to say. Haven't seen him in years. Not since I left London.'

'He came in useful once, didn't he, your friend?' said Jessica.

'What do you mean?'

'You and him watching football together while Milner

robbed that supermarket.'

'It was true. I was with him.'

'So, I ask again, why did Mr Milner say different?'

'Because he was a vindictive bastard.'

'So who was with him that night of the robbery?'

He rubbed his nose. 'No idea.'

'Where were you Monday night, Mr Turner?' asked Benedict.

'Here. Like I am every night. Me and the wife, we don't go out much. We prefer our own company. The boys go out a lot but you'd expect them to; they're teenagers.'

'Mr Turner, we need you to provide your DNA.'

'You can't make me.'

'You're a suspect, Mr Turner, so if you wish to be eliminated from our enquiries, I'd strongly advise you to provide us with your DNA.'

'Bloody hell.'

Benedict heard a car arriving. Turning, he saw a green Vauxhall coming into view.

'My wife and the boys,' said Turner. 'Weekly shop. The boys usually help. Is there anything else?'

Benedict and Jessica exchanged looks. 'No,' said Benedict. 'I think we've covered everything.'

The woman, a short, rounded woman with dyed orange hair, approached. 'This is Juliet,' said Turner. She nodded at the detectives. Turner explained who they were. The two boys appeared, strong-looking lads, both carrying tote bags of shopping, both tall, one dark, one fair. Turner introduced them, the darker, slightly taller boy was Felix, his brother Kelvin.

'Are you from Sevenoaks?' asked Kelvin.

'No, Camden in London,' said Jessica with a warm smile.

'London?'

'Go on, boys,' said Juliet. 'We need to get the stuff in the freezer before it melts.'

The boys traipsed off towards the house, their mother following them.

'OK,' said Benedict. 'We'll be off. I fully imagine we'll be in touch again, Mr Turner. So don't go anywhere for the foreseeable.'

Chapter 43: Benedict

Benedict's mobile rang. Unknown number. But he answered it nevertheless and was surprised to hear the voice of Alan Milner's mother, Sheila. He began by thanking her for coming in and identifying her son's body, saying he knew it was never an easy thing to do. She dismissed it, sounding sanguine. 'So, how can I help, Mrs Milner?'

'I remembered something. I should have mentioned it but I forgot until just now. Someone came around looking for Alan on Tuesday morning. She said her name was Jane but I reckon she was lying. She said she was an old mate of Alan's but I didn't believe that either. She was a little mousey woman in her fifties or sixties. There's no way the likes of her and Alan would be friends.'

'OK. And did this Jane say why she wanted to see your son, Mrs Milner?'

'No but I said he'd be on his boat. I even told her the name of it. *Crazy Lou*. I shouldn't have done that, should I? But she didn't look the type to go around murdering people.'

'It takes all sorts, Mrs Milner. Was she tall, short, white, black?'

'Short. White. Grey hair. She wore a necklace with a large cross on it. Oh, almost forgot, she drove a Fiat Panda. A blue one. Normally, I wouldn't know about these things but my ex used to drive one so I recognised it.'

Benedict thanked her. That sounded suspiciously like Patricia Godwin. 'DC Prowse, a job for you, if you please?'

'Boss?'

'I need you to visit a woman we interviewed yesterday and take her fingerprints. If she asks whether she's a suspect now, then tell her that yes, she is.'

*

Benedict and Jessica returned to Regent's Canal, the sun bearing down on them. It took a while but eventually, they found the barge they were looking for, *Lazy Suzan*. Benedict couldn't help but think back to his canal boat holiday in the weeks following his father's death. His teachers knew about his situation, having been forewarned by his mother, and they treated him kindly. He loved the locks, watching the water rise and the slow parting of the gates. The sun shone that whole week. It was many years before mobile phones so he had no contact with his grieving mother. Yes, he thought about his father all the time but somehow, here, many miles from home, his grief was suspended. Halcyon days indeed.

'Here we are,' said Jessica. '*Lazy Suzan*.'

'Nice boat,' said Benedict. It looked sleek and well-cared for, its green stern reflecting in the water.

Jessica stepped on the boat and knocked on the little door. A woman appeared, dark hair, wearing dungarees. 'Beth Whitehead.'

'Are you coppers?'

'Yes.' The detectives showed her their IDs. 'Can we come in?'

It was cosy indoors, thought Benedict, a red rug on the wooden floor, a gas stove, a sofa and a pouffe in the shape of a frog.

Jessica started by telling Beth Whitehead that Alan Milner had been found dead, not more than half a mile from here. 'We understand that Mr Milner was asking for you, Mrs Whitehead. Did he find you?'

'Actually, I don't use that name any more. Me and my husband separated. I use my maiden name these days – Pearson. But you can call me Beth.'

'You live here alone?' asked Jessica.

'Yes.'

'So, Beth, did Alan Milner find you?'

She took a moment to answer. She sighed before answering that yes, he had found her.

'How long had it been since you last saw him?' asked Benedict.

'Before he went to prison. So, eighteen years.'

'What did he want to see you about?'

'He was looking for my ex. Kris. Alan didn't threaten me but I felt threatened nonetheless. I almost called the police but then Dan appeared.'

'Dan?'

'My son. He lives nearby, he comes around quite often. Probably less so now. He's just become a father.'

'Oh?' said Jessica. 'Your first grandchild?'

'Yes.' She smiled. 'A little boy.'

'Congratulations. What else did Mr Milner want?'

'Nothing. That was it.'

'Did you know where your ex-husband was?' asked

Benedict. 'Or is?'

She shook her head. 'I did but I didn't tell him. You see…'

'Yes, Beth?' said Jessica. 'You can tell us.'

'Before he went to prison, Alan and Kris were… sort of mates. I hated it. You see, Kris was a bit weak. Always has been, and Alan exploited that. Got him to do things that made Kris uncomfortable. I mean, nothing major, but he was bad news, that man. And now you say he's dead and, you know what, I don't care.'

'Do you know whether Milner found your husband?'

'He hadn't the last time I spoke to him.'

'Can we have Kris' number and address?'

'Sure.'

'Beth,' said Benedict. 'In 2005, your husband, as he was then, was interviewed as a possible suspect in the supermarket robbery Milner carried out.'

'Yeah but nothing came of it on account he didn't do it.'

'Beth,' said Jessica. 'I know this is going to be painful but–'

'I know. You're going to ask me about Harry.'

'Yes. Is that OK? We read up about it and–'

'You know, when I opened the door to you just now, just for a moment… just for a moment, I thought you had some news for me.' She looked down. 'But you didn't.'

'I'm sorry, Beth.'

'Oh, it's fine. It's not your fault. I'm used to disappointment. I've had to get used to it. It's hell, you know, this life of not knowing. It's what drove Kris and me apart. I could see Harry in Kris and after a while, I couldn't bear it. But the real reason is that I blamed Kris. I did then, I still do now. And he knows he's to blame and funnily enough, I actually feel sorry for him. It's a heavy burden to carry.' She wiped her eyes with the back of her hand.

'You OK, Beth?'

'I mean, he's out there somewhere, my son, my eighteen-year-old son. He's still alive, I know he is. I still look for him. I know Kris and Dan do too. Harry had a birthmark, they call it a port wine mark, on the back of his leg, near the top. Every time I go out, my eyes are on stalks looking for him. I've run up to boys and young men in the past, stopped them in the street just so I can take a look at them, look them in the eyes. People think I'm mad, of course. Wouldn't you? But I'm bound to be unhinged, aren't I, after all I've been through. A parent's worst nightmare. That's what they say, the cliche they use in the papers. Well, I've lived it. Every day for eighteen years.' She rubbed her eyes.

'I hope you don't mind me asking,' said Benedict. 'But do you have a photo of Harry and perhaps one of his birthmark?'

'I suppose, yes. I'll find it for you. You know, I went to Benidorm once, convinced I'd find him there, I don't know, working in a bar or something, happy, the life and soul. Would he recognise me, his own mother? I'm sure he will when the day comes. Because... Oh, hell...' She whipped a handkerchief from her sleeve. 'I'm sorry.'

'No,' said Jessica. 'Don't be. There's no need to say sorry.'

'I still believe, you know. I'm convinced he's going to walk back in one day as if he'd just popped out for an hour or two. You never get used to it, you know.' She started shaking, the tears coming. 'It doesn't get easier with time, it's not like grief. God no, this is so, so much harder, that constant hoping and wondering – what happened to him, why did someone steal my baby, what did they do with him? It's these questions...' She tapped her temple. 'They never go away, they're always there demanding answers and no one knows the answer and it drives you insane. And Dan, my poor boy, was affected even worse. You saw the files, yes?'

'We did.'

'He was on the boat all alone when that... that bastard took Harry. Dan was ten at the time. Can you imagine the effect it had on him? It didn't help that I shouted at him about it, so he thought it was all his fault.' She put her head in her hands and sobbed.

'I'm sorry this is so difficult for you, Beth,' said Jessica in a whisper.

'I hate myself for the way I talked to him back then.'

'You were in shock, Beth.'

'Yes, I know. I lashed out. But it wasn't fair on him. I almost lost him too. It took a long time for him to... Actually, no, he's still not recovered. He goes to therapy. I think it helps but I think Erik will be the best medicine.'

'Your grandson?'

She flashed a smile through her tears. 'Yes. Erik. We've all been so damaged, so fractured but Erik will help us mend. Little Erik. No pressure, Erik.' She laughed. 'It's been a shit life, you know, these last eighteen years. It was Harry's birthday last month. Eighteen years old. He's a man now. I bought him a birthday card, wrote it out and sealed it up. Then I put it in the box file I have along with the seventeen other birthday cards I have and all his Christmas cards. He'll be able to open them when he comes back. His bed is made and ready. I've always got enough food for two – just in case, you know.'

'Beth,' said Benedict. 'Your husband pointed the finger of blame at Alan Milner.'

'No. Like me blaming Dan, he was lashing out, trying to deflect the anger I had for him. Alan was a lowlife but he had nothing to do with Harry's disappearance. I knew that from the start.'

They sat quietly for a while, the silence broken only by Beth's sniffing. After a while, Beth found some photos of Harry on her phone. 'Dan got them digitalised,' she said. 'Here's one of him in his nappy. You can just about see his birthmark. Do you want me to forward them to you?'

Benedict thanked her and nodded at Jessica. 'Beth, we're going to make a move now. Thank you for your time.'

Beth nodded. 'He will come back one day. Maybe not today, maybe not tomorrow but one day, one day, he'll be back.'

Chapter 44: Benedict

'Boss?' DC Prowse looked up from his computer.

'Yes? Your tone of voice, DC Prowse, suggests you've found something of interest.'

'Yeah. Lots of things about that money we found on Alan Milner's boat.'

'Oh yes?'

'Firstly, Manish Patel withdrew £500 from his savings account on five consecutive days.'

'Did he indeed?'

'Yeah, £2,500 in total.'

'That's the amount we found on Milner's boat.'

'Exactly. And, related, you know that fifty-pound note Alan Milner gave Lana… Lana…'

'Kozlowski.'

'That's the one. Well, its serial number shows it's from Milner's stash.'

'Aha. Thought as much.'

'And there's more, boss. Patel's fingerprints are on Milner's money. And no one else's – just Patel and Milner himself.'

'Crikey. OK, that's super interesting. Thanks, DC Prowse. I think another chat with Mr Patel is in order.'

*

Using the address that Beth Pearson had given them, Benedict and Jessica found Kris' flat, a basement in West Hampstead. A short, bearded man answered. It was Kris Whitehead. 'Have you found him?' he said.

'You mean your son?' said Jessica. 'No, I'm terribly sorry but that's not why we're here.'

'I know why you're here.' He showed them through to his living room, a squalid place, the coffee table piled high with the remnants of a couple of takeaways, two crushed Coca-Cola cans under the table. 'Excuse the mess,' said Kris. 'Will this take long? I'm about to go out.'

'We've just come from speaking to your ex-wife, Mr Whitehead.'

'Oh yeah? How is she?'

'I think, like you, she thought we'd come bearing news about your son.'

'Yeah, well, stands to reason.'

'Yes. I wish we had but we're here about Alan Milner.'

'Ah yes. The bastard's dead. I heard.'

'Had you seen him or spoken since his release?' asked Benedict.

'No. Beth said he was looking for me but, luckily, she pretended she didn't know my address or anything.'

'No one we've spoken to,' said Benedict, 'has had a good word to say about him. Why is that, Mr Whitehead?'

'Because he was a bully, a crook, a thug? Need I go on? Put it this way, you won't be seeing me at his funeral.'

'You were questioned about the supermarket robbery.'

'Yeah, briefly, but I wasn't involved and they knew that.'

'Why do you think your name was in the frame?'

'Because they knew I was an associate of his.'

'Meaning?'

'Meaning nothing. I tended to avoid him.'

'Did Milner involve you in any of his illegal activities?'

Kris laughed. 'I'm hardly gonna tell you that, am I? But I will tell you about an incident that *didn't* happen. A few days before the robbery in that shop, Alan wanted to kidnap a girl.'

'Oh? What happened?'

Kris walked off and returned a few seconds later with another can of Coke. 'I'm a bit addicted to these,' he said, opening the can. 'Still, beats smoking, I suppose.' He said using air quotes. 'So, yeah, I'm telling you this so you get a picture of what sort of man Alan is. Or was. Nothing happened, the plan was aborted. If something had, I wouldn't be telling you.

'What was this plan, Mr Whitehead?' asked Jessica.

'Alan had this stupid plan to kidnap this girl, a teenager, the daughter of a local business owner. He owned… something, I forget now, some big company. And… if it wasn't so stupid, it'd be quite funny. So, me, Alan and someone else who will remain nameless were going to kidnap this girl and hold her in a squat or somewhere that Alan knew until her old man paid up. Simple. On paper. Luckily, like I said, nothing came of it and the girl was none the wiser. Thank God.'

'Mr Whitehead, you accused Mr Milner of stealing your baby. Did you have reason to think he had?'

'No. I was panicking. But it wasn't a far stretch was it –

kidnapping a girl to snatching a baby. The only difference was Beth and me weren't exactly well off. Alan knew that.'

'It must have been difficult for you,' said Jessica.

'Yeah. You could say that.' No one spoke for a few moments. Kris drank his Coke. Then he began to talk. 'A couple of years ago, I thought I saw him. I was in Camden market on a Sunday afternoon, the busiest time there. I saw this lad in a long leather coat with a girl and I did a double take. I thought, Christ, that's Harry. I couldn't move at first. I was, like, rooted to the spot. My heart, God. He and his friend walked off. And then I sprang into life and chased after them. Problem is, I'd already lost them. You know what it's like, that market is like a rabbit warren. I kept bumping into people. I saw some bloke with a similar coat and I grabbed his arm and spun him around. It was someone else. I thought the bloke was going to lamp me. I called Harry's name out even though I knew it'd be pointless. He wouldn't be called Harry no more. That set me back, that did.' He slouched in his chair.

'What do you mean, Mr Whitehead?'

He grimaced. 'I sort of got used to Harry missing over the years. I mean, don't get me wrong, I never stopped hoping he'd come back one day, but I'd sort of calmed down about it. But seeing him that day, and I'm sure it was him, just got me fired up again.'

'Did you tell Beth?' asked Jessica.

'I almost did. I wanted to but in the end, I didn't.'

'Can I ask why not?'

'I thought about it. Actually, I agonised over it. In the end, I knew how it was affecting me so I thought why put her through it? Why give her false hope.'

'Did you mention it to the police? They could have

checked their CCTV.'

'Nah. I couldn't face it. Look, I know what you're thinking but remember back in 2005, Beth and me had the police around all the time. We knew they were working on the case and trying to help but it did our heads in. Every other day, they'd say we might have a sighting or someone says they know someone who knows someone. It never stopped, and these little eruptions of hope just kill you when they come to nothing. I couldn't go through that again. And I certainly couldn't put Beth through it again.' He put his head in his hands.

'Can I ask, Mr Whitehead,' said Jessica. 'How do you and Beth get on these days?'

He looked up. 'Better actually.'

'We hear congratulations are in order.'

He smiled for the first time. 'Yeah. Little Erik, our little Viking. Bless him. Dan, my son, will make a good dad. I'm sure of it.' Under his breath, he added, 'Better than I ever did.' He scratched the back of his head. 'Beth never forgave me when Harry went missing. I didn't blame her. It destroyed our marriage but I still... I still have feelings for her. I know we're not gonna get back together, not ever, but I'm hoping Erik will help heal us a bit, you know?'

'Yes, I understand,' said Jessica.

Kris stood and went to stand at the window. Staring out, he finished his drink. 'Whatever happens, Beth and I are tied forever, whether we like it or not. We have this link, this terrible thing that happened to us, the sort of nightmare you wouldn't wish on your worst enemy. It destroys you. It eats at you from within until you feel... hollow.' He turned around. 'And they're still out there. Both of them.'

'Both of them?' said Benedict.

'Harry, my son, and…' He returned his attention to the outside world. 'And the bastard who stole him.'

*

Back in the office, Benedict received a call from Adrian Collins. 'Ben, you'll be pleased to know we've got a match for one set of fingerprints found on the canal boat. They belong to a woman you've just interviewed – Patricia Godwin.'

'Really? Wow, that does surprise me.'

'I've made a list. Her prints were found on the door handle of the door leading inside and on the frame of the bedroom door and on the bedroom light switch and, finally, on one of the bedroom walls.'

'What about the mallet? Do Patricia Godwin's fingerprints appear on the mallet?'

'Don't know yet. Forensics have still got the mallet, testing it for DNA.'

'OK. Interesting. Thanks, Adrian.' He rang off.

Chapter 45: Benedict

'Have you remembered the DNA kit?' asked Benedict.

Jessica patted her handbag. 'Of course.'

Benedict did not expect to see Patricia Godwin again so soon. And it was evident by her expression on opening the door to her pebble-dashed home that the feeling was mutual. 'Inspector Paige? Detective Gardiner. You're back. How can I help?'

'Can we come in?'

'I w-was about to go out actually. I have a meeting with the funeral director.'

'I'm afraid it'll have to wait. This is important.'

'More important than my father's funeral?'

'Yes, well, I'm sorry but we need to have a conversation.'

'Oh, OK. Erm, yes, come in.'

The detectives sat down in her living room while Patricia hovered. 'Would you like coffee?'

'No, thank you. Why don't you take a seat?'

She sat, perching on the edge of an armchair, her hands clasped on her lap. 'One of your officers popped around yesterday and took my fingerprints. I assume you sent him, Inspector. Why did you do that?'

'I'll get to that. Ms Godwin, when we spoke to you two days ago, you categorically said you hadn't seen Alan Milner since his release.'

'That's right.'

Benedict paused. He almost felt sorry for her; her father had just died, but she was going to have to face this. 'Ms Godwin–'

'Please call me Patricia.'

'Patricia. Alan Milner was found dead in a canal boat called *Crazy Lou*. What we need to know is why are your fingerprints all over that boat?'

Her hand went to her mouth. She let out a little anguished cry.

'We've found your prints in several places, including in the bedroom where Milner was killed.'

'Oh dear me.'

'What sort of car do you drive, Patricia?'

'Is that important?'

'Just answer the question, please.'

'A Fiat.'

'A Fiat what?'

'A Panda.'

'Colour?'

'It's… it's blue.'

'Right, so that leads me to my second point. Alan Milner's mother told us a woman called Jane called for Alan on the morning he was found dead. Her description matches yours. Plus, this woman, according to Mrs Milner, drove a blue Fiat Panda.'

She pulled on a thumb.

'Patricia,' said Jessica. 'Did you kill Alan Milner?'

'No.' She shook her head as the tears came. 'No, as God is my witness, I did not kill that man.'

'So, explain the fingerprints, please.'

She stood and, going to one of the pictures of Jesus on her wall, straightened it.

'Patricia? You need to answer the question because, if you don't, you will have to answer at the station.'

She sat again. 'OK, I may not have been entirely honest with you both. I did go to that boat. I might as well tell you I also saw him a couple of days before.' She stopped and leaned back in her chair.

'Can you tell us, Patricia?'

'The first time, I simply wanted to see what he looked like after eighteen years in jail.'

'Why?'

She shrugged. 'I don't honestly know. Morbid curiosity, I guess. I remembered him from the trial. I suppose I wanted to know if he looked like a man who'd suffered. Most unchristian of me, I know. I don't know how else to describe it.'

'Did you see him?' asked Jessica. 'Did you speak to him?'

'I, erm, parked the car near to where he lived and yes, I saw him walking towards the car. I got out and asked him where the post office was. Why I did that, I have no idea. I suppose it was like poking a bee's nest. He recognised me and called me a vile name. So, I got back in the car and drove off rather sharpish after that.'

'And that was it on that occasion?' asked Jessica.

'Yes.'

'And the second occasion, when you spoke to Mrs Milner?'

'I wasn't thinking straight. The funeral directors had just taken my poor father. You must understand, my emotions were all over the place. Milner may not have killed my father but, as far as I'm concerned, he was directly responsible for his death.'

'But what did you hope to achieve by confronting him?' asked Jessica.

'I simply wanted to tell him.'

'That your father had died?'

'Had *just* died, yes. I wanted him to know that the man he hurt all those years ago had suffered every day since and now he was gone.'

'Instead, you lost control,' said Benedict. 'You didn't mean to kill him but you saw him and something snapped–'

'No.'

'You picked up a mallet and you hit him on the back of the head with it.'

'No! No. Absolutely not.'

'We found the mallet that killed him. Now, people who live on boats usually have a mallet in their possession so I don't believe you took your own mallet but you saw one on the boat and you picked it and–'

'Please stop, Inspector. Please. You've got it totally wrong.'

'Have I? So, tell me, what did happen?'

'He was…'

'Yes?'

'He was already dead, Inspector.'

'OK.' Benedict considered her for a few moments. 'So, you saw him there in the bedroom. What did you do?'

'Do?'

'As in, did you try to revive him or…'

'No. I-I didn't. I suppose I should have but I was, I don't know, I was in shock. It's not every day one sees two bodies in quick succession.'

'So, what did you do?'

'I have no memory. I guess I simply left. I walked back the way I came but I was in a haze.'

'Did you see anyone on the towpath?'

'I probably saw lots of people but I don't remember a single one. I didn't see anything unusual or anyone acting suspiciously. I was in a state, Inspector. My brain was a fog of emotion and upset.'

'It was you who made the anonymous call to the police, wasn't it, Patricia?' asked Jessica.

She nodded. 'Yes. That was me. I'm sorry, I was too frightened to use my mobile or leave my name. Cowardly of me, I know.' She pulled on her crucifix. 'What will happen now?'

'You were on that boat, Patricia. You have no witnesses to collaborate your version of events and you had a motive. You are a suspect.'

'Oh dear, oh dear.'

'Would you like a glass of water, Patricia?' asked Jessica.

'No, I'm fine. But thank you.'

'Like I said, we found the mallet that killed Milner,' said Benedict.

'I swear, Inspector. It wasn't me.'

'We haven't had it back from forensics yet but hopefully today. So, what we're going to do now, we're going to take your DNA and send it off for analysis. If your DNA or your fingerprints match what's on that mallet, we will be arresting you for the murder of Alan Milner. Do you understand?'

She didn't answer.

'Patricia, I said, do you understand?

'Yes, Inspector. I understand. But I'm not worried.'

'No?'

'No.' She sat up and looked him in the eye. 'Because I know your analysis will clear my name. Now, if you don't mind, I really must see the funeral director. We have a lot to discuss. I have my father's cremation to finalise.'

Chapter 46: Benedict

Benedict and Jessica arrived at Barclays Bank in Brent to be told that Manish Patel was seeing a client and was due to see another client straight after that, so he wouldn't be free for an hour. Benedict asked the clerk to book an appointment with the busy manager for an hour's time. Meanwhile, the detectives went to a local café and each ordered a fried breakfast. 'So, what are we thinking, boss?' asked Jessica, as she tucked into her vegetarian sausage. 'Do you see Patricia Godwin as a killer?'

'It'd be hard to credit, wouldn't it?'

'Her father had just died that morning and she said herself that her head was everywhere. Like you said, she may not have sought him out with the intention to kill him but the anger got the better of her, she saw the mallet and wallops him from behind. You can see it happening.'

'The mallet will tell us everything.'

'We hope. And what about Beth Pearson or her ex, Kris Whitehead, or Ian Turner?'

'They all had the motivation and any of them could have

the means. How's your breakfast?'

'It's alright. The sausage is like sawdust but the mushrooms are nice. I did like Ian Turner's place out in the woods. I could see myself living somewhere like that, slightly off-grid.'

'You do surprise me, Jessica. I had you down as too much of a party girl.'

'Yeah, as long as I had a car and it wasn't too far, I'd be OK. Best of both worlds.'

An hour later, the detectives were back at the bank. This time, they met Mr Patel in his office. Patel looked worried, as well he might, thought Benedict. He started: 'Mr Patel, could you tell us why you withdrew £500 from your savings account on five consecutive days last week?'

'Oh, erm. I'm sorry, it's a tax dodge. I'm-I'm having some work done to the house and the builder said he'd take cash. I-I shouldn't be telling you this.' He laughed.

Benedict looked at Jessica. 'Did you know, DS Gardiner, that Alan Milner was a builder?'

'No. News to me.'

'Milner?' said Patel, a tremble in his voice.

'Yes, Alan Milner. We found just short of two and a half thousand pounds on the boat he was occupying – five bundles of fifty-pound notes, all of them brand new. So new they only had two sets of fingerprints on them. Mr Milner's and yours, Mr Patel. Why were you paying Mr Milner five hundred pounds a day, Mr Patel? Was he friends with this builder of yours? Be very careful how you answer, Mr Patel. Perjury, in other words, lying to the police, is a serious offence, as you're about to find out for yourself. Tread carefully now and tell me why you were paying Alan Milner such large sums of money on a daily basis.'

'I-I, er, I owed him.'

'You know I'm going to ask you for what? After all, you have told us that you'd never met Mr Milner and yet that's quite a hefty IOU, isn't it?'

'It's a long story.'

Benedict waited but nothing else was forthcoming. 'Indulge us, Mr Patel. We have all day.'

Patel's eyes shot between the detectives, a bead of sweat showed on his upper lip. He opened his mouth and then shut it again.

'Is it to do with your friend Ian Turner, perhaps?' asked Jessica.

Patel's eyes widened but he kept his silence.

'OK, Mr Patel,' said Benedict. 'We currently have enough with which to arrest you. We could make this more formal and take this back to the station. You can inform your solicitor. If you don't have a solicitor, we can–'

'He was blackmailing me.'

'I'm sorry? Blackmailing you? Who was? Alan Milner or Ian Turner?'

Patel rubbed his eyes and stared up at the ceiling. He looked close to tears. 'Actually, both. I've been carrying this guilt for eighteen years. I've never told a soul.'

'The last time we spoke, Mr Patel, I accused you of providing Ian Turner with a false alibi. I was right, wasn't I?'

He looked down at his lap. 'Yes. Ian caught me in a… compromising position at work and he threatened to tell my bosses if I didn't do as he said. So he forced me into telling the police that he was with me that night watching the football.'

'The night of the supermarket robbery in which an innocent man was bludgeoned.'

'Yes.'

'Man City v Liverpool, if memory serves.'

'I think so.'

'So what was this compromising position, Mr Patel?' asked Jessica.

'Do I have to say?'

'You will have to at some point.'

'I was… I helped myself to an IOU from the company where we worked. It wasn't much, it really wasn't, and I fully intended to pay it back. But Ian caught me and threatened to tell them and I was scared. I'd only just started my first managerial position. I… I thought it'd be the end of my career so when he said all he wanted me to do was to lie for him, I thought OK, no big deal. So I did.'

'But it was a big deal, Mr Patel,' said Jessica. 'Ian Turner took part in a violent robbery that night. A man's life was ruined, a man who died, funnily enough, on the same day as Alan Milner. Ian Turner may not have struck the blow but he was very much part of that robbery and thanks entirely to you, he was never brought to justice.'

'I know that now. Don't think I don't regret it because I do. The stupid thing is that had I owned up back then to my bosses, I'd probably have got away with a rap on the knuckles. Instead, I've had to carry this burden for these last eighteen years.'

'Much more than that, I'm afraid, Mr Patel,' said Jessica. 'Perjury can result in seven years in prison.'

'Oh God.' He looked as if he might faint. 'Worst case scenario,' said Jessica in a lighter tone.

'And Alan Milner knew about this,' said Benedict.

'He, erm, forced it out of me.'

'That was why he was so keen on finding you. His silence

cost you two and a half thousand.'

'Yes.'

'But then he asked you for more and you, panicking, killed him.'

Patel leapt up from his chair. 'Hell no! I didn't kill him. Honest to God. I may have wanted to but I didn't. I wouldn't…'

'Yes, Mr Patel?'

'I wouldn't have the balls.'

'You don't have an alibi for Tuesday morning–'

'I told you, I was working. I was here,' he added, jabbing his desk.

'Yes, but you don't start until half eight. Alan Milner could have been killed at any time in the hours before.'

'I didn't kill him. You have to believe me.'

'Have you got many more appointments today, Mr Patel?' asked Benedict.

'Three or four. Why?'

'I'll give you a couple of minutes to rearrange–'

'Why? You're not arresting me, are you?'

'I'll let you make your arrangements first but then, yes, I will be arresting you as a suspect in the murder of Alan Milner and for perverting the course of justice as defined by the Perjury Act of 1911. Now, we had to wait a whole hour for you this morning already. Please don't keep us waiting any longer.'

While the detectives waited for the flustered bank manager to make alternative arrangements, Benedict phoned DC Prowse. 'DC Prowse, I got a job for you and DC Kelly. I'll text you over the address but I want you both to drive down to Sevenoaks in Kent and arrest a man by the name of Turner, Ian Turner…'

Chapter 47: Benedict

Saturday morning. Benedict and Jessica found Ian Turner waiting for them in Interview Room 1, sitting next to a duty solicitor Benedict had met before, Mr Newman. Sitting down, Benedict said hello. He switched on the tape recorder and introduced the four people present. He started by recapping why Turner had been arrested – namely, having been an accomplice in the 2005 supermarket robbery, being a suspect in the murder of Alan Milner and lastly for blackmail.

'I see your face is clearing up, Mr Turner.' He didn't respond. 'OK, let's make a start. We found the weapon that killed Alan Milner. It was a wooden mallet made out of beechwood. It'd been discarded in some undergrowth not more than a hundred yards or so from the canal boat Mr Milner was killed in. We're expecting any evidence from that, ie DNA and fingerprints, to be available today. If your DNA matches, we will be charging you.'

Mr Newman scribbled on his A4 pad.

'So, when we spoke to you a couple of days ago, we asked you a number of questions. I'd like to revisit those topics now. First of all, regarding the supermarket robbery in 2005. In his original statement made to the police eighteen years ago, Manish Patel said he invited you around to his house to watch a football match on the night of the robbery. Therefore, even though Milner named you as his accomplice, you had an alibi.'

'Yes, exactly,' said Turner.

'Yesterday, DS Gardiner and I spoke to Manish Patel. He has now withdrawn his statement–'

'What?'

'He says you blackmailed him into providing a false alibi.'

'He's lying.'

'In other words, Mr Turner, you were not at Mr Patel's house watching football. You were, as Milner said, robbing that shop.'

Mr Newman cleared his throat. 'And you believe him, do you, Inspector, this Mr Patel? It's his word against my client's.'

'No, I don't think so. By admitting he lied, he knows he'd be arrested for perverting the course of justice. So, Mr Turner?'

Turner shrugged. 'OK, I admit I got Manish to lie for me. That's because I didn't have an alibi but that doesn't mean I was there. I was at home, watching that match on TV but apart from my missus, I had no one that would vouch for me and I knew that wouldn't be enough for you.'

'My client has a point. How are you going to prove it now, Inspector? You had no evidence at the time and you still don't apart from the dubious testimony of a notorious thug who is now dead. Patel may have thrown himself under a bus but his change of story doesn't implicate Mr Turner. You had and still have no CCTV, DNA, fingerprints, witnesses…

nothing. Unless you're keeping something from us perhaps?'

Benedict didn't answer. He knew Newman was right. 'OK, moving on. It wasn't until after we spoke to you that we realised you know Beth Pearson–'

'Who?'

'Beth Whitehead, as she was, and her husband, Kris Whitehead.'

'I've not seen them in yonks.'

'You were friends at the point their baby went missing.'

'No, not friends. I barely knew them. I'd only met Kris a couple of times.'

'Kris Whitehead pointed the finger at Milner. Do you think Milner stole the baby?'

'Is this relevant?' asked Mr Newman.

'The abduction of Harry Whitehead remains an unsolved case, Mr Newman. So, yes, it is relevant. Mr Turner?'

'It's possible, yes.'

'It is? Why do you say that?'

'Because Alan was always coming up with stupid ideas. He once mentioned to me this idea of stealing babies and selling them to a third party who, in turn, would sell them in China. He reckoned there was a big demand for white babies in China. Those were his words.'

'Did you report this to the police at the time?'

Turner looked down. 'No.'

'No?'

'Just because he mentioned it in passing, didn't mean anything. Like I said, he was always coming up with mad ideas. Nothing ever came of them.'

'Like kidnapping a teenage girl, the daughter of a local business owner?'

Turner looked at him. 'I don't know anything about that.'

'Did you steal the baby, Mr Turner?'

'Don't be daft. Of course, I bloody didn't.'

'OK, so let's talk about the murder of Alan Milner. We found a tea towel on Milner's boat smeared with blood. We had it analysed its DNA and we found it belonged to two people – Milner and…' He paused for effect. 'And you, Mr Turner.'

'Me?'

'Hmm. How do you explain your blood on that tea towel, Mr Turner?'

He didn't answer.

'Is it related to those nasty-looking cuts on your face?' asked Jessica.

'I told you I fell into a ditch in the woods near the house.'

'We're conducting a murder enquiry here, Mr Turner. You need to be honest with us.'

He stared into the distance. Turner drummed his fingers on the tabletop. 'OK, I admit I saw him.'

'Milner? When?'

'I don't know. Sunday, I think.'

'Why?'

'Why? Because he…'

'Yes?'

'Because he wanted me to do a job with him. He wanted to rob a bank. He–'

'Which bank?'

'Erm, a Barclays.'

'Is that the one on Brent High Street, by any chance?'

'I don't know. He may have said, I can't remember. I wasn't interested. You saw my house. I've got a decent life there. I'm not about to jeopardise that for some half-brained idea to rob a bloody bank so I told him where to go.' He shrugged. 'We got into a fight. I came off worse.'

'That's quite a fight you had as it involved a hammer.' The surprised look on Turner's face told Benedict that he'd got it right. 'Mr Milner was killed by a blow to the back of the head with a wooden mallet but we also know he sustained an injury to his left shoulder with, what we believe, was a hammer. You make it sound like a fisticuffs type of fight, Mr Turner, but you hit him with a hammer. You struck his shoulder. I reckon you were aiming for his head but you missed. In other words, you tried to kill him.'

'No, no. I-I j-just wanted t-to scare him but it…'

'But?'

'He was too strong for me.' He looked down, as if ashamed by the admission.

'So, Milner thought he'd dealt with you. But he was in pain, having had his shoulder hit. Maybe he turned his back on you. You, seeing a mallet, hit him on the back of the head with it—'

'No.'

'And killed him.'

'No, you're talking bollocks.'

'You didn't mean to kill him, after all, it was only a wooden mallet but—'

'I did not kill him. Alan was a scumbag but I'm telling you, I didn't kill him.'

'You need to wait for that DNA, Inspector,' said Mr Newman.

'Indeed. We shall detain you here, Mr Turner, until we have the test result. Shouldn't be long and if you didn't kill him, as you say, you'll be free to go unless of course we need to charge you for any other offence, like lying to the police perhaps, or blackmail. We'll let you know.'

Chapter 48: Benedict

Benedict sat at his desk. Jessica pulled a chair up. 'What do you think, boss?'

'I think we may well have our man, DS Gardiner. Yes, we still have Manish Patel and Patricia Godwin in the frame but I can't see it. Possibly even with Beth or Kris Whitehead. But let's be frank – our money has to be on Ian Turner. We'll know soon enough.'

As it was, Benedict was right – the wait was brief. Diana Pettigrew from forensics came to see him in person. 'Results just in, Ben,' she said. 'I know everything hinges on this so I thought I'd come tell you face-to-face.'

'Thank you, Diana, I appreciate it. So, go on, don't keep me in suspense.'

'First of all, I can confirm that the mallet we found is indeed the instrument that killed Alan Milner. The mallet penetrated the brain tissue and caused a traumatic brain injury. So it's what's called a penetrating brain injury, in other words, there was a break in the skull. The victim suffered a diffuse axonal injury, as in the tearing of the brain's long connecting nerve fibres. This happens when the brain is injured as it shifts and rotates inside the skull. All this means the killer wasn't messing about. He hit him from behind with as much force as he could muster. It took a person of some strength to inflict quite so much damage. But of course, if Milner's back was turned, the killer did have the element of surprise on his side.'

'OK.'

'We do have a DNA match from the mallet. And it's not Ian Turner.'

'No?'

'But it *is* someone related to him.'

'I'm sorry?'

'The DNA is a fifty per cent match for Turner.'

'Heck.'

'Does Turner have a sibling or a parent?'

'I don't know but he does have two sons.'

Diana placed her hand on Benedict's sleeve. 'You'd better find them pronto, Ben. One of them could well be your killer.'

*

Benedict found Ian Turner in a holding cell. A uniformed officer unlocked the cell door. Turner stood on seeing Benedict. 'Mr Turner, you're free to go for now.'

'I am? Ha, told you. Bloody hell. I'm going to speak to my solicitor. I'm going to sue you. I've got rights, you know.'

'I'm aware of that, Mr Turner. And so have we while a suspect remains a person of interest. And I warn you, we will be revisiting the other offences, the blackmailing and the perjury. Now, if we could talk practical matters. DC Prowse and I are going to give you a lift home all the way to

Sevenoaks.'

'Hey? No, I'm fine. I'll catch the train.'

'It wasn't so much an offer as an instruction.'

'What for?'

'I'd like to speak to the rest of the family.'

'Why? They've got nothing to do with this. Nor have I. Leave us alone.'

'This is not open for discussion, Mr Turner. Will everyone be in?'

'Juliet will be. Don't know about the boys.'

Benedict handed Turner back his mobile. 'If we leave now, we should be there by five. Please phone your wife and tell her to make sure the boys are there for then.'

'But what–'

'Just do as I say, Mr Turner.'

A brief phone call later, Turner was finished. 'They'll be there,' he said.

'Good. Thank you. One last question before we go – do you have any siblings or a surviving parent, Mr Turner?'

'No. Why are you asking me that?'

'Now, have you got everything? Would you like to visit the gents before we go?'

Turner continued grumbling, saying he had a right not to be escorted home by police, but he didn't resist as Benedict escorted him to the pool car.

The hour-and-a-quarter drive south to Heaverham, five miles north of Sevenoaks, was painful. DC Prowse sat in the back with Ian Turner. Apart from a couple of comments about the weather and traffic, no one spoke. Benedict could feel Turner's anger and resentment.

It was late afternoon as he parked the car up at the end of the track. He and DC Prowse followed Turner back to his house. Juliet came rushing out of the house, her concern clearly etched on her face. 'What's happening?' she asked, breathlessly.

'Ask them,' said Turner.

Benedict and DC Prowse followed the couple indoors. It was, thought Benedict, certainly a cosy place – wooden floor, wooden beams, colourful rugs, a large fireplace stocked up with wood.

The two boys stood up on seeing the detectives. 'You alright, Dad?' said the eldest, Felix.

'I'm alright but they want to speak to you.'

'Individually, please.'

'What for?' asked Juliet.

'We're conducting a murder investigation, Mrs Whitehead. We have to investigate every possible avenue.'

'But us? My sons?'

'It won't take long.'

'No, not Kelvin. He's seventeen. I have a right to sit in.'

'Fair enough. Shall we start with Kelvin then?'

Ian and Felix made themselves scarce. The four of them sat down, mother and son together.

'Kelvin,' said Benedict. 'Did you know Alan Milner?'

'No.'

'Had you ever met him?'

He glanced at his mother. 'Only when he came around recently to see Dad.'

'And that was it? Did you speak to him?'

He shook his head. 'No. I mean I guess I said hello, and that was it.'

'Where were you Monday afternoon just gone?'

'Monday? I was at college, I guess.'

'What's the name of the college?' asked DC Prowse. 'And

what are you studying?'

'Agriculture at West Kent.'

'What time–'

'Why are you asking all these questions?' barked Juliet. 'You surely don't suspect Kelvin of murdering that man.'

'We're trying to eliminate both your sons from our enquiries, Mrs Turner,' said Benedict. 'That is all. Kelvin, what time did you finish on Monday?'

He shrugged. 'Normal time. Half three. And then came home.'

'Can you vouch for that, Mrs Turner?'

'Erm, no. I work Mondays. But he's not lying. He always has loads of homework and stuff, don't you, Kel?'

He nodded.

'OK, fair enough. That was it.' He could see Juliet's shoulders relax. 'Now, if we could see Felix?'

'Sure,' said Juliet.

After Kelvin and Juliet had gone, DC Prowse leaned over and asked, 'Aren't you going to ask for his DNA, boss?'

'All in good time, DC Prowse.' He tapped his nose. 'I have a plan.'

A minute later, Felix appeared, sat down and answered the same set of questions. Benedict thanked him. 'Felix, could you ask your brother and parents to come through?'

'Haven't you finished with us yet?'

'Not quite.'

Felix called them through. Everyone stood in a circle as if they were at an awkward party, not sure what to talk about. Benedict broke the silence. 'Thank you, Kelvin, Felix, for answering my questions. I hope you didn't find it too onerous. Thank you too, Mr Turner, for having helped us with our enquiries. I apologise that we had to detain you for so long.' He turned his focus on Juliet. 'We'll be off but before we go, can I ask you, Juliet, for your DNA sample?'

'Really?'

'Hang on,' said Ian. 'Why do you need her DNA? You can't suspect my wife.'

'Just procedural,' said Benedict. 'Also, Kelvin and Felix, we need your DNA too, please.'

Juliet blanched. 'What did you say?'

'We need to take the boys' DNA. DC Prowse, would you mind?'

DC Prowse stepped towards Felix.

Juliet blocked him. 'No. You can't.'

'It's fine, Mum,' said Felix.

'No. They have to have my permission.'

'No, they don't. I'm eighteen—'

'Shut up,' said Ian.

'I don't want to do it,' said Kelvin, edging towards his mother. 'Don't let them do it, Mum.'

She put her arm around him. 'Leave us alone,' she screamed. 'Just fuck off out of here, leave my family alone. Please.' She began crying.

'Don't you have to have a warrant or something?' said Ian.

'We can require you to give a DNA sample if we've arrested you for a criminal offence or if we intend to charge you with an offence.'

'And do you?' Turner shouted. 'Do you intend to arrest one of my sons?'

'The DNA we got from the weapon that killed Alan Milner is a fifty per cent match for yours, Mr Turner.'

'Meaning?'

'You told me earlier you don't have any siblings or parents so it means the DNA belongs to one of your sons.'

He staggered back.

Juliet was sobbing loudly now. 'No, that can't be.'

'Well, I'll tell you this for nothing,' said Felix. 'I didn't kill no one.'

'Nor did I,' said Kelvin, his eyes welling up.

'I'll do your test for you,' said Felix.

'No, Felix,' screamed his mother. 'You can't. You can't.'

'But, Mum–'

'Listen to me, Felix, for God's sake, you can't take the test.'

Next moment, Kelvin bolted for the door. 'Kelvin?' screamed Ian.

DC Prowse gave chase, charging out of the door.

Ian looked as if he might run too. 'Stay where you are,' shouted Benedict.

'What the fuck?' said Felix.

'He'll be back,' said Benedict. 'Now, enough of this – Felix, your DNA now, please.'

Felix said something in return but Benedict didn't hear it over Juliet's sobbing.

Chapter 49: Benedict

The following morning, the whole station waited on tenterhooks pending the DNA tests on Felix and Kelvin Turner. But while they waited, Benedict received a new update from the CID's technological forensic team – they had in their possession Ian Turner's mobile during his brief incarceration, and they took the opportunity to have a look at it, and they found that someone had installed a bit of tracking software. Therefore, someone was following Turner's movements. The question was – who? Meanwhile, Benedict asked DC Kelly to ring West Kent College and then asked both DC Kelly and Prowse to start on the tedious task of viewing CCTV.

It hadn't taken long for DC Prowse to catch the younger Turner boy the previous day. He'd made a run for the quad bike. He managed to get on it, slam the key into the ignition and start it. But by the time he'd engaged the gears, DC Prowse was on him, pulling Kelvin off the machine and securing him in an armlock. Prowse dragged the sobbing boy back to the house. His mother hugged him. 'Kelvin, my baby.'

'Get off me, Mum.'

'Kelvin,' said Benedict. 'Have you got anything you want to say to me?'

'Keep your mouth shut, Kel,' said his father. 'Don't say a word.'

'He has to give us your DNA, Mr Turner. There's no getting away from that.'

'OK,' screamed Juliet. 'Take his but not Felix's. You don't need Felix's.'

'I'm afraid we need both, Mrs Turner. I'm sorry.'

The DNA results arrived late the following afternoon having been speeded through the system.

Benedict sent DCs Prowse and Kelly to Sevenoaks to bring all four Turners to the Camden nick.

*

The following morning, Benedict found all four Turners sitting in Interview Room Three with Mr Newman appointed again as solicitor. Benedict asked Felix Turner to wait in the reception area.

Benedict moved them into Interview Room One, the biggest room, but with six of them, it was still a squeeze: Benedict, Jessica, Newman, Kelvin and both his parents. Benedict had to borrow a couple of chairs from the next-door room.

'OK, let's make a start. I'll get straight to the point. Kelvin's DNA matches the DNA we found on the mallet.'

The announcement was met by audible gasps from all three Turners. Ian shook his head. Juliet's eyes moistened.

'Kelvin, did you kill Alan Milner?'

He glanced nervously at his mother. Benedict could tell

they were holding hands under the table.

'Kelvin?'

'No.'

'So, how do you explain the DNA?'

'I-I don't know.'

'I killed him,' said Ian Turner. 'Like you said, I had a fight with Alan and I hit him on the shoulder with that hammer and then–'

'Mr Turner,' said Benedict. 'Please stop. You may have assaulted Milner but we know, and you know, you did not kill him. We know Kelvin did.'

'But he was at college,' said Juliet. 'He told you. He'll have people there who saw him, his friends, the teachers.'

'But he wasn't, Mrs Turner,' said Jessica. 'One of my colleagues spoke to the college this morning and it appears Kelvin left college at half past one on Monday. The students and staff at West Kent have to tap in and out with their lanyards so we know Kelvin left at…' She consulted her notes. 'At one thirty-four that afternoon. How did you get to London on Monday, Kelvin?'

'I didn't.'

Benedict slid a sheet of paper across the table. 'Have a look at this, please, Kelvin, and tell me what you see.'

He saw Juliet and Ian's shoulders slump. 'Is that you at Sevenoaks station at two thirty-one on Monday afternoon, Kelvin?'

'This doesn't mean he's going to London,' said Mr Newman. 'This is taken in the ticket hall, he could have been going south.'

'We are currently viewing CCTV at both Charing Cross and London Bridge stations where the Sevenoaks trains terminate. I'm confident we'll find Kelvin there. Did you pay for your ticket by cash or card, Kelvin?'

'Card,' he muttered.

'And when you found Mr Milner, what did you say to him, Kelvin?'

'I didn't see him.'

'Hang on,' said Ian. 'He wouldn't know where to find him. I didn't even tell Juliet.'

'He did. Your son installed a piece of tracking software on your phone, Mr Turner. I'm sure when we check Kelvin's phone, we'll find the other end of it there.' Turning back to the boy, Benedict was about to ask his next question but paused on seeing Kelvin breaking down in tears. His mother placed her arm around his shoulder. Kelvin leaned in towards her.

After a while, Benedict asked, 'Why did you do it, Kelvin?'

'You don't need to answer that,' said Mr Newman.

'Because he was threatening my family,' said Kelvin between sobs.

'How?'

'Kelvin, shut up,' said Ian.

'No,' said Juliet. 'He has to. Let him talk.'

'I heard Mum and Dad talking. He was blackmailing Dad. He wanted Dad to sell the house and give him sixty-seven thousand pounds. I couldn't let him do it.'

Ian put his head in his hands. 'Oh, Christ no.'

Juliet hugged her son. 'Oh, my poor love. Kelvin, you didn't have to… Oh God, no, no, no. Kelvin, why didn't you just speak to us?'

'I was frightened, Mum. I didn't want him to hurt us. I only wanted to speak to him, man to man, but…'

'Oh, my poor love. Why? Why? You're only seventeen…' He may have been seventeen, thought Benedict, but right now, he looked every inch a small, frightened boy.

'I was only trying to help. I didn't mean to… I found him on his boat and I told him to leave Dad alone but he just laughed at me. I said he was a horrible man for threatening to steal our home and he called me a 'little boy', and then I saw that hammer lying there, the mallet, and my mind went blank and next minute…'

'Oh, Kelvin.'

'I only meant to hurt him but he fell like a… like a sack of potatoes and I tried to… to wake him up, Mum, but he wouldn't wake up. I shook him and shouted at him to wake up but he wouldn't and he just lay there, all limp, and there was all this blood everywhere and… and I just… I panicked so I ran away. I'm sorry.'

'Kelvin, my darling boy.'

'I'm sorry, Mum. I'm so sorry. Will they send me to prison? I can't go to prison, Mum. Help me, Mum. Help me…'

Kelvin fell onto his mother's lap and sobbed uncontrollably.

Chapter 50: Benedict

Benedict sent DC Prowse to visit Beth Pearson and Kris Whitehead and ask for their DNA. He gave the Turners time alone but now he needed to speak to Ian and Juliet Turner. A uniformed officer led Kelvin away.

'What will happen now?' asked Juliet.

'We'll need to interview Kelvin again and go into detail about what happened on Monday,' said Benedict. 'Then, we will present the case to the CPS–'

'The…'

'Crown Prosecution Service and they will decide if there's enough of a case to take it to trial.' He stopped himself from apologising. As much as he felt sorry for them, it wasn't for him to apologise. 'This all stems back to the supermarket robbery in 2005. It is my belief that you were the second man that night, Mr Turner–'

'Hang on–'

'Let me finish. Milner knew Patel had given you a false alibi and Milner took the opportunity to blackmail both him and you.'

Ian bowed his head. Was that shame he was feeling, wondered Benedict. Juliet inched away from him.

'You idiot,' said Juliet. 'You bloody, bloody idiot.'

'I'm sorry, Jools.'

'What good is that?' Ian reached his hand out for his wife, wanting to offer warmth.

'Don't touch me,' she snapped. 'Don't ever touch me again, you bastard.'

'Please, Jools–'

'They'll try him as a kid, won't they?' asked Juliet.

'Yes. He's already shown a lot of remorse and if he pleads guilty, a judge may treat him with a degree of leniency.'

'I need to see him,' said Juliet. 'I need to see my baby.'

'Not yet,' said Benedict. 'We now need to speak about Felix.'

'F-Felix?'

'Felix is not your son, is he, Mrs Turner?'

Juliet let rip a howl of agony. Ian swore.

'Your DNA and his are entirely different.' He waited while Juliet cried. Ian placed his arm around her shoulder but she swore at him.

'However,' said Benedict. 'Ian *is* Felix's father.'

'Christ!' Ian shot up from his chair.

Juliet blanched. 'What... I-I don't understand.'

'Sit down, Mr Turner.'

Ian did, his hand pulling on his hair. 'No, no, you mean after...'

'Yes, Mr Turner? After what?'

'He's my son *too*,' said Juliet.

'Emotionally, yes but biologically, he isn't. He *is* Mr Turner's biological son though.'

'But...' She looked at her husband, her eyes filled with

confusion, fear possibly. 'No, no. That's not...' Her eyes widened. 'Oh God. Tell me.'

Ian shook his head, his eyes filling with tears.

'Tell me!'

'I can't...'

'I think I know what happened,' said Benedict, addressing Ian. 'Would you like me to say, Mr Turner, or do you think, after all this time, it'd be better coming from you? Your wife deserves it.'

Ian put his head into his hands. 'I was only...' He looked up at Benedict. 'I didn't mean it to go so far. I...'

'Mr Turner, I think you should be addressing this to your wife, not me.'

'The truth, Ian,' said Juliet. 'I need to know the truth.'

'Felix is Harry. Beth's and Kris's. I found him one night on the boat all alone and I was worried for him, so I just...'

'Beth's?'

'You were grieving over Toby and—'

'No, don't you dare, don't try to blame this on me.'

'I only wanted to help you get over the loss, Jools.'

'Did you know he was your baby?'

'No.'

'So you... you screwed Beth and...'

'I'm sorry.'

'I don't believe I'm hearing this. After all this time. All this time, you've been Felix's dad, after all.'

'I didn't know.'

'You didn't know?'

Ian shook his head.

'How could you not have known?'

'Mrs Turner—'

'I brought him up,' she screamed. 'I gave him a decent life.

He's never wanted for anything. I love him and he loves me.'

'But it wasn't for you to deny another woman her child,' said Benedict.

'Felix would never have the life he's had,' said Juliet.

'Through your actions, you subjected a mother to eighteen years of agony. We're waiting on Beth Pearson's DNA. If it matches Felix's, as I imagine it will, we will have to inform Felix as well as his biological mother.'

'No, you can't. He can't know.'

'He has every right to know, Mrs Turner.'

'You've taken one child from me, you can't take both. Please, I beg you, Inspector, don't do this to me, to us.'

You did it to yourselves, thought Benedict.

*

Having checked the CCTV, DC Kelly found Kelvin Turner at Charing Cross station at three thirty Monday afternoon. Meanwhile, Beth Pearson's DNA results arrived at the end of the day. Felix Turner was indeed her son. So now, Benedict needed to speak to Felix. He scrolled through his phone, finding the pictures Beth had sent him showing Felix, or Harry, as a baby. First, he rang Kris Whitehead and asked him to go to his ex-wife's boat and wait there for his visit.

Felix had just returned from a fast-food restaurant. The officer on reception phoned through to Benedict. Benedict asked the officer to escort Felix to Interview Room 2.

'Felix,' said Benedict. 'I'm sorry to have kept you waiting for so long.'

'What's going on? What have you done with Kelvin?'

'Felix, do you have a significant birthmark?'

'What sort of question is that?'

'Where is it?'

'It's… it's on the back of my left leg. On my thigh. Why?'

Benedict showed Felix the pictures of him as a baby, including the one that partially showed his birthmark.

'Yeah, that's it. Why have you got these photos? I've never seen them before. Did my mum send them to you?'

'Felix, I've got something to tell you and it's going to be difficult for you to process.'

'Shit, what is it?'

'In 2005, your father had a relationship with a woman called Beth Whitehead. They had a baby. That baby was you.'

'No…'

'When you were just three months old, your father stole you from your biological mother. Beth and her husband, Kris, have been looking for you ever since.'

Felix put his hands over his ears. 'I'm not listening to this.'

'Your father stole you, Felix. The sad thing is, he didn't know he was stealing his own son.'

'No. This is bullshit.'

'Beth never told Ian that the son she gave birth to was his. Maybe she didn't know herself.'

Felix stared at Benedict as he absorbed the detective's words. 'No. No way. You've got it wrong. I don't believe you.'

'I'm sorry to have to break this to you. Your mother is not your biological mother.'

'That can't be right. Why would he do that? Why would he steal me? It doesn't make sense.' Felix's eyes reddened. 'I can't believe I'm hearing this. Shit. Christ.'

'I'm sorry. These photos were sent to me by Beth.'

'Shit. Really? My real mum? She sent you those?'

'Yes.'

'What… what about Kelvin?'

'Kelvin is your parents' biological child, yes.'

'Oh, Christ. I can't believe I'm hearing this.' He wiped his eyes. 'You're actually telling me Mum isn't my mum and that Dad stole me from my real mum when I was a kid?'

'A baby. Yes. I'm sorry.'

'Oh my God.' He stood and paced the interview room. 'So my whole life's been a lie, a great big sodding lie.'

'Felix, I have to tell you that I now need to go see Beth and Kris Whitehead–'

'Kris? Kris who? Who's Kris?'

'Beth's ex-husband. He may not be your real father but all this time he has always believed he was. This will be difficult for him as well.'

'This is unreal. Oh God, what's my name? It's not Felix, is it?'

'I think for now, we'll stick with Felix.'

'So my name isn't even my name. This gets better by the minute. This is doing my head in.' He sat down again.

'It's a shock and I'm sorry to have to tell you but I had to. You need to know.'

'What are you saying? You want me to feel *sorry* for you?'

'No, no. Not at all. I didn't mean to give that impression.'

'So, what do I do now?'

'Felix, there's a lot for you to take in here and so I think it'd be appropriate now to refer you to the social services–'

'You mean like a shrink?'

'No, nothing like that. But you need someone with the suitable training on your side. There will be a lot for you to absorb, Felix. Too much for now. But give it time and with the help from social services, they'll help you piece everything together and help you with the way forward. At some point whenever you're ready and only if you want to, social services can arrange a meeting with your biological mother.'

'God, no. If they were stupid enough to let me get stolen in the first place, then I don't want to see her.'

'I understand and it's totally your prerogative but maybe, when you've had enough time—'

'No, I said. Not now, not ever. She's not my mother; she's nothing to do with me. I don't want to see her. End of. You tell her that, right? You bloody tell her, I'm no son of hers.'

Chapter 51: Benedict

Benedict needed to go see the Whiteheads on Beth's canal boat. He braced himself; this wasn't going to be easy.

It was a pleasant evening as he approached *Lazy Suzan*, the sun dipping but the day retaining its warmth. He stepped on the boat. The door opened and there was Kris. 'Come in,' he said.

Benedict ducked as he entered and was momentarily taken aback by the vision of the famous Three Monkeys on the kitchen shelf looking at him.

Beth stood on seeing him. 'You've got news, haven't you?'

Benedict nodded and waited for Kris to follow him inside.

'We've found Harry.'

Beth screamed, her hand went to her mouth to muffle it. 'You found him? You've found our baby?'

'Yes. Yes, we have but–'

'Kris, they've found him, they've found him.' She hugged Kris. 'I knew it, I knew this day would come. Is he here? Where is he?'

'Can we sit down?' He waited a moment. 'Beth, Kris, I've

got something to tell you and I'm afraid, it's not going to be easy for you.'

'What is it?' said Kris.

'Kris, I'm sorry but Harry is not your child.'

Kris stared at him as if he didn't understand before bursting out laughing. 'Of course, he's mine. I mean, come on.'

Benedict waited.

Beth's eyes moistened, her hand to her mouth.

'Oh, Christ no,' said Kris. 'I'm not Harry's dad? No, I don't… You mean, like…' He turned to his ex-wife. 'So, if Harry isn't mine, Beth, whose is he?'

Beth didn't answer.

'I said, who's his father, Beth?' shouted Kris.

'Ian's.'

'Ian's? Ian Turner?' He shot to his feet. 'Oh God, this is too much. First, you tell us you've found him only to tell me the kid I've been looking for all these years isn't even mine. This is so fucked-up. Wait, what about Dan? Oh no, please tell me Dan is my son, Beth.'

'Of course, he is.'

'Hell, thank Christ for that.' He sat down, looking exhausted.

Beth turned to him. 'I'm sorry, Kris. I'm so sorry. But he *is* your son really. He's *our* son.'

'You slept with Turner?'

'I'm not proud of the fact.' Turning to Benedict, she said, 'I need to see Harry.'

'He's not quite ready to see you–'

'I must. I have to.'

'I do understand that but it's come as a massive shock to him, to be told his mother isn't his mother. After all, before today, he didn't even know you existed. Give him time. It's a lot for a young lad to take on board.'

'I know how he feels,' said Kris.

'Oh, God, no,' said Beth. 'I can't bear it.'

'Who took him?' asked Kris.

'I can't tell you that yet.'

'I want to see Harry. Please, Inspector, talk to him again.'

'We've waited eighteen years, Beth, another–'

'No. I have to see him. He's my son. *Our* son, Kris.'

'I told…' Benedict stopped himself from saying Felix. '…Harry that he has a brother and a nephew.'

'What did he say?' asked Beth. 'Was he pleased?'

'Yes but I think he was too much in shock to take it in. We're referring him to social services. They will work with him, answer his questions, and support him emotionally. And, when he's ready…'

Beth nodded.

'What did these other people call him?' asked Kris.

'No,' said Beth. 'I don't want to know. Not yet. He's Harry. He's always been Harry. I'm sorry, Kris. Me sleeping with Ian, it was a mistake, it shouldn't have happened. Please forgive me. But they've found Harry, Kris. Isn't that the main thing? They've found him after all this time.'

'I know.' Kris squeezed her hand.

'Thank you, Kris. Thank you. I just want to see my baby.'

'And we will, love. Like the Inspector said, it's a lot for him to digest. He'll be in a state right now. He'll need time.'

'I'm sorry, Kris.'

He rubbed his eyes. 'It's just a bit of a shock, you know.'

'I will speak to him again,' said Benedict.

'Please,' said Beth. 'Tell him… tell him his mummy is waiting for him, that she's desperate to see him.'

Benedict smiled. 'Social services will look after him.' He stood. 'Look, I'll leave you now. You also need time to process this.'

'I'll see you out,' said Kris.

The two men stood on the towpath. 'I don't know how to thank you, Inspector.'

'It's fine. I just hope Harry comes around soon.'

'God, so do I.'

Benedict smiled and nodded. He walked away, knowing his presence was no longer needed. He looked at the canal boats as he made his way back along the towpath. He remembered looking for the last time at the boat that had been home for those five days when he was fifteen in the weeks following his father's death. Five days but it had felt like so much longer. His mother had been right – it had helped him with his grief, being part of a gang, having fun, steering the boat, playing games. He'd loved every moment.

He remembered his mother meeting him at Euston train station. She thanked his teachers and then, turning to him, hugged him which in itself was a rarity. 'How was it?' she asked. 'Did you have fun?'

'Yeah. It was great. Brilliant.' He smiled a big, warm smile. He dreaded asking her but he knew he had to. 'How are you, Mum?'

She placed her hand against his cheek, tears forming in her eyes. 'I've just seen my son smile for the first time in weeks. And that makes me so happy.'

Epilogue
Six months later

Beth Pearson's life had been on hold for eighteen long years, ever since the day that bastard, Ian Turner, had stolen her baby.

Every day had been a torture. But now, knowing that Harry had been found, that he was safe and sound and living nearby, the torture had ramped up a thousandfold. She couldn't get Harry out of her mind from the moment she woke up to the moment she fell asleep – and therein lay another torture – she couldn't sleep for thinking of him. She couldn't put her mind to anything, couldn't think of anything but Harry. At times, the sense of longing manifested itself into a physical pain; she could feel it like a stone in the pit of her stomach, the continuous pounding of her heart. Every time she heard footsteps on the towpath, someone approaching, her heart lurched. Oftentimes, she feared it was going to overwhelm her.

She'd lost so much weight. Her hair needed cutting and

her complexion had turned dreadfully pale. She couldn't face cooking, couldn't face eating. Merely keeping the boat tidy had become such an effort; *everything* was so much of an effort.

Kris came to visit every day after work. Back then, eighteen years ago, she hated him, blaming him for allowing Harry to be stolen. But now, she needed him so much. She feared she'd driven him away now that he knew, now that she knew, that the baby wasn't his after all. Instead, he'd become a permanent fixture in her life and for that she was grateful. She often hoped he'd stay the night but he never hinted at it and Beth was too fearful to mention it. But even Kris couldn't take away the anticipation and pain of knowing that her son could turn up any day, at any hour, out of the blue.

Dan visited often, a couple of times he brought Helene and Erik. Beth loved seeing her grandson but it pained her so much that Erik, now at four months old, was already older than Harry the night Turner stole him.

The days of summer turned into autumn, the clocks changed and the nights drew in. And still, Beth waited, hoping that *this* day, finally, might be *the* day.

She and Kris had learned that it was indeed her former lover, Ian Turner, who had stolen Harry. Turner was now on remand, awaiting his trial. Beth hoped they'd send him down for a long, long time. He deserved nothing less. Kelvin, Turner's son, was on remand for the killing of Alan Milner. He was just a boy still, surely the court would treat him with a degree of leniency. But frankly, it wasn't her concern.

Fifth November, a bitterly cold day in London. Kris insisted they attend a firework party being held early evening in Regents Park. Beth resisted, not wanting to go. 'I have to stay here, Kris. He could turn up now, tonight.'

'No,' he said. 'Not during the evening. If... I mean, *when* he turns up, it'll be during the day, won't it? Anyway, we don't even know whether he knows your address or not, do we?'

'Social services will have told him, surely.'

'We don't know that. Come, come to the party. You need to get out, Beth. You can't just sit here, waiting for him forever. And it'll be fun. You love fireworks.'

'I hate fireworks.'

'You need to see people, Beth. You need to get out.'

'No. I don't want to.'

'Dan said he'd come too.'

That made all the difference.

In the end, Beth allowed Kris to bully her into going to the bonfire night party. Wrapped up with gloves, scarves, woolly hats and heavy coats, they made their way to the park and joined the throngs of happy, expectant people anticipating a glorious display of fireworks. She remembered taking Dan to displays like this when he was a boy. Even then, she kept scouring the crowds, hoping to see Harry. So many years later and nothing had changed; Beth scanned the crowds, hoping to see him, sure that he'd be here somewhere. Would he be with his other mother? A girlfriend, perhaps?

Sure enough, Dan turned up. He hugged his mother. Helene and Erik, he said, were doing fine. He looked tired. Knowing that his brother had come back from the dead had shaken him too.

The crowds were immense and Beth had never felt so lonely. She took Kris' hand and refused to let go. But it was a jolly crowd that cheered and applauded as the fireworks exploded, blazing a multitude of colours across the night sky, piercing the blackness above.

Kris bought her a red wine in a plastic beaker. She didn't want it and hadn't touched a drop of alcohol for months but she drank it. She could feel it stamping down on the pain a little, anaesthetising it; it was still there but slightly numbed. She leaned into Kris, needing his warmth and comforting presence.

The firework display continued for such an age, each explosion greeted with delight. After an hour, Beth, lightheaded and cold, had had enough. She could tell that Kris didn't want to leave so soon but he accepted it with good grace. She kissed Dan goodbye and together, Beth and Kris caught a bus home.

It was still only nine o'clock by the time they arrived back at Beth's boat.

'Do you want a coffee?' she asked once they'd stepped inside, rubbing their hands to get warm.

He hesitated. 'Erm, no. Thanks but I guess I should head back. Early start and all that.'

This, thought Beth, was the moment to say it – that she didn't want him to leave, that she wanted him to stay with her, to keep her company through the night, to help keep the demons at bay. But she couldn't bring herself to say it. Instead, she thanked him for a pleasant evening.

'Yeah. Sure.'

She forced a smile.

'I'll pop in tomorrow if you like.'

'Yes, that'd be nice. Thanks, Kris.'

He kissed her goodbye and Beth resolved herself to another night spent alone, listening to the silence of the night, hoping that come the new day her son would return.

Kris had only been gone a few seconds when she heard him calling her name. 'Beth? Beth, come here.'

Beth was out of the boat in a shot. She stepped onto the towpath. 'What is it?'

She followed Kris' gaze and saw a figure half illuminated by the lights of a neighbouring boat. Was that…? She squinted through the darkness, her heart threatening to explode. She glanced at Kris. Kris nodded. Yes, it was him, it was her son. She let out a shriek. She took a step forward. She and Harry locked eyes. Beth tried to call out but the words wouldn't come. Gingerly, they approached each other.

'Hello,' he said in a surprisingly deep voice.

'Harry?'

'Yes. Are you…?'

'Yes,' she cried. 'Yes, it's me, Harry, your mum.'

They both paused, taking in the image of each other. Beth started shaking on seeing the man before her, her handsome son. She edged forward, a step at a time. 'Harry. Is it really you?'

They stood opposite each other within arms' reach.

'Hi… Hello… What do I call you? Mum?'

Mum. He said Mum. Her heart collapsed on itself. Never had she heard such a wonderful word, never had she envisaged what effect it'd have on her. 'Harry. You look… you look exactly as I imagined. Can I… have a hug, please?'

He looked away for a few seconds as if unsure. He took a small step back. *No,* she thought, *don't leave me, don't go; I couldn't bear it.*

Then, with a flicker of a smile, he nodded.

Beth stepped up to him, hesitated a moment, then gently put her arms around her son. He too was shaking. He stood erect as a statue, his arms at his side, his eyes shut. Beth tried so hard for his sake not to cry but she had no control over it as the tears seeped down her face. She wanted desperately to hug him as tight as could be but again tried to restrain herself. Slowly, Harry lifted one arm and gently put a hand on his mother's back.

'I've been waiting for this moment,' she whispered, wiping her tears.

'I'm sorry it took me so long.'

'You're here now.'

Beth could have held onto him forever but, knowing she had to take this slowly, let go of him. He glanced beyond her and saw Kris standing behind her, near the boat.

'Are you my other dad?'

Kris stepped forward. 'Hello, my son. Welcome home. It's good to see you.'

With tears forming in his eyes, Harry reached out for Beth's hand. She took it and had to stop herself from crying with the joy of touching his flesh. 'This is so weird,' he said.

'I know. For you and me both.'

He smiled and all the upset and trauma that Beth had carried all these years simply melted away all at once. She had her son back, her gorgeous, beautiful son, and that was all that mattered.

THE END

Novels by Joshua Black:

The DI Benedict Paige Novels

Book 1: And Then She Came Back
Book2: The Poison In His Veins
Book 3: Requiem for a Whistleblower
Book 4: The Forget-Me-Not Killer
Book 5: The Canal Boat Killer

To obtain Joshua's short story, *The Death of The Listening Man*, and join his Mailing List and be the first to know of future releases, etc, please go to:

rupertcolley.com/joshua-black/

Rathbone Publishing

Printed in Great Britain
by Amazon